FATED TO BURN

EMMIE HAMILTON

FATED TO BURN

FOR MY OLIVER GRAYSON—

I know what you're thinking. "Really, mom? Again?"

But my first book was for you—my baby— for being the foundation of everything I am and the constant source of motivation to keep going.

This book, however, isn't for my sweet little Ollie Gray.

This is for my Oliver Grayson. My teen as heck kid of the future, who is well on his way to becoming the person he was always meant to be.

Right now you're playing with your toy dinos and still pronouncing the world purple like "purkle," but one day, you will grow up. You'll be filled with so many new emotions and it will be overwhelming. I will 3inevitably be the source of your angst and hate, as that's what the teen years are for: blaming your parents for your misfortunes. You're going to be confused and lonely and feel like no one really understands what you're going through.

So this book is for future you, the one that maybe feels a little alone and doesn't quite know how to say it. I am here for you, my love. Through whatever happens in the passage of time, our innulum will never break. We will always find our way back to each other.

NOTE TO THE READER

Dear Reader,

I must once again thank you so very much for purchasing this copy of Fated to Burn. If you're here, that means Chosen to Fall left you in enough of a bother to want to continue, and you have my endless gratitude for giving *The Destined Series* a chance. The hours it took to create and expand this world was devoted solely for the purpose of escaping into another place in time. As such, it is always my responsibility to make you aware of the content contained within this story.

This is a transitional book from Upper Young Adult Fantasy to New Adult Fantasy, so you can find much more serious and mature content than the first installment. Adult language, sexual content, torture, inferences to sexual assault, brief mention of miscarriage, and death are all contained within this story. As before, this series as a whole may not be suitable for those under the age of sixteen, but I will leave it to your discretion based on your personal traumas and triggers, along with maturity level. Please consider this information before proceeding. I would never want to cause undue harm onto any of my readers and want to provide as safe a space as possible for all who are willing to give me a chance.

Thank you, once again, for showing interest in my book. I hope this leaves you with a sense of resilience, hope, and gratitude.

Yours always,

Emmie

Sea of
Aurelia
FORBIDDEN CONTINENT
The Fores
of the Dar
Athinia
Mentage
ANI
Mercy Bay
Crescent Poin
THE BARREN PLAIN
WENDORRE

North Sea
City of Farrah
Carenek Peaks
Tuluk
TRA
THE BONE ISLES
Widow's Passageway

THE ETERNAL FLAME

One of the closest-kept secrets of the Val is that of the Eternal Flame. According to ancient lore, the Flame was the last remnant of power from the gods with the ability to render its owner immortal and the lands they rule forever prosperous. It is said to be hidden in the center of an inactive volcano in a secret fire realm, protectedv by *Drogosterra* and firelings. The bite of a fireling, a dragonfly-sized sprite, can boil blood and peel skin, thus killing all who dare enter. No one alive at the time of this writing has succeeded in finding that realm or capturing the flame, and according to prophecies of the Ancient Originals, one capable of such a feat will not exist for nearly one thousand more years.

PROLOGUE

DARROC

·ONE YEAR AGO·

The salty sea air mixed with arid winds and a blast of searing heat as the rocky shore gave way to dry lands. The boundary between Wendorre and Anestra was nothing more than a festering wound: a stretch of dead grass and the memory of blood, centuries gone.

A millennia ago, the Ancient Originals used the last of their gifts to create the deadened boundary as a place of remembrance for the Great War's fallen.

Darroc L'Azare, last surviving member of Warlock Royalty, crossed the dividing line, relishing in the land's echoes of pain. Knowing that he would soon cause more only spurred him further.

It had been years since Darroc needed to hold his glamour as a normal warlock in place for so long, although he found he rather liked being out of the shadows in the open sunshine. He had taken years to perfect his glamouring spell and knew it to be infallible.

He hadn't always been the monster he now was.

It was the reason behind all of it; why he dedicated his life to such atrocities for the salvation of his people. Ultimate power would bring back the vitality Wendorre had been missing for so long. It would ensure that his people thrived and that their land would prosper. It would ensure that he ruled the way he wanted and no other would ever step in his way again.

I must be the one to fulfill the prophecy.

Darroc traveled night and day, no longer needing sleep to provide him energy. All those long years of using dark magic had turned him into something else, something other. Perhaps he was not a known race at all.

The thought jolted his blood. To be the first of his own kind, soon to be breeding with the female that would help the prophecy come true.

They didn't know what he knew. Faria was just a tool; it was the offspring that was important.

Darroc's offspring.

He hadn't spent centuries creating unspeakable horrors and planning for the siege of Anestra to be anything but absolutely sure that Faria would bear his child. A child with their combined magic whom, under his direction, would ensure the world bowed to him alone.

Nearly a week passed after crossing The Barren Plain before Darroc came upon them. Warlocks. His kind, if he truly belonged to a "kind" anymore.

Darroc recognized their scent and hid his sneer as he steered his horse through their fields. He carefully avoided their crops; keeping the disguise was not just about looks, but complete appearance. He didn't want to cause unnecessary damage to their main source of food and risk suspicion.

A weathered man with a crooked back stood up from where he gathered beans, and a woman with leathery skin came to stand by him, a basket balanced on her hip. They both wore cautious smiles as Darroc jumped off his horse and adjusted his tunic made of deep azure silk.

"Hello, Grand-Mother," Darroc addressed the woman in the traditional warlock greeting, placing his right hand over his heart. "Sir, hello. I am Darroc L'Azare, Royal Liaison from our home of Wendorre."

The woman's shocked expression melted into suspicion while a smile spread widely across the man's face.

"Hello, Sir. I'm Jed, this is Nora." The man bowed at the waist but the woman did little more than nod in his direction. "What brings you so many leagues away from our homeland?"

Anger flashed through Darroc as he heard their human names. "I have important business at *Mentage*, but I'm afraid I still have such a long journey." The feigned politeness in his voice grated on his nerves.

"I wasn't aware our people had a Royal Liaison anymore," Nora said, staring boldly into his own violet eyes—the one true mark of a royal warlock. "There hasn't been a royal warlock for centuries." The way she challenged him while staring at the one piece of evidence that he might have been telling the truth called to something primal in him. Something that made him want to shred her throat with his teeth.

Swallowing his bloodlust felt like nails clawing his insides. "Please, if you can spare little food, I would be more than happy to help with the rest of your harvest."

Jed looked disbelieving at Darroc's clothes, as if wondering if he had ever done a hard day's work in his life. He paid particular attention to the silks shining off of the mid-afternoon sun.

"These are nothing," Darroc said, noticing where Jed's eyes traveled to. "Really, I don't mind."

He removed his travelling cloak and outer tunic, revealing plain underclothes and exchanged his expensive riding boots for a pair that were worn with age, before placing his belongings in the pack on his stallion. He led the horse over to a fence and tied her up before facing the old man again.

Jed looked appreciatively at Darroc's muscles. "Okay, then. You can help me finish this section and the next. Time we're done, we'll be ready to eat."

Nora quickly excused herself and the men worked in silence until the sun drew long shadows on the ground. Darroc didn't mind the grunt work as much as he thought he would. After centuries of hiding away, it was almost cathartic to perform manual labor in the sunlight and it gave him time to begrudgingly appreciate the land of Anestra.

The land that would soon be his.

A child darted out from behind large stalks of corn a few feet away, no more than seven or eight years old by the look of her. Dirt streaked the girl's face. The sight of the girl gripped Darroc with surprise; warlock children were rare. He hadn't heard of a warlock child surviving into adulthood in nearly twenty years and this girl seemed relatively healthy.

"My granddaughter, Moira." Jed motioned the girl forward. "Her mother, my daughter, died from sickness two summers ago."

Darroc stared harder at the child, subtly trying to scent the air to see what else she was. Her appearance was not typical of pure-blooded warlocks. She had the sun kissed coloring and bright blue eyes known among their race, but her curly red hair gave her the appearance of being on fire. She had some warlock, yes, but something else, too. "And the father?"

"Never knew," Jed replied. "We hadn't known our daughter was pregnant until she came home with a child."

"D-dinner is ready." Moira curtseyed before running away.

"Strange," Jed said. "I normally can't get her in at night."

The two warlocks walked toward the little cottage that Moira ran into, and Darroc mused on how much personal information he should share to learn what he needed to. It had been a long while since he'd needed to prove himself trustworthy, and he decided to use this as an opportunity to test his deceit before arriving at *Mentage*.

The inside of the cottage was little more than destitute. A few shelves lining the back wall held broken pots and well-used dishes, and the chairs at a worn-out table looked barely able to hold his weight. An adjacent room held two beds—or rather, straw and blankets on the floor. At least it was clean.

Darroc's blood boiled, thinking of where his people were now. Centuries ago, it would have been unheard of for a warlock to be taken by sickness. If he hadn't spent so much time hiding and experimenting across the realms, he might have been better attuned to the squalor his people had fallen into.

They were once a wealthy, revered people. They used to hold huge markets where people of all races would trade rare fabrics, fine jewelry, and nearly impossible-to-find spices. Now, they had nothing. Granted, Jed and Nora chose to leave Wendorre, but he could hardly fault them for it.

They weren't the only ones to do so. This was arguably a better life than what they would have had if they stayed, and that thought only increased his anger.

I should have killed my father sooner.

How dare the queen not take better care of his people? Did she even know his subjects were this far out on her land?

She had much to pay for.

Nora poured bits of stew into each of the bowls laid out on the table and bread was divided amongst them. He almost felt sorry for eating their food, because along with no sleep, he did not require sustenance in the traditional sense. He needed information though, and had already asked them to share their meal.

Jed motioned Darroc to the seat at the head of the table; a sign of respect. He gloated inwardly at the gesture. Avoiding eye contact with Darroc, Moira seated herself as close to Nora on the side opposite him as she could get. Jed took the remaining chair and sat with a grunt.

"We follow no deity here, but if you need to say prayers or offerings, please feel free to do so."

Darroc almost scoffed at the absurdity. The only offerings he needed were the ones his minions laid before him, not the other way around.

"No, thank you," he replied, taking a modest bite of stew. It was only a few root vegetables, but it was flavorful enough, not that he cared either way. "Tell me, Jed, do you often hear news out here of what goes on up north?"

"Well, we are a week out from *Mentage* and the capital, so we usually hear of things several days after it has passed, when travelers come out this way."

Darroc nodded, figuring out how to word his next question. "Anything…unusual?"

Jed shared a quick look with Nora and swallowed. "Unusual in what way?"

"Anything out of the ordinary. You see, I have particular business with Queen Amira and her daughter." Darroc stared hard at Jed before continuing. "Business that would have a direct impact on Wendorre, and its people. If there is something amiss, I would need to prepare before making my final leg of the journey to *Mentage*."

"Ah," Jed stared back down at his bowl, tapping his spoon against the bottom of it. "Well, we have heard several strange rumors of late."

Nora choked on a sip of water and glared at him, her ire coming off her in waves.

"Please, I have been traveling nearly three weeks already and you are the first of our kind I have encountered." Darroc paused a moment before subtly shifting his voice to a command. "Tell me."

"Well, these are just rumors, of course, we won't know the truth of it until later," Jed hedged. "It seems as though young Faria has started to come into her gifts."

"And what do we know of these…gifts?" Darroc tried to keep the excitement out of his voice. If Faria proved powerful, then their offspring would be, too. He would mold their daughter into the weapon he would need on his way to total domination.

To save his people, of course.

"Only rumors, but something strange happened in the Forest of the

Dawn, as we heard it. Some foul magic was there, burning that ancient forest."

"No!" Feinting shock and alarm were almost as difficult as being polite and maintaining the glamour.

"Yes. The queen could not stop it, and from what we hear, Faria flew out to the fields and she poured her essence into the land, creating water and fire where there was none. And was able to douse those strange flames."

"Flew?" Darroc had already suspected that Faria's powers had begun to overtake his, but this confirmed it. He'd felt when she stopped the black flames from consuming the forest. It was how he knew it was the right time to accept the queen's invitation.

"Oh yes, as a bird in flight as we heard it told," Jed whispered conspiratorially with a wink.

"Elves cannot fly."

"Yes, strange rumors we heard." Jed sat back in his chair and took another bite of stew. Nora stared hard at her untouched food.

"And what about you, Nora? Have you heard anything else?"

She clenched her jaw shut. For a moment seemed as though she wouldn't answer, before pushing out the word, "No."

"Oh, come now," Jed said. "There is one other bit of interesting news."

"I'm sure this man," Nora spat the insult toward Darroc, "does not care for more rumors and false stories."

Darroc didn't know whether to laugh or sneer. Nora was bold in her obvious distaste of him, though he couldn't imagine where it came from. Neither of them was old enough to remember him. No one alive should remember who he used to be.

"Well, we don't know how false they really are," Jed said.

"No," Darroc cut in, trying to keep the desperation and anger out of his voice. "On the contrary, I care very much indeed of what you have to say, truth or not. I am here for Princess Faria. The queen has struck a deal with me, offered me a chance to court her daughter. I intend to make Faria mine."

Silence hung in the air, sticking to the walls, quieting the fire. No one moved.

Interesting.

"Ha!" Nora's barked laugh broke the silence. "I'm afraid that won't be happening."

Darroc stilled, the challenge in her voice calling to that primal place in him, and his control was quickly slipping. Sweat broke down his neck as he tried to keep his glamour in place. This would not be the time to unleash his claws. "What," he squeezed the word out with visible effort.

"Well, *Darroc*," Nora sneered. "It seems as though our Faria has chosen her partner already. So, I'm afraid you came all this way for nothing."

"Nora!" Jed said, slamming his hand on the table. Moira flinched at the sound. "Show some respect!"

"There is something not right about this creature sitting at our table!" Nora said. "Moira felt it, and so do I." She took a breath before continuing, fire in her eyes. "You may once have been a warlock, but you are no more. I don't know what you are doing here or what you really plan, but you cannot have our Faria. She is the Chosen One and she has chosen who is hers. It is not you. I suggest you leave and don't come back."

Darroc's glamour slipped, anger and hatred spitting out of him. How dare she say Faria was hers? His face elongated, his unholy canines coming loose from their hidden prison. The world around them shook with violence while clouds gathered outside, and thunder rumbled menacingly over the shack.

Moira screamed as Jed pushed back from the table, horror staining his features. Nora's face blanched, but she held her ground, refusing to avert her eyes.

Darroc could almost admire her foolishness. After several deep breaths, he was able to control himself enough to change his face back but the damage was done and a storm still threatened the air.

"Who has she chosen?"

Jed only shook his head, his mouth opening and closing like a fish on dry land, his voice lost to him. Moira cowered under the table, as if that could save her if Darroc really meant her harm. No, his wrath was all for Nora. Women were precious to his race, which was the only thing keeping him from tearing her heart out.

A triumphant smile slid over her face, her eyes shining with victory. "A. Human." She said each word distinctly, making sure Darroc heard her clearly.

The words echoed in his ear, barely audible above the sound of his blood pumping furiously as the pressure in his body rose. Darroc took a moment to process that impossible information. He let out a roar, his glamour completely disintegrated. He felt freer than he had in weeks, but the ease in his body did nothing to calm the rage that overtook him.

Before realizing what he was doing, Darroc reached for an obsidian bone knife hanging from his belt, sliced his palm down the middle, and allowed the blood to flow out on the table.

Black.

"You-you are the evil one?" Jed stammered as he pressed his back against the front door, as if he had anywhere to run from the predator Darroc was.

"Yes," he replied simply before turning back to Nora. He watched as his blood drifted slowly toward the old woman. She was rooted to the spot, her face contorted with a scream that would not free itself from her body.

Once it reached her, the blood lifted into the air, hovering inches from Nora's face before lazily entering her mouth as a snake to its den. Within seconds she changed from pale to purple, her eyes pleading for mercy.

There was no mercy to be had.

With a flick of his wrist and a brief exhale of breath later, Nora's body exploded. Pieces of her rained down around them, oozing down the walls, and landing in a bloody pool on floor.

"Nora!" Jed cried out, but it was too late.

"You understand, Jed, that you know too much now." Darroc stalked closer to his latest prey. "I could have liked you. Tolerated you," he amended. "I am doing this for our people. They must be saved and this is the only way."

Jed's painful cries were the only reply he could give.

"I'll make this merciful, for the kindness you have shown me." Swifter than light, Darroc slashed Jed's throat, stepping back as his body thumped to the ground.

Wiping his knife on the back of Jed's tunic, Darroc's ears perked at the mewling noises coming from under the table.

"Ah, yes. Moira."

Darroc knocked the table over without preamble, pieces of Nora flinging to the walls and sizzling in the fire. The scent of cooked meat and boiled blood pervaded the air.

Moira was curled in the fetal position, vomit spread around her. Darroc inhaled deeply, savoring the moment before considering his next move. To kill Moira would be unfortunate, as there were hardly any warlock children anymore. Besides, if he killed her, who would help to spread fear among the people of Anestra?

Decisions, decisions.

Darroc threw a gold coin at her feet, landing in a puddle of sticky fluids.

"I will have mercy on you, child, because you are precious to our race. Contrary to what it seems, I *am* doing this for all of us."

Darroc stepped back toward the door. "I will be setting fire to this shack soon. I suggest you leave." He turned the handle before glancing over his shoulder to give her one last demand. "And if you survive the trip to *Mentage*, you tell them what happened here. Tell them what I will do to all of Anestra if they do not heed me."

Darroc stepped out into the open air, taking in a deep breath to clear his nostrils of the stench of fresh death. Then, he called a simple fire spell and set the roof in flames.

Darroc's horse pawed nervously at the ground at the sudden appearance of fire. "Easy, girl."

He climbed onto the beast, urging it forward. He had little more than a week to make it to Anestra, and if those rumors were correct, he could already be too late.

He was hardly worried, though. A mere human was nothing compared to Darroc, but he would have to play it smart. Faria was the future queen of Anestra, and while she was not the Chosen One as everyone believed her to be, she was still an essential piece in his game.

The most important piece, if his plans played out the way he intended.

Galloping off into the distance, leaving the smoldering shack behind, Darroc made his way toward the heart of Anestra, forging each piece of his plan as the leagues closed in.

Soon. I will have what I want, soon.

⋅PRESENT DAY⋅

"Begin."

Screams rent the air, echoing off the trees whose leaves shook in the breeze as if they were laughing, entertained by the sight laid out before them. Darroc smiled to himself. Yes, even the nature of this land recognized what needed to be done and gave its approval.

He took a deep breath, savoring the flavors of the screaming shapeshifter bleeding out at his feet. If only the shifter had not disagreed with Darroc...but alas, now he got to appreciate the tantalizing bouquet of fear and sweat as the screams of terror clanged throughout his mind.

"Again," Darroc commanded his second. He watched as the young man selected a long, thin blade from the selection of weapons. He walked over to the shifter, running it under the prisoner's fingernails.

The sound was a sweet harmony that sang through Darroc's blood. He longed to sink his teeth into the traitor, but that would be a mercy.

And he wasn't feeling merciful.

The screams of the shifter sent shivers of ecstasy down Darroc's spine. He looked down at his second's handiwork, satisfied by what he saw, but he needed to make sure the message was driven home.

"Again."

PART I

ONE

HUNTER

The scent of fire and ash permeated the thick air, blanketing the trees, the ground, any life form unfortunate enough to be hit with the blast of dark magic. Silence kissed the branches, its stillness worse than death, worse than the broken promise of infinity.

The unmaking of light and life was the first sign of his awareness. The emptiness, the lack of almost everything save oxygen reminded him of what happened in that forest. Of how he died.

Waiting for his vision to return, Hunter felt the charred earth against the exposed parts of his back beneath him, felt the skin of his fingers brush against the ground as it sewed itself back together. No scars would be visible. Ravenous hunger raked through him as his body healed itself, though he knew he wouldn't have time to eat for hours yet, maybe more.

His hearing faded in and out, and it wasn't until he thought he heard an anguished scream rent the air that he tried to yell back, but his vocal cords weren't ready. The precious minutes it would take for him to heal would be too long to get her attention, to let her know that he was fine.

If only the Elders hadn't prevented him from telling her more about what he was, about his healing ability, that the only way for him to die would be for someone to unmake him. The thought of having his muscles tear away from his bones as his cells popped out of existence one by one would have made his heart race, if it were ready to beat again. It was a long-kept secret of the Val, a spell known only to a select few, and able to be wielded by even fewer.

Shaking hands tore at him, searching for the secret pockets where he held his daggers. He thought of all the ways he would tease her, if he could, for robbing him blind. He willed her to look closer at him, to see that his neck wasn't twisted an impossible way, that the burns on his thighs were now surely just angry patches of skin. He knew she wouldn't look at his injuries any more beyond confirmation of his death. He could already feel her walking away from him.

Wait! He wanted to yell. *I'm still here, Princess.*

He was trapped inside himself, at the mercy of his healing body and the forces of fate.

The connection the Elders had put in place as her protector was still there and he felt her fade away as the minutes went on. The blast from Darroc had taken away everything in the clearing, including the light from the moon and stars. He was grateful, at least, that he would find her quickly. Finally, his vision returned, though if he had been human, he still would have felt blinded.

But thankfully he wasn't human, he was Val—a race of people created by the Fae millennia ago to be protectors of their elven children. He used to be Prince and sole heir of their race—a mighty soldier—and would have been king, if everyone were not wiped out after the Great War. Now, with him the last of his kind and the Fae virtually non-existent, the Elders had seen to it to give him the status of protector to the Elven Royal Bloodline.

It was absolutely forbidden to fall in love with a charge or to have any relations at all. But when it came time to protect Faria, he felt something he had not in years. He felt a kindred spirit, both chosen ones in their own way, both the only ones of their kind, both knowing what it felt like to be trapped in a cage of expectations and responsibility, when they wanted to be anything more than what they were destined to be.

For months, he did what he could to hold his feelings at bay. He knew the role Faria would play in saving not just her race, but all who lived in Anestra. He knew the bigger picture, of how the human realm would be involved, how the humans would eventually depend on her to do her part. He couldn't jeopardize his position and more than anything, he couldn't begin to try to change fate.

But the Fates had another plan, one no one could have foreseen when They encouraged him and Faria to be together, when they cleared the path for them to be unable to deny each other, to finally lay together as lovers.

It was then that he knew they were mates. He felt the cord of his connection to her settle deep within his bones, as if it were written within his soul, and perhaps it was. He hadn't known, or hadn't remembered any Val mated with elves, but surely that's what it must have been. But the

Elders had forced him away to the human realm. They didn't know what had happened. They couldn't see it and he was grateful for that. It would have been his unmaking day for sure. But they knew it was something. The entire realm heard the gong of fate play and fade out.

He needed to catch up to Faria. He had to let her know he was still alive and would do what it took to protect Anestra. He still wore his heavy armor and though his skin had healed, the armor had seen better days. He thought about removing it so he could run quicker but still didn't know what he might run into. The pull of his protector's bond led him in the direction of the Gate. He willed his body to heal quicker so he could see her before she left this realm.

A twitch in his leg was good enough indication that his body was ready for him to move. Gingerly, Hunter rose, slowly stretching his new muscles, careful not to irritate his fresh skin. He rolled his neck, getting used to the ability to move again. He needed to get to Faria as fast as possible and do whatever it took to save their son.

An incessant buzzing noise rattled his eardrums. Irritated, he shook his head and did what he could to ignore the Elders. They must have felt him come back to life and didn't waste a moment before summoning him as if he were a dog. They used to be his guides, *his* protectors. Now they acted like gods, as if their word was law. He quickened his pace, coaxing his muscles to warm up so he could use the speed of his race to defy them and reach Faria. They would punish him but that didn't matter; they had punished him many times over the centuries and he survived. No, the only thing that mattered was getting to his family.

Finally, a sliver of moonlight penetrated the darkness, and he knew he had reached the edge of the blast zone. Crossing the threshold, he was overwhelmed by the frenzy of activity that assaulted his senses. Life in the forest was frantic. He heard wicked growls and hissing unlike any he had encountered before. He figured it must be a few hours until dawn, maybe later, but the terrified screams let him know most, if not all, the citizens in this area of Anestra were awake, fighting, and seemingly losing against whatever foul beasts were attacking them.

His return from the human realm with the memory of evil creatures he saw there. On Earth they were still months from being ready, but the snarls echoing in the forest were eerily similar. The screeches of those other worldly creatures sent a chill down his spine. Hunter knew that whatever Darroc had cultivated—whatever creations he'd once made and stowed away on Earth—would be used in the coming war.

When Hunter was sent to the human realm, he thought he was gone only a day or two at most, but if he had returned on the night of his son's birth, it meant he had been gone for months. He was supposed to tell the Elders what he discovered in the human realm, but then he had felt Faria's need for him as he stepped out of the Gate and, well. Then he died.

Was the war they were afraid of already here?

The pulsing ache from his body reforming and the Elders summoning him was almost too much to take. The compulsion would eventually force him painfully heed their call.

The King of Anestra expected him to defend *Mentage*, though he was not an official member of his army. The skills he possessed could help shape the course of battle, especially having trained all the Royal Guard. He paused, uncertain of what he should do, needing more time. He wanted to go after Faria, after his son, his *son*, goddesses above. He didn't know why he felt so torn; he was a father, something he never thought in all his centuries alive that he could ever be. What more did he need to think about?

He took two steps toward the Gate before his body squeezed, suffocating in the sudden darkness. He felt as though his insides would explode, that his head might shear from his body. Then, he was thrown to the ground.

Sputtering a breath, Hunter glanced up and saw through watery eyes a fire and seven hooded figures standing around it, and him. The sand burned beneath him, smelled the mixture of ocean air and burning driftwood, and beyond the flickering light, a cavern of darkness. He knew immediately that he had been transported to the Forbidden Continent, a faraway land across the Sea of Aurelia where the Elders had secretly resided for almost two thousand years.

The ocean waves crashed against the surf and competed with the sound of beechwood crackling in the fire before him, its loud pops echoing off the cavern just beyond the flames. A drugging incense permeated the air, putting a stay on any magical abilities he might have recovered from his recent death. Fear rushed through his veins and all thoughts of getting to Faria or saving *Mentage* flew out of his head.

The Elders surrounded him, their power keeping him on bended knee. Incensed, he tried to fight their compulsion. To his surprise, he felt his leg shift, something he never had been able to do before, but their magical grip was too strong. How dare they trap him here, when his life and his love were in the grasp of the evilest creature he had ever known?

Hunter opened his mouth to speak but was immediately silenced.

"We know, *princeling*," one of the Elders said. He tried and failed to recognize their cold, punishing voice. "We know that which we couldn't see before."

Hunter felt his newly beating heart stutter as his breathing quickened. The only thing he knew the Elders were unaware of was exactly how far his relationship with Faria had gone. For beings who acted as gods, they were surprisingly left in the dark. It seemed that the gods—the real gods—had given him a reprieve, though that time seemed to have come to an end.

"I don't know what you mean," he lied. He did know. He knew exactly what they meant.

"We saw nothing, for a time," another voice hissed from the shadows of the flames. "The world went dark last year. It was so empty, the strings of fate that wove around you, not even our gods would enlighten us. At first, we thought perhaps someone had ended you for good but then we heard the gong of the Fates. We knew something had been done to change that which had been foretold for centuries."

He tried to pay attention to what the Elder said, but his thoughts snagged on something else. They expected their gods to control or intervene with the Fates' design?

"So we sent you on a mission to the human realm, to get you away from the princess," another Elder continued. "Until we could figure out what you had done with Faria. Until we knew if she still required your protection, or if it was you that she needed protection from."

Rage surged through him at the implication. He tried and failed to rise from his knees. The magic of their gods kept him tied to the ground.

"I would never harm her," he said through clenched teeth.

"Wouldn't you?" Another Elder spoke up. "You were forbidden to interfere. You were supposed to keep her safe." The fire in front of him suddenly blazed, sending sparks into the air. Hunter held up an arm to shield his eyes then stared horrified at the image that appeared before him.

Faria, fighting for her life among trees that looked the same as those he had left only hours ago. She must have been in the human realm, then. Thank the goddesses for small miracles. Horrible monsters attacked her and her face was splattered with blood and gore. The image changed to one of *Mentage* under attack by the same beasts, then of a boy, with a white bow and arrow, hate in his green eyes and a clawed hand gripping his shoulder.

Hunter panicked. He didn't know if what he saw was the present or future, or even if it was set in stone, but it didn't matter. "I must go to her," he said. "Release me."

A collective hiss erupted from the circle around him. "You do not command us! You have disobeyed beyond comprehension. You did that which was not allowed. You sired her child and changed the course of fate."

Pain seared down his neck, his vision blurring. He needed to get them to see reason before they decided to take his torture to a level that could not be undone.

"You should have told me more!" he shouted. "I did not bear a child in all my thousand years as a protector, nor as a Val Prince." He didn't want to press his luck, knowing the precarious situation he was in, but Fates be damned. He had the goddess-blessed blood of the Fae running through his veins and he would not let these creatures control him anymore. "I will go. I have to protect her. Them. All of them."

"No."

The word chilled him, the finality of it ringing through his ears, but he would not let it deter him. He bared his teeth at them. "You can punish me all you want, but there is nothing you can do that will stop me from going to Faria."

A drum sounded in the night and Hunter felt a sharp pain rip through his abdomen. He panicked and a cold sweat broke across his forehead. The drum sounded again and he felt something crack near his wrist. The figures stepped closer as one, the firelight casting sinister shadows where their faces should have been. He peered at the one closest to him and with his sharpened eyesight recognized Jacobi—Jacobi, who was like a father to him—scowling down at him with no sign of remorse.

It couldn't be. But another drum beat paired with the pain of fire that seared through his head, and a faint chanting rose from the Elders. His worst fears were becoming realized. There was nothing else it could be.

The Elders, the ones meant to protect him, allegedly appointed to him by the gods themselves, were now unmaking the last surviving Val.

TWO

NELLIE

There were few times in her life when Nellie Glazer had been struck with pure, abject terror.

Like the time she and her mother were on a cross-country road trip, traveling Route 66 and their car broke down somewhere in the vicinity of Kansas. A group of bikers decided it would be fun to harass a young single mother while her child watched. Mother took care of them quickly, hiding their bodies miles into the desert.

Then there was the time, later that same trip, when they had finally reached California. Nellie had thrown herself into the ocean at Santa Monica Pier, the sound of laughter and music filling the air as carnival games whirled nearby, and the intoxicating scent of sweet fried food rumbling her starving stomach. She had never been in the Pacific before and she was eager to jump in, to feel the salt in her hair and the current run between her toes. But the undertow quickly grabbed Nellie and yanked her under, barely allowing her to release a strangled cry before her lungs began to fill with salt water, its abrasive nature forcing its way down her throat. Nellie nearly received a thrashing after her mother was forced to shift form underwater to save her life, though they couldn't risk the locals seeing what she was.

And the time she had found her mother murdered. Her ripped throat. Her missing heart. Her blood soaking the ground.

Nellie shuddered, suppressing the images deep into the recesses of her mind.

Now, standing in the shadow of darkness in the human realm, fear once again smothered her. A blanket of stars twinkled overhead, a silent witness to her impending death. Her former clan—her adoptive family in all their beautiful and terrible forms—surrounded her, weapons at the ready. The Gate of All Realms shocked the area into silence once its grating humming ceased, leaving Nellie to hear every throbbing beat as her heart sped up in unadulterated fear.

"What's going on, Nellie?" A voice whispered, startling her from her defensive position. She'd nearly forgotten that Faria Agostonna, Queen of Anestra, stood beside her and that they had a critical mission: find Ander. "Where are we?"

Nellie scanned the eyes of the beasts and humans before her. Her banishment meant a murder sentence for her if she ever returned here. A confrontation was inevitable.

"Earth. We are in the human realm. On Earth."

As if her voice broke some kind of spell, a horn trilled off in the distance and a drum beat steadily. None other than her former clan leader, Garret—the very same who had banished her all those years ago—pushed his way to the front of the line. She almost rolled her eyes at the dramatics, and would have, if she didn't feel as though she would pee herself at any moment. She was dressed in her elven suit of armor, further marking her as different from what stood before her. She could still change into any beast she needed to, and she could still fight, but Faria…not only was she a mere shell of herself at the moment, but Nellie doubted whether Faria could access her powers on Earth. It was Nellie's sworn duty to protect her best friend, her queen, now. It was the only thing that kept her feet planted firmly on the ground as she forced herself into a relaxed, unassuming stance, trying to ignore the weapons and beasts surrounding her.

"Nellie Glazer," Garrett's gruff voice rang out, putting his authority as clan leader into her name. "You do not belong here. You were banished. And yet, you thought to return. The punishment is death."

A flutter of activity at his proclamation filled the air with various growls and squawks. Nellie kept her face blank as she casually searched the crowd for anyone she might recognize. She needed someone on her side before it became violent. Faria stiffened next to her, and Nellie brushed her shoulder against Faria's lightly as a signal to stay quiet.

Nellie sucked in a breath as her eyes fell on Thomas Selwyk— Tommy, to her—her former mate. Nearly six feet tall, he stood shirtless, with scars she had never seen before running along his arms and chest. They looked old, as if they had been there for years, and she wondered briefly how he could change so much. She had last seen him when they were seventeen, and nearly six years had passed. He was in his twenties, then. Her heart gave a twist at how much she had missed. She pleaded with her eyes for him to do something, to say something to intervene. She knew the mate bond wasn't there anymore for either of them, but she hoped some sense of loyalty remained.

He glanced down at the wolf crouched in front of him, then back at her, slowly raising his bow. Devastation filled her. She didn't think he would shoot her, but she knew where his devotion lay, and it wasn't with her. The wolf in front of him growled and bared her teeth. Its protective stance brought a sour taste to Nellie's mouth. Tommy had found a new mate.

"Tie them up!" Garrett's gravelly voice dripped with hatred.

Hands grabbed at Nellie's arms and body, trying to disarm her of her elven weapons.

She kicked into action. Though it hurt more than it should, they weren't her family anymore. The years she spent pining after her life and her former mate were wasted on creatures filled with hatred. Faria was her family now and she needed to get her out of danger so they could find Ander.

Nellie whipped her elbow at the nose of the shifter closest to her, smiling with satisfaction at the crunching sound that accompanied it. She punched another in the gut before someone grabbed her from behind. She stomped on their instep and tore away once their grip loosened. A quick glance told her that Faria was holding her own against three shifters. She looked like a mighty warrior queen, unwilling to succumb to her assailants.

A blow from someone's fist threw Nellie's head back, and a spurt of blood gushed from her nose. "Son of a fluffing kitten. Are you *kidding* me?" she yelled as she rushed at her attacker and knocked him down. She could have shifted into anything she wanted but the attacker stayed in his human form, and it would have been dishonorable of her to shift if he hadn't. But that didn't mean she couldn't play dirty. She punched his ribs, his face, his sides, over again until hands ripped her away. She shrieked as a rope seared against her chest, pinning her arms.

Nearby, Faria snarled at the group that had overtaken her. "Stop."

The command was short, simple, and laced with power, ceasing all activity. Even Nellie stopped struggling at the sound of Faria's voice.

Garrett's mouth dropped as he looked at Faria with equal parts disgust and bewilderment. The hands that had tied her up fell away as if they were burned. Jaws dropped and a flutter of activity waved throughout the clan. Some fell on their knees, finally noticing and recognizing Faria for what she was. Nellie understood their reaction. Before her banishment, she thought elves and Fae were just legend, and it wasn't until she appeared on their land after going through the Gate of All Realms that she realized how little she actually knew about anything outside of Earth.

Garrett noticed some of his pack on their knees. "Stand up immediately," hissed at them through his teeth.

"We will speak," Faria said quietly, though each word was sharp as a knife's edge, cutting them down to size. "As if we were *all* civilized creatures." She spoke eloquently and confidently, not as though she were trussed up, though Nellie could feel and hear her grief behind each word she uttered. "We did not choose to come here. The Gate brought us here. We seek something—someone—extremely valuable to my people. It is a matter of life or death. I must speak to all who are in charge here, immediately."

"I am the only one in charge, and I decide when I am spoken to." Garrett puffed his chest, his hand on his bow tightening as if he considered raising it against her.

Nellie bared her teeth at him. "You will show my queen respect."

Murmurs broke out; not only was an elf in their midst, but a queen. Others stared at Nellie, bewildered at her violent reaction. She ignored them. Maybe once she'd been more amenable, more eager to be liked. But she wasn't the same girl as when she left. That Nellie did die, exactly the way they intended. This one wouldn't take crap from anyone.

Tommy stepped around the wolf crouched in front of him, lowering his bow. "There are several whom the clan looks to in decision making." He gave a pointed glare in Garrett's direction. "We can gather at the main cabin."

A chill wind swept through the darkness, and though she didn't shiver, it sent an urgent unease through Nellie. She turned as gracefully as she could while tied up without falling over, and Faria followed closely behind her, trailed by those who dared to bind her. She gave them a haughty glare but continued, unaware or perhaps uncaring of the dangers that lied behind her.

Though, perhaps when one faced the worst terror across the

realms, "dangerous" was a matter of perspective.

Nellie knew where they were headed. If memory the Earth Clan's territory served, the main cabin was only about a half mile away. Nellie used the time to think of how they were going to get out of this situation. They needed to find Ander, and fast. Earth was huge, and just because they were deposited at the Gate in her former clan's territory, didn't mean that Darroc and Ander were there. Or that they were on Earth at all. They might have been brought there for an entirely different reason, but she really didn't want to believe that. She had to hold on to the hope that everything would soon get back on track.

Getting back on track also meant explaining to Faria why everything had gone wrong between them. Nellie didn't know how Faria would ever forgive her for lying to her all those years, or for their blow-out fight, or for disappearing in the months that Faria had needed her the most. Once they were as close as sisters, and now they were little more than a queen and her protector. Regret curdled Nellie's stomach. She knew she had to listen to Queen Amira when she was ordered not to reveal herself during those long months that Faria suffered through a pregnancy and marriage she didn't want, but for once, she wished she hadn't listened. There was so much hurt between them, and now they were stuck on Earth for who knows how long while Anestra was under attack or worse. That they had no communication to the other side made their strained situation nearly unbearable.

They traipsed through a copse of trees and approached a ramshackle cabin, its warped, moldy wood peeling off the sides. The roof looked like it wouldn't endure even the lightest of storms. Nellie remembered this cabin. She recognized this area of the woods as a campground her clan would rent in the summers, so that they could spend time together as a family, rather than living separately the whole year. None of what she remembered seemed right. It all felt off, diseased, and most certainly aged.

The door creaked open as they walked up a few rickety steps and someone flicked a light on. Given the state of the campground, it was a wonder they still had electricity out here. Inside, the threadbare rug was moldy and ripped. It used to be green or maybe a dark blue, from what Nellie could remember, but was now brown.

Her eyes zeroed in on a man with delicious muscles and full tattoo sleeve on display who led Faria over to the fireplace. To keep an eye on her, of course. Nellie found it hard to look away and wondered if he was new to the clan because she certainly would have remembered someone like him.

Nellie reeled it in and was almost ashamed she allowed herself to be distracted. She focused her attention on Faria. She couldn't decipher the emotions that flickered across Faria's face. Fear? Grief? She wondered how her queen was taking it all in: the humans, the shapeshifters out of her elven bedtime stories. Nellie would often speak of human inventions like electricity and cars and technology, but she knew it was different to see it all in person. Faria turned around and Nellie scooched closer to her, as much as her captives would allow, watching as flickering shadows danced across the strangers in the dimly lit room.

Then Faria spoke.

THREE

FARIA

The fire ripped feelings of remorse, guilt, and longing from the very core of her body. Faria tried to bottle away any emotion other than what she needed to complete her task of vengeance and redemption. As she stared into the flames, she couldn't help but recall the events that led her here, to this moment, standing in a room full of strange smelling shifters, unable to trust anyone. Not even Nellie. Her heart clenched. The empty ache of where the *innulum* she had shared with her mother pulsated, as if taunting her and her pain. She had so many regrets, so many things she wished she knew before the late queen's time had come to an end.

But this was not the time for sadness. They needed to find Ander, and this delay incensed her. She swallowed down every warring emotion she felt as she looked around what appeared to be a common room in a ramshackle cabin. Stained paper peeled down the walls, and she was unable to tell what color the carpet originally was. The wood floors were all scratched up and worn through and a damp smell radiated throughout the house.

Colors seemed muted, even at night, everything a dull gray hue. Faria hated it here. This was Earth? This was what humans lived in? Why didn't more of them jump through the Gate of All Realms, as surely anything would be better than this? It infuriated her that they were not properly cared for and she vowed to do better by the humans in her care when she returned home.

She tried again in vain to call her power to her. It simmered beneath her skin, as if it, too, were agitated at being locked inside. Her head ached from the lack of food or water, from all the tears that had poured out of her, from the adrenaline that slowly trickled away. And there was so much noise beyond what lay in the forest. They must be near a village or town because in the distance she could just hear weird honking and screeching, a strange mumble of many voices. The smells were wrong. She just couldn't bear to think what else was out there, what other obstacles stood in her way besides this infuriating clan leader standing in front of her. Yet another person to tell her what she could or could not do.

But she was a queen now. No one told her what to do.

Nellie stood beside her, facing the clan leader that she assumed was responsible for her banishment. She almost wanted to thank him, for without that brutal punishment she never would have known the spitfire, but she knew it wouldn't be wise to give these people any indication what

Nellie meant to her. She had to figure out a way to escape from their clutches before they followed through on their murder threat. Faria hated the look of the clan leader, his cocky sneer, the way he seemed to look down on her. If they were back in Anestra, Faria would incinerate him with one glance. Try as she might, her powers didn't seem to work in this land. She felt it as a phantom limb, its well achingly empty. She longed to get this over with and find Ander so she could return home.

A man strode forward and Faria noticed Nellie flinch. He was tall with dark hair and blue eyes that reminded her of the color of the ocean surrounding Mercy Bay. He was not overly muscular but he seemed strong, and though he appeared only a few years older than her, his face was drawn and haggard. He held a rough-hewn bow loosely at his side, staring Nellie down with an unreadable expression on his face. Faria wondered if there was history between them. In all the stories she'd been told as a child, shifters always found mates. Of course, she hadn't known shifters were real at the time, and now she wondered if that were true. Was that who he was to Nellie? It was a hard thought to reconcile. To her, Nellie was still a sassy thirteen-year-old, not this stranger standing next to her. The only person she had left.

The pain in her heart radiated as she thought of Hunter. His death was because of her. Just as her mother had died because of her. Just as her people were dying because of her.

She needed to get out of this place. She was drowning. It was too much, too soon.

A log popped in the fire behind her and for a moment Faria was back in the Forest of the Dawn under attack by Darroc's dark magic. She had the urge to flinch, but she would not show any fear or weakness in front of these people. The clan members who had followed them into the cabin shifted from foot to foot, as if unsure of how to feel about their uninvited guests. Faria took in their ragged clothing, the exhaustion etched on their faces. Few looked at her curiously, though, and she suspected they weren't as apt to kill her and Nellie as their idiot leader seemed to be.

The clan leader pushed through to stand before the girls, angry spittle forming on his mouth. "This is my home, my land that you're invading. And you dare to take my people into a room and fill their heads with what? Lies?" The clan leader looked at Nellie. "Not that I'm surprised, given your company."

"Enough. You will not speak like that to one of my own."

His chest inflated as he made to interrupt her but she held up her hand. She thought back on the history of the human lands and everything Nellie had told her about Earth. There had to be something she could connect with him on.

"I do not have time for your petty drama or reasons on why you think we are invading land you do not own and was not gifted to you. If I recall correctly, humans stole this land from others long ago. But that is neither here nor there. There is an enemy on your Earth and it is not me."

"There's more than one enemy," someone murmured with a few chuckles in reply. "No one likes us."

"I am talking of an evil being. A warlock. His name is Darroc L'Azare and we have reason to believe he is here along with a child he stole from my people." She thought it best not to tell them the child was hers. She didn't want to give them any leverage over her. "He's only a baby. A newborn.

Golden skin. Deep green eyes." She swallowed the lump in her throat threatening to choke her.

"What makes you think he's here?" Nellie's maybe-mate asked.

"The Gate would not have led me here if he were not."

The leader, Garrett, she thought his name was, scoffed. "How do you expect us to know your warlock? Do you know how many people there are in this country? In the world?"

"He looks like a man. Tall. Dark hair. Darker skin with purple eyes. You would know if you had seen him. Are purple eyes a common trait on Earth?" She stared each of them down, swallowing a huff of breath. Patience. She had to practice patience. The group collectively shook their heads.

"I'm sorry," Nellie's maybe-mate said. "I think I speak for everyone when I say that we have not seen a man with purple eyes with a child. We've had enough going on here but certainly would have noticed that."

Nellie spoke up, then. "What's happening? Last time I was here… this place didn't look like this. It was lively and well cared for. And we all marathoned Game of Thrones on this TV. How could this happen in just a few years?" She gestured to the room as a whole.

"Nothing is as it was."

"That's enough, Thomas," Garrett growled. A quick glance at the clan leader let Faria know that he wished Nellie's maybe-mate would stop speaking.

The young man—Thomas—ignored the interruption, his eyes fixed on Nellie. "There is something going on this year. A wasting disease killing shapeshifters. Some humans have even been affected."

"A wasting disease?" Nellie asked. "But we don't get sick."

"This is something else, something more complex. It takes away our ability to shift, like it's feeding off the essence of our magic. We don't know we're sick until it happens. And after our magic is gone, it continues to feed off us until there is nothing left." He paused and Faria's jaw dropped, dismayed at the reality the people of Earth faced. She couldn't imagine something she couldn't see or defend against feeding on her powers. "And it has been a tough year otherwise. The economy crashing, businesses closing, protests. Not to mention all the effects of climate change."

"Sorry," Faria cut in. "I don't mean to interrupt, but we really don't have time to talk about your issues with the economy. If you cannot help us then Nellie and I must find someone who can. We cannot delay. At the risk of sounding melodramatic, the fate of the world is at stake."

"That's what I mean. It is for us, too." He picked up a rectangular device that seemed to be made of some special plastic and aimed it at a metal box on the wall. "Look at what's happening."

The smooth flat surface on the front of the box suddenly changed with flashing images. They looked much like her visions did in her head. Was this someone's vision? Someone's prophecy? If so, how could they all see it? There was so much noise, so much flickering light, so many images filled with things Faria had never seen before. An ocean in flames, protests, large insects devouring entire farms, fire tornados, bodies in mass graves, terrifying weapons she didn't have a name for.

This was the human realm? No wonder her parents had never let her travel to the other realms. It was too dangerous. Her overwhelming homesickness for Anestra threatened to undo her. But not yet. She could still get more information from these people. Faria glanced at Nellie's horrified face. What must it be like for her to return home, only to find it in such disrepair, ready to rip apart at the seams? Hot tears prickled Faria's eyes, but she refused to let them fall. Instead, she relished the burn. If she went home to nothing but destruction, she would have to take care of it.

"Do you see what you stumbled into?" Garrett said. "We have more important things to worry about than this warlock of yours."

Faria took a deep breath to control the rising need to set this person on fire. Not that she would be able to anyway, but still, she could still put him in his place. Whether she was tied up or not didn't matter. She could have loosened herself from her bindings if she wanted to. And now she really wanted to. She was done playing nice.

"If you could stop it, would you?" Faria asked in a low voice, anger emanating from her every word. "If you could cure the disease, heal the earth, if you had the means to save your home, you would do anything, would you not?"

Garret crossed his arms. "Of course I would. But I can't and neither can you."

"No, I cannot save your home, but I know how to save mine. And I will do whatever it takes to make it happen."

With a flick of her wrists, the ropes that held her fell to the ground. The clan leader rushed forward as if to grab her. She smirked at him and planted her feet on the ground, ready to take the impact of the hit. But before that could happen, they were interrupted by a door slamming open as an enraged screech filled the room.

An irate half-naked female stomped in the crowded space, pushing shifters aside until she could point a crude bow and arrow at Nellie. It was all Faria could do to not roll her eyes at the interruption.

"You traitorous bitch!" The newcomer screamed. She made a move toward Nellie, but Thomas held her back. "You murderer!"

Faria raised her eyebrows. She would love to hear the story behind that, because as far as she knew, Nellie wouldn't hurt a fly.

"How dare you think to return here! You deserve nothing but death."

Faria couldn't take it anymore. She had had enough of everyone's misplaced emotions, of pandering to the needs of other beings. She stepped in front of the arrow, ignoring Nellie's command to step out of the line of fire.

"I do not know what your issue is, nor do I care," Faria's voice barely overshadowed the woman's, but she quieted all the same. She had her mother to thank for her commanding tone, she knew that. She had her mother to thank for so much more than she ever realized and the pain of it seeped into the dark chasms inside her. "Nellie was already punished by you. She could have ended up anywhere when she went through the Gate. She is now one of mine. My family. My subject. A citizen of Anestra. She no longer belongs to your Earth and does not need to follow your outlandish and barbaric rules."

Out of the corner of Faria's eye, Nellie stood taller and gave a small smile. Faria found that she couldn't look at her friend for long, though. She still had not accepted all the lies and secrecy.

"Enough." The clan leader tried to take back the control. As if he could overshadow a queen. "I have allowed your insolence for long enough. You have no say here. We owe nothing to you. We won't help you." He turned to leave. "Tie the elf back up and grab Nellie."

No one moved for a moment and Faria felt a quick sense of satisfaction that they hesitated to follow his orders, though she did notice that several gripped their weapons tighter. She raised her chin, daring anyone to be brave enough to make a move against her. She wanted nothing more in that moment than to incinerate every one of them. The thought turned her blood to ice. Never had she felt so unapologetically violent before, and she wondered whether the potion Darroc had fed her nearly a year ago her hadn't somehow planted the evil seed he once hoped would nestle into her.

"I will go willingly, my queen," Nellie said from behind her. Faria hesitated. It was Nellie's choice whether or not she wanted to be thrown to these wolves. Nellie bent close to Faria's ear. "I will find the answers we seek. Please don't do anything without me." Several hands reached for Nellie, dragging her out of the room.

Thomas blocked Faria as she made an unbidden attempt to follow. "You have said your piece, but you are still in our territory. You need to let us do what we need to do."

"How can you? How can you treat her so unfairly? She didn't ask to leave or to return."

"I don't know this person. She isn't my Nellie anymore."

Hmm, sounds familiar.

"The bond broke when she went through the Gate. It felt as if she had died, so I mourned her and moved on. I have another mate now. I'm sorry, but I have to do what is best for the clan."

Hm, so the lore back home wasn't entirely accurate. They could find new mates as other species could. Shifters filed out of the room now that the excitement was over, but the furious woman stood her ground, staring daggers at Faria. She nodded her head in the woman's direction. "Your new mate, is she that shrieking madwoman?"

His mouth drew in a straight line and said, "You may call me Thomas," before he turned away and closed the door. Faria was alone in the dampened room, with the strange box still flashing horrible images, causing light and shadow to flicker along the walls. A log snapped in the hearth, as if the fire taunted her into action. To access her abilities. To do something great. To live up to the expectations of her people. To not surrender to these strange creatures.

She pressed her back to the wall and slid down until she collapsed in a pile on the floor and finally gave in to the sinking grief that had threatened to overwhelm her all night, tearing open the cracks she barely held together. The kernel of darkness embraced her as closely as her lost lover and she finally cried.

FOUR

NELLIE

The Fates-forsaken room was freezing and the air felt thick with moisture. A single light bulb dangled from the long-broken ceiling fan, the propellers hanging limp and forgotten. There was no evidence of the creature comforts of a former life; no rug, nothing on the walls, and no furniture save for a single chair in the corner. Apparently, this was some kind of holding room, one that hadn't been there when Nellie last stepped foot in that cabin.

Time passed. She paced in circles in the dark. She tried failed to open the locked door. It was impossible with her arms bound at her sides as they were. She considered turning into some manner of creature that would allow her to leave, but she knew that wouldn't earn the trust of her former clan.

After she was well and truly annoyed, the door creaked open and a sliver of light from the hallway turned the person who stood in the doorway to shadow.

A whisp of a woman walked in. She smelled of fresh fruit, a welcome change from the mold Nellie had been breathing in. The woman closed the door behind her and walked closer to the stream of light, her brown hair making her already pale face even lighter. Large round eyes met Nellie's, and for a moment it was all Nellie could do to not gasp with disbelief. She stared at her former best friend from another life, someone she never thought she would see again. Callie.

"Wha-what are you doing here?" Nellie breathed, allowing her friend to engulf her in a hug. Strong arms tightened around her shoulders. Nellie breathed in the smell of strawberries and cream, the lotion they used to be obsessed with when they were kids.

"Nellie, what are *you* doing here? How are you alive?" her friend whispered back at her, careful to keep her voice low. "No one here knows how I know you," she said in explanation.

"Why are you here? It's been what, at least ten years since I last saw you?" Nellie said, quickly doing the math in her head.

"I've only just arrived the other day. There is so much to tell you, but we haven't got a lot of time. I've asked Tommy to let me speak with you. He isn't as harsh as Garrett."

She scoffed at that. "I would think not."

"Anyways, I've been looking for you for years and by the time word got back to me that you were gone, I didn't know what else to do. Something didn't feel right so I made my way here, and only just arrived the other day and here you are. It's fate."

"Is that right?" Nellie hated the thought of the Fates almost as much as Faria did, and while she was glad to see her friend again, she couldn't make sense of what Callie was saying. Nellie eyed her friend, wondering if the feeling she had was her intuition at work. Callie was one of the rare humans with a true psychic talent: visions of the future. She'd had them since they were kids, and when Nellie saw her last, she was just starting to hone her ability. "So, fill me in, quick! Last time I was here, Jon Snow won the Battle of the Bastards and life was…different? Now I feel like I landed in some kind of upside-down world."

"We don't have time to discuss pop culture, but that episode was just about the last good one of the series. You're better off not knowing what happened." Callie smiled at her. "Seriously though, the world is turning to ruin. There has been a lot of talk from all the spiritual leaders of the world that the apocalypse has started, and I didn't believe it until about a year ago."

"What happened? Is it because of everything I just saw on the news?"

"There are so many bad things happening at once. There's only so much you can blame on climate change. Plus, this wasting disease that's going around…it's strange."

"Tell me more about it. Shifters are losing their magic?"

Callie shuffled on her feet and twisted her hair around her hand. Anxious eyes looked back at Nellie as she said, "It isn't only that shifters are affected by it. It's that it *started* with the shifters and has since mutated and is killing humans now. We're approaching thousands of deaths, and it's all the shifters' fault!"

Nellie gasped. "What? How can that be?" She tried pacing the room but stopped as the rope pulled at her sides. Callie noticed her wince, then moved to untie her. "Stop! I don't want to get you in trouble."

Callie rolled her eyes. "Tommy is gonna come in here soon to untie you anyway, and plus they don't scare me."

"Why not? You're just a human. They could hurt you and I couldn't stand it if I were the cause."

Callie put her hand on her hip. "I'm twenty-two years old and a grown ass woman. They can try to hurt me if they want to, but I do have some tricks up my sleeve if you recall." Nellie had to give her that. In addition to visions, Callie can speak to the souls of those gone into the Beyond. The process to do it was terrifying, to say the least. "Anyway, it's this wasting disease we all have to worry about." She swallowed hard, and Nellie braced herself for whatever new information she was about to learn. "I don't even know where to begin."

"Spit it out!" Nellie said after a minute. "Jeez Louise, don't keep me in suspense."

"Okay," Callie sighed. "It took me a while to find your clan. I was guided toward the one in the south."

"The Fire Clan?" Nellie asked, surprised. Each of the four clans in the US took after the elements: earth, air, fire, and water. The Air Clan all turned into creatures that could fly. The Earth Clan, the one she used to belong to, all changed to earth-bound creatures. The Water Clan were water shifters, and the Fire Clan were fire shifters—specifically dragons— which she was under the impression had died out.

"There were so few of them, maybe ten or so," Callie said. "I asked if they knew you or where to find you, but they were all so weak and looked malnourished. One of them directed me to their clan leader, who was in the worst shape out of all of them."

"What is it?" Nellie asked after Callie paused for a moment too long.

"I never knew a shifter to get sick, let alone as sick as he was. The room smelled of death. He had a high fever, could barely breathe, and was hallucinating. He kept saying, 'Not again, please, not again.' Then he would scream as if he were being tortured. No matter what I said or did, he wouldn't calm down. He tore his clothes off and just as that frenzy stopped, he died."

"That's weird, but I don't really see how that's apocalyptic. I mean, fire tornadoes and locusts are one thing. A disease? It could have just been bad luck."

"No, it wasn't luck at all. It was intentional. There was a mark on his stomach. An imprint. I don't know how to describe it, because I'd never seen anything like it. There was a handprint, and some symbols that looked as if they were burned through his flesh. And the skin around it was black and festered. It was unnatural, and certainly the work of something evil."

Nellie narrowed her eyes, her brain trying hard to process Callie's words. "Do you mean to say that someone intentionally set this sickness upon the shifters?"

"Whether it was meant to be punishment for just him, or for the whole clan, I don't know. What I do know is that the entire clan is gone, now. None are left. And I heard rumors that it had spread to shifters in other countries, and gifted humans like myself were a carrier for it. Humans are so much weaker than the shifters and are dying at an alarming rate. I'm positive it's all connected."

"But why would anyone do that? Surely there couldn't be a reason to justify so much death?" But as soon as Nellie said it, she thought of the result of any war. The only sure things were death and destruction, with little victory in between. Was this a strategic move? Could it have been Darroc, or did they have to worry about someone else?

"I don't know. I don't even know why I was guided to find you, when I hadn't been able to see you for years, but this feels important. Like you're involved, somehow. I just knew that I had to follow the Angels of Fate. They led me to you. I'm relieved to see you alive, but I'm worried for you, too."

Angels of Fate? As if the Fates needed their own protectors? Nellie shook her head. She needed more time with Callie. She wanted to share with her the truth of how they ended up in the human realm and who exactly Darroc was, but judging by the increase in footsteps she heard out in the hallway, she knew they'd be interrupted soon.

"How are you involved in anything, Callie? Why did you track me down? Is there something you aren't saying?"

The door burst open and Tommy entered, a severe look on his face. Try though she might, Nellie couldn't help but yearn for what was lost between them.

"I need to talk to Faria," she said before he could get a word in. "It is my duty to protect her."

"She has nothing to fear from us," Tommy's gentle voice rumbled. He glanced down at her loosened restraints and narrowed his eyes at Callie. "Did we give you permission to free our prisoner?"

"Prisoner?" Callie snorted. "You know as well as I do that Nellie could have shifted to release herself from her restraints if she wanted to. I'll catch you later, Nellie." Callie gave her a meaningful look before leaving her alone with Tommy.

The air felt charged with all the things left unsaid, all the ache that tumbled into the empty space between them. He looked her slowly up and down and she fought not to squirm beneath his scrutiny. It didn't feel like that of a lost lover, but rather that of one sizing up his enemy. She did the same to him. He was still annoyingly shirtless. The scars that marred his chest and arms looked like the result of a fight gone wrong. She wondered the story behind them. She wondered if he cared about her story, too.

"You can't come here and expect you and that elf to change our ways. As if we could drop everything to help you look for an alleged man with purple eyes. You have no idea what we are going through. A civil war is right on our doorstep."

Anger surged her veins. The nerve of him! "*That elf?*" was all she could think to say.

"You left!" he said, pointing a finger at her. She wanted to bite it off and spit it back in his face. "You left and you don't get to come back and decide what our people need to do as if you still belong here."

"In case you forgot," Nellie said through gritted teeth, "I didn't leave of my own choosing. In case you forgot, it was me walking to my *death* when I went through that gate. In case you forgot, I lost a mate, too, while you remained behind to find someone else. Did you even wait a day before replacing me?"

He looked affronted, but Nellie didn't let him get another word in. "I never wanted to leave you and for the past five years, while I was *hiding,* while I kept my identity a secret for fear of being persecuted like I was a

Salem Witch, I ached for you every day. So don't tell me that I don't have a say in anything. I never asked to come back. And just an FYI, we only want information you might have and we will leave as soon as we get it."

She turned away, intending to walk out the door but his hand gripped her arm, holding her in place. He closed the distance between them and she felt his eyes boring into her back. She inhaled his scent of woods and rain and was flushed with memories of him. The way his boyish locks used to hang loosely around his face. The way he laughed with his whole body as he clutched onto her arm, as if he could transfer his laughter into her. Now, his fingers were rough and calloused, and they tore her from her memories as he kept her rooted to the spot.

"We are on the cusp of a civil war, Nells. There are rumors about our origin and everyone is split about what to believe. That, paired with the disease that is killing us means that no one trusts each other anymore. The peace treaty between our clans is all but dissolved. You have no idea what we've been through." His breath tickled the whispers of hair along her neck. Tiny fissures in her chest cracked open. "You being here is bad timing, especially with you being…what you are. It will instill more fear and mistrust within our clan all over again."

Of course he had to mention the one thing that was different about her. The one thing that always kept her separate from everyone else. The thing that encouraged the vote to condemn her to the worst punishment a shifter could receive when they accused her of murdering her own mother.

She turned and stared at Tommy. Seconds passed as she searched for some recognition for the person she once knew. Nellie cursed whatever type of hell-demon that was in charge of her life. How could they put her in this position? How could they make her see all that she had missed, all that she could not have again?

Tommy broke away from her stare and brushed past her, leaving her in that holding room. As he lifted his arm to shut the door, Nellie finally saw something that made her stomach bottom out. Mate tattoos, the same pattern as the she-devil psychopath that had screamed for her execution. He had not only mated again, but to *her*.

A sob threatened to tear through her as her exhaustion and fear and heartbreak finally caught up to her. Nellie shook, silently releasing the energy that had been pent up since the moment Darroc destroyed the Forest of the Dawn and stole Ander. She gave herself only a minute to feel her grief before she straightened, then swallowed hard and cursed herself for caring so much about someone who wouldn't—couldn't—do the same for her.

Enough of this. We are on a mission, and heck if I'm just gonna sit around and wait for something to happen.

She tried the doorknob again and was relieved to find that Tommy had left it unlocked. She didn't know why, but she wouldn't question it. She was eager to find her queen and figure out what they would do, and figure out if an apocalypse across two realms was more than what they could handle in what precious little time they had.

to convince an Angel of Fate—protectors to gifted humans—to give him this information, and he needed it passed on before he was gone for good.

"It appears that some evolved so much that they turned into what we now know as shapeshifters." He groaned as another wave of agony crashed through him.

Whispers sprang up around him as the Elders spoke amongst each other. He could tell this information excited them, though he didn't know why.

"Are you saying he created shapeshifters?" Hunter cringed as he recognized Azeen's voice. Azeen took himself to be the leader of the Elders, and he was by far the cruelest. "They were hunted in Anestra for hundreds of years, much longer than any potential threat of a warlock takeover. There is no way that they were so evolved back then as they are now."

"I don't know." Hunter winced as he tried to stop the world from spinning as the pain made him too dizzy to see straight. "I was unable to extract more information. I was only there for perhaps a day before I returned."

"Why did you leave so quickly then?"

"To warn you of what was to come, to warn Anestra. To protect Faria." He didn't know why he was explaining himself to them. He almost hit his breaking point. "You must let me return to her. The time change, the different powers of the world, all will affect her abilities. I must protect her and save my son."

One Elder stepped up and addressed the others. Hunter recognized the voice belonging to Jacobi, the one who had guided him most since his entire race had gone extinct.

"There is something to consider, brothers," Jacobi said. A rumble of dissension went through the circle. They had no desire to hear anything other than what they wanted. "Perhaps the gods did not allow the Fates to tell us all that was to come and we should see how their vision for the future plays out. Perhaps he was meant to have a child with Faria. I daresay his mate mark is telling."

"My what?" His pulse ratcheted up a notch. Mate mark? He had been alive for over a thousand years, stuck in the body of a twenty-five-year-old human. Never had he thought…but his kind didn't get mate marks, did they? He couldn't be sure. It had been too long, the memories blurred in the shadows of the past.

"That lovely intricate design settling itself across your brow," Jacobi said, a smile in his voice, as if they were having a pleasant conversation over tea or mead.

"I will do anything you ask of me. Please, just let me go to her." He was disgusted with himself for begging, the very thing he just said he would never do again, but what did it matter? He was the last of his race. He was Prince of No One. They already stripped his flesh from his body, already suspended his life in the realm of the pain he was in. Who cared if they stripped him of what was left of his dignity?

Their fevered whispers reached a new pitch as they discussed it among themselves. Perhaps they didn't want to intervene with whatever design the Fates had laid out for him. "We will not unmake you, for now," Azeen said. "Disobey us again and we will not be so merciful."

"And," another named Sundi added, "you will prove to us that you will do anything we ask of you. You will not be protecting Faria but rather the home she needs to return to. We will send you to *Mentage*, otherwise it will be done for. Try to abandon them, and we will not hesitate to finish what we started here."

"You will never," Azeen said, stepping closer to the fire so Hunter could see the sneer dripping from his face, "be allowed alone with Faria again."

The ground rumbled beneath him before he felt the shift of time and place suck him into the void once again.

"Wait!"

He felt his body fling back from the sand before it collided with gore-soaked grass. His shout was lost amidst screams and battle cries as he appeared in the thick of chaos. All around him, beasts fought amongst appalling carnage, unlike anything he had seen in hundreds of years. The scent of putrid flesh and rotting blood assaulted him.

He was thankful to feel his body whole and unharmed, though livid once he realized the Elders had not replenished his energy. To fight against Darroc, then die, then to be partially unmade meant he had nothing left to give. He needed a hot meal and days of sleep to fully recover. It was as if he meant absolutely nothing to them, that they would risk him dying in battle again just because they knew he would return. He had to find a way out of their control.

A vicious snarl sounded from behind him. Hunter jumped to his feet as fast as he could and tried to summon a fireball, something that had taken him years to master, only to realize he wasn't in his Val body. He cursed the Elders for not allowing him that added protection and grabbed the nearest weapon off the ground.

The sword he snatched sliced through the belly of a rabid wolf, its poison spittle sizzling on the puddles of blood soaking the earth. He carved at the creature, and though blood spilled to the ground, it seemed otherwise unaffected. He slashed at the monster's belly, expecting it to be disemboweled, but nothing happened. It took Hunter a moment to realize the creature wouldn't die from a regular weapon. He spotted something glinting in the moonlight: a dagger protruding from a pile of gore, its rainbow sheen at odds with carnage. He tossed the wolf off him and jumped over a shredded body on the ground before landing with a squelch in the muck next to the dagger. He raised it without pause and stabbed the wolf just as it tried to latch onto Hunter's arm. The wolf let out a yelp of pain then shriveled, its blackened shell of a body falling on top of the countless other corpses already littering the ground.

Those fucking Elders. They thought to leave him defenseless, in the thick of battle, with no energy or access to his magic. He cursed them again, along with Darroc, the Fates, and even Endo. Endo had been as much of a friend as Hunter ever had during his Protector assignments, and his betrayal still stung.

There was a break in his line of sight, and Hunter spotted King Dennison fighting a huge, rabid bear. The king just barely kept the beast at bay as it tried to maul him in a storm of spittle that sizzled where it landed on his armor. Hunter ran toward them, parrying an attack against a half-bear, half-human form, its deranged look reminding him of something out of a horror movie he'd seen on Earth.

"I'm so sorry, my king," he yelled over snarls and the clash of weapons. "I'm sorry for not getting here in time!"

"Hardly an hour has passed since Faria fled," the king said, barely winded. He was fierce, every bit the warrior Hunter knew him to be. He deflected an attack easily against a smaller creature. "Queen Amira is dead. The Guard are all fighting. Faline is as well, though I advised against it. All able-bodied people from Athinia are here, though I worry for their fate." Hunter and King Dennison synchronized their moves as they stood back-to-back, attacking any monster who came at them. "We must protect Anestra for Faria."

Hunter was surprised at the king's lack of emotion over the death of his love, but in that moment, Dennison was a soldier—there was no time for emotion, for any moment's hesitation could result in death.

Pools of blood and guts saturated the ground, and the complete darkness in the hours before dawn didn't help the humans who tried so hard to fight. It was in vain. They would all be dead before the night was over. There just weren't enough of them and the beasts were proving difficult to kill.

Hunter allowed all thoughts of Faria, of his son, of severing his ties from the Elders, to trickle out of his mind as he became the warrior Anestra needed him to be. *I am a ship on the sea. The crashing waves move for me.* He repeated the calming mantra with each inhale. With each exhale, he blocked out everything other than the fight at hand.

He might not be able to save Faria or Ander at that moment, but he could do whatever it took to protect her Queendom. Hunter attacked the next beast and then the next, praying for a miracle. They needed back up.

He knew, however, that the only back up was him.

SIX

NELLIE

The steady ticking of a clock somewhere in the cabin and random creaks of the wind against the rooftop kept Nellie company as she stood outside the door to the living room, wondering how she should approach Faria. She didn't know how to talk to someone who could barely look her in the eye.

She was thankful Tommy left the door open for her and really couldn't understand what the point in separating her and Faria was, other than it being some lame attempt at an intimidation tactic and wasting their time.

They would soon find out that once someone faced an evil creature like Darroc, it would take a lot more than being locked away in separate rooms to be intimidating.

Taking a deep breath, Nellie crossed the threshold, her eyes quickly falling to the person huddled in front of the fireplace. Faria sat on her knees, unmoving, staring into the flames. It was strange to see her so empty, so alone, when Nellie was used to seeing her full of life and curiosity about the world.

Grief manifested itself in many ways; in the shocked stillness of a quiet house, in the darkened torrent of words left unsaid, in the manic permanence of the empty echoes loved ones left behind. Faria had lost Hunter, her son, and her mother all in one night. And now she was queen—surely the fate of her people sat heavily upon her.

Approaching carefully so as not to startle her, Nellie sat down next to Faria and said, "Can we talk?"

The fire flickered in Faria's eyes, giving the impression that the flame blazed within her.

"Faria?" Nellie said again, waving her hand in front of Faria's glassy gaze.

Unsure of what to do but certain that Faria was in no immediate danger, Nellie decided to wait. It was nice to sit together, in almost companionable silence, like they used to do when they called each other sisters. Now they were strangers. The past year had severed what Nellie thought was an unbreakable bond. There had to be a way to mend the frayed edges between them.

Finally, Faria shuddered and shook her head.

"Oh, hey." She gave Nellie a cursory glance, then checked to see that they were alone. "Did they harm you?"

"No, they left me locked in a room. I think it was just a power play." She took note of the tear stains along Faria's cheeks. "Are you okay?"

The silence between them stretched. Nellie cleared her throat. "Listen,

I wanted to thank you for standing up for me. For claiming me as yours and not theirs."

"You are a citizen of my land. I would have done it for any of my people." The response was robotic, unfeeling.

A citizen. "You seemed like you were in a trance."

"Oh, just meditating." The way Faria glanced back into the flames let Nellie know that wasn't entirely the truth, but she let it go. Her queen continued, "We need to find Ander. We have been delayed long enough."

"Yeah…what I wouldn't give for a magical room behind the tapestry of the Val."

Faria's eyebrows scrunched. "What tapestry of the Val?"

"In your wing of *Mentage*. The one with the Val Prince and his… sacrifice…" She trailed off as Faria stiffened, and Nellie silently cursed herself. How could she bring up any reference to Hunter or his recent sacrifice at a time like this? *Stupid.*

"Anyways…" Nellie dragged the word out. "I can hear people outside the cabin. I don't think they're just going to let us walk away, especially not me."

"There are only eight people outside, hovering outside the windows and doors, judging by their footsteps. Idiots. As if they could stop us. You can shift into anything, right? I thought that's what I heard one of them say. They're scared of you. Do whatever it takes to leave."

Nellie's gut clenched at the thought. There was still a small part of her that cared about what they thought of her. She couldn't stand knowing that they feared and hated her. She still longed to be thought of as one of them. It was a foolish thought, one she would have to quickly rid herself of. "What about you?"

Faria smirked. "I still have all my elven abilities. I'm faster than them. I just don't know where I'm going or the rules of this land. I need you to come with me."

The words stung. *Am I only good as a navigation device now?*

"First chance we get, we're running."

"Actually, Faria, there's something—"

A scream tore through the quiet house. A flurry of activity sounded outside the cabin as shouts erupted and the metallic screech of weapons rang out. Nellie jumped to her feet, landing with a dagger in each hand, looking for the quickest way to get Faria to safety.

Faria was *smiling,* of all things. "Looks like the Fates agree with me." And with that, she leapt to her feet and sprinted out the door. They descended into chaos.

The entire camp area was in disarray. Shapeshifters—some in human form, others in their wolf, bear, or stag forms—ran in between several lit fires, grabbing weapons wherever they could. Shrieking, roaring, growling, and children crying echoed in the night. Shifters grabbed buckets to put out the fires. Tommy ushered the younger and less skilled fighters to safety, while others started to line up near the path toward the Gate.

Nellie felt torn between staying to help or following her queen's orders, but Faria had already escaped into the forest line.

Dang it! Nellie sprinted after her. Just as she made it onto a barely used path, she made eye contact with Garret. His face filled with rage and she smirked at him, giving him a little finger wave before catching up with Faria.

"What way?" Faria asked as Nellie fell in stride beside her.

"I'm not sure." Nellie didn't want to lead Faria toward any cities, especially not while they were both still dressed in armor and carrying weapons.

Nellie shifted her eyes to those of an owl so she could see better in the dark. The two of them sprinted through the forest over fallen trees, and through thick briars, along paths that hadn't been used in years. "I think we're reaching the edge of this campground," Nellie huffed. A whooshing sound followed by a loud snap crackled through the air as Faria lunged to the side; right above where she'd been, Nellie glimpsed the bright fletching of an arrow embedded in the tree closest to them.

"What in the world!" Nellie shouted. She turned around to see Garrett, nocking another arrow in his bow, and a giant bear sprinting after them. "Are you psychotic?!"

Nellie upped her pace. Nearby, Faria ran backwards with her own bow and arrow aimed at the bear charging toward her. "Do not make me shoot you," she threatened.

"Faria—"

In her distraction, Garrett tackled Nellie to the ground, his putrid breath huffing against her neck. "I didn't say you could leave."

"Get off of me," she said in a low voice. "You do not want to mess with me."

"I sent you to your death once. I can be sure it happens again. Permanently."

His knee dug into the center of her back as he yanked her arms behind her and bound her hands in…*iron cuffs?* What the heck kind of wacko carried iron cuffs? Nellie looked over at Faria. The bear held her down with its giant paw, its snout hanging dangerously close to her face.

She didn't want to do anything to provoke the bear, but Nellie cursed to herself and vowed to end that person's life for daring to treat her queen that way. *Ugh, back in the human realm for an hour and I'm already the murderous, bloodthirsty wench they tried making me out to be six years ago.*

"Get off of her before I turn into something with no morals that will eat you in a single bite," Nellie said through clenched teeth. Diplomacy be damned. She might have been insecure about what she really was, about the hatred and fear that poured off the clan, but she was two seconds away from decimating them all. She searched for the glimmer of magic that resided deep within her, but felt nothing but hollow emptiness. *What the heck?*

Garrett lifted her to her feet and pushed her back in the direction of the camp. "You really love to talk," he said in her ear. "But I'm going to play with you later."

The bear shifted away from Faria and she dusted herself off before picking her weapons back up. Faria glanced behind her then back at Nellie, as if she were contemplating abandoning her. She sent a scathing look to Garrett. "You have nothing better to do than abuse a person you claim is no longer tied to your clan? Uncuff her."

Garrett chuckled darkly. "Not a chance. She—"

"Quiet." Faria cut him off and tilted her ear back in the direction they had just run from. Whatever she heard sent a glimmer of recognition over her face. "Your people are going to be slaughtered," she said with a horrified look on her face. "You dare abandon them to that terrible fate just to capture us? Are you insane?"

Not waiting for an answer, Faria sprinted back toward camp and whatever fight the shifters were about to get into. Nellie looked at Garret's expressionless face. The bear whined next to them until Garrett finally clenched his teeth and said, "We shall return, then."

Garrett pushed Nellie into a run, which was difficult with her hands awkwardly tied behind her. Pain wrenched through her arms with every dip in the ground. She tried to shift, but the magic she usually felt brimming under her skin wasn't there. Her eyes were still those of an owl, but she couldn't change them back to human either. What archaic iron cuffs had the ability to render shifters useless? And why did Garrett carry them around?

Nellie racked her memory, trying to find an explanation. She remembered hearing about how the clans had an arsenal of old weapons and items to help keep a dangerous shifter at bay, but she'd never seen any before. Even when she was accused of murder, they hadn't used iron shackles to stop her use of magic.

Once they reached the edge of the encampment, the bear ran ahead of them, roaring. Garrett staved off to the left while Nellie ran right to the action. She needed to find Faria—or anyone who could remove her restraints.

A warning horn from a lookout sounded in the distance, one low steady note that seemed to prompt the camp into renewed frenzy.

The ground beneath her rumbled. Nellie shrieked as she lost her balance and the floor raced up to hit her, but strong hands grabbed onto her waist before she could eat dirt.

"What the hell are you doing?" Tommy yelled, dragging her to her feet.

"Help me out of this thing, will you?" Nellie asked quickly, glimpsing the chaos around them.

Tommy looked down at her wrists and hesitated.

"Um, now! I need to shift and I can't with this thing on me."

Tommy whipped out a ring of keys from his pocket and found the right one to unlock her cuffs.

"You just happen to carry around keys to this archaic piece of crap?" Nellie asked. "Were you in on him restraining me like this?"

Tommy rolled his eyes. "No, I had copies made a few years ago. He shouldn't have exclusive access to items like this."

A rush of magic flowed through her veins as her as the power heated her, and she swiftly shifted into an eagle. It was only for a few moments, but Nellie never wanted to feel powerless again. She could only imagine what that wasting disease felt like to the shifters who fell victim to it.

With one last glance at a worried-looking Tommy, she cawed and soared up into the night sky. Her wings ached, remnants of the pain from being bound, but all thought of her discomfort left her when she saw hordes of rabid looking beasts down below, who appeared to be accompanied by a flock of hawks.

Not hawks. *Shifters.* But why would the Air Clan attack them? Something about those beasts, the noises they made, seemed familiar to her, but her memory was fogged over.

She veered back toward the campsite and landed in front of Garrett, quickly shifting back to her human form. His eyes widened at her sudden appearance. "It's the Air Clan, along with a boat load of beasts. They're almost here."

"Like I would trust you," he sneered at her. "You probably set this up."

Nellie's jaw dropped. "Are you kidding me? You just shackled me with iron cuffs! When the hell would I have had time to organize an attack?" Nellie yelled back. "They're coming from the opposite direction. Hurry, tell people to fall in line over here."

"I also caught you running away."

Stupid, impossible, ungrateful, slimy, son of a— "Yeah, and you followed me, you psychotic wackadoo!"

"Enough!" Tommy broke in. "Now is really not the time. We need her," he said to Garrett. "We don't have enough people or resources."

"Whether we help or not is up to Queen Faria, and if we do help, then we will leave as soon as we are done here."

"Looks like your elf has already decided," Garrett said, his eyes narrowing on a spot over her shoulder.

Nellie followed his glare and saw Faria with her bow drawn, shooting arrows into the sky at the first crest of hawks that dove over the Earth Clan. She hit each target she aimed for, much to Nellie's dismay. The ear-piercing shrieks of the shifters rent the air as they fell, landing in their human forms.

"Stand down, Faria! They're shifters!" Nellie yelled as Faria circled around, calmer than anyone else. It was as if she needed this fight, as if she had something to prove. Nellie knew by one look at her that there was little chance Faria would stand down.

"There are more coming from the opposite way!" Nellie said, giving her attention back to Tommy. Garrett continued placing his people haphazardly in a line facing the wrong direction. If she didn't act, they'd lose this fight. "Please, Tommy. Tell him to change the lines."

He looked down at Nellie, concern rivaling anger on the sharp planes of his face. "Damn it!" he yelled. Turning away from her, he yelled to his clan mates. "Turn around. Form here! Dem, over here! Ranc, here!" Nellie recognized the hottie with tattoos as Tommy shoved the one named Dem in the area she had indicated. An unwanted rush of affection for Tommy flooded her. She swallowed it down and joined him, yelling at the females to join the males, to fill in the gaps. She called out formations, correcting the positioning Tommy put them in.

"No, to the left! Watch that flank!" Nellie let out an exasperated breath when no one listened to her directions. She glanced at Tommy for help, willing him to defend her in this.

He hesitated for only a moment. "You heard her, get to it!"

Grateful to feel useful and wanted for once, Nellie felt like she could somehow make up for the hatred her former clan felt towards her. She silently thanked the Fates that had led her to Anestra, a country that believed in equal training to all their citizens, and eventually the Elven Royal Guard, allowing her to learn from the best.

"Bows!" she yelled at them. To her surprise, the clan members listened to her that time.

Faria ran up to her. "Where do you want me?" she said, scanning the lines. It was hard to choose. No one save for a handful looked like they knew how to properly handle the few weapons they had. A young girl held up a thick branch as if it were a bat. A middle-aged man, who looked better suited for a corporate office than a battle in the middle of the woods, held a gun at the ready. Nellie shook her head.

"Nowhere. I need to protect you, Faria. You are my first priority. You should defend the others that are too weak to fight. I can find you after!"

"I am not abandoning them," Faria ground out.

Another horn sounded, this one trilling a lower beat than the other. It came from the direction of their enemies. Thick pine trees began to fall in front of them, and the ground rumbled as snapping branches cracked through the air. Around them, shapeshifters yelped and growled as they popped into their animal forms. A stag, a wolf and a bear formed a triangle of protection around the clan members who remained in their human forms.

This isn't enough, Nellie thought frantically. *Come on, think Nellie. Think.*

She turned in circles, pulling at her hair, wondering what they could possibly do. There were maybe twenty who were able to fight. She knew she couldn't leave Faria out. They didn't have the numbers to allow it. Cursing Garrett for not encouraging unity between clans, for not properly training his shifters in any sort of fighting technique, she did the only thing she could think to do.

A prickle of heat started at the base of her spine then spread upwards and outwards as she thought of the intricate details of a beast she'd once seen on a tapestry in *Mentage*, next to Faria's tapestry of the Val. Pain erupted between her shoulder blades as she felt her cartilage and bones expand and reform. Her lungs worked overtime as she warred with her brain, trying to breathe through the pain, though the temptation of passing out was almost too much to ignore. She grew taller, wider. A fire seared her belly as her vision turned sharper, clearer, as if someone had turned on stadium lights in the camp clearing. She landed on four legs, talons digging into the dirt as rows of sharp teeth ripped through her jaw. New muscles formed around large wings and she took a moment to flex them, getting used to the new sensation. It was by far the most painful transition she had ever made—one she didn't even know was possible until that moment. She felt powerful towering over everyone and ready to take on whatever hell was heading their way.

For where once a small twenty-two-year-old woman stood was now a gargantuan dragon, quadruple the size of the largest shapeshifter. Nellie tossed her head from side to side, making sure everyone was in proper formation, or as close to it as they could get.

She felt rather proud of herself when she saw frightened looks of wonder staring back at her. Even Faria's dropped jaw. After a second, Faria nodded her approval and turned toward the impending chaos.

Nellie stretched her wings and dug her talons in the ground, ready to see what kind of damage this beast form could do.

Then waves of monsters broke through the trees.

SEVEN

FARIA

Stark disbelief rippled through her as Nellie transformed into a *Drogosterra*—dragons of the Forbidden Continent. Val soldiers used to ride on their backs and use weapons dipped in their blood, imbuing them with magical properties. They had disappeared along with the Fae after the Vals' ultimate sacrifice during the Great War. Nellie's brilliant coat gleamed in the darkness, the scales catching the moon's light with every turn. Thin, black wings shot through with deep purple veins sprouted from between Nellie's shoulders. They expanded what must have been at least twelve feet, their thin webbing etched with beautiful designs. Her sharp teeth jutted fiercely from her jaw. The ground shook as a long tail with spikes at the end slammed into the ground. The hair on Faria's forehead whipped back as Nellie's new form huffed a hot breath in her direction.

Nellie took a talon and scraped it along her own front leg, letting a pool of blood well. She motioned to Faria with her head from her weapons to the blood. Faria quickly understood what Nellie wanted. She dipped her arrow in the blood and watched it seeped into the metal and turned to black. She did the same with two daggers and the rest of her quiver of arrows.

A low growl rumbled in Nellie's throat seconds before a hoard of monsters tore their way out of the trees. Fire blasted from her mouth, stopping the first wave from reaching them.

All around Faria, no one knew where to run; whatever ramshackle weapons they had were either lying on the ground or tossed about without care. It was clear these people had never been trained properly—or if they had, it hadn't stuck. Despite what Nellie did for them, the enemy was upon them within seconds.

Faria aimed her bow at the monsters. She felt badly for hurting so many shifters, even though she made sure not to hit anything vital. These creatures, however, wouldn't get any mercy.

Though it was yet another distraction from her finding her son, she was grateful for something to do, for a way to get all her repressed energy and anguish out. She squared her shoulders and released an arrow into the eye of a snarling wolf that had lunged straight toward her. And then another. And then another, unleashing her pent-up anger, anxiety, and grief onto those wretched monsters.

Never again. She slit the throat of another rabid wolf. *Never again will I hide or beg the Fates to rescue me. Never again will I wait to be saved or have someone fight for me.* Though she had no magic, she still had her natural elven abilities. In addition to her hearing, she had low light vision and she was an exceptionally skilled fighter. And it seemed her elven accuracy consistently worked.

Pity engulfed her as she took in the mangled face of her latest kill, at the broken teeth, the holes in the cheeks where the flesh rotted through. She looked at the deformed paws, the sores visible through patches of fur. A hissing sound drew her attention as she watched pus and blood hit the ground. She mourned the life of these creatures. No being should have to live like that.

Sounds of dying filled the space around her. She swallowed her bile and nocked an arrow, going after a rabid bear. And then another wolf. A stag. Anything that looked unnatural she aimed at. She needed to compartmentalize her feelings and get these people to safety. The sooner this was over with, the sooner she could go back to finding Ander.

Pained screams erupted from behind her and Faria whirled to find huge eagles and falcons swooping down to attack members of the Earth Clan behind her. The damage they dealt were evident by the bodies injured on the ground.

Beside her, Nellie chomped down on a wolf, crushing it, while Thomas had turned his attention to the birds. Something hiding in trees behind them caught Faria's eye: Garrett.

Useless, pathetic excuse of a leader. She would never understand how he was alpha enough to lead an entire pack of shapeshifters.

A bloodcurdling scream came from behind Faria. A rabid boar had clamped its jaw on a man's arm, and even as he—Faria thought Thomas called had him Ranc—swiped the throat of the beast with a dagger, the creature showed no sign of letting up. Past them, another monster feasted on a shifter, his bloodied axe laying on the ground next to him.

Horror filled her. Their weapons weren't working. *They needed Drogosterra blood.*

She dove on the beasts she had felled and collected her spent arrows before shooting them again and again at the monsters surrounding her. As if by magic—which she figured, it was—they dropped as soon as they were hit.

There was nothing she could do for the dead and injured except keep going.

The stench of pus, guts, and infected things quickly added to the air already tainted with blood and death. The sounds of the dying, the snarling of the creatures, and the blood-drenched ground were sure to add onto the nightmares she already suffered from the past few months. She just needed to end it, end the fight, end the battle, end this war before it truly began. She couldn't lose hope, though she felt it in her bones. They needed more weapons, more people. Whatever this was, if it wasn't Darroc, was sure to be a wrench in her plans to get Ander, not to mention whatever battles she would have to face once she returned home to Anestra. The ache of the empty well of magic that longed to fill her pressed against her skin, but she tried not to think about it. Tried not to listen to the screams. Tried not to feel the burn of her muscles. Tried not to feel anything at all as she poured her grief and agony into each attack on the onslaught that seemed to never end.

Just keep going. End this. End this all.

EIGHT

NELLIE

There were few things in life Nellie found more enjoyable than using her new body to tear down enemies. Dramatic? Yes, but she had felt so hopeless the past few days and finally, she could free herself from her human half and let the beast inside take over.

Glancing around, she smirked with some satisfaction at the creatures that were torn to pieces where she killed them. Faria managed to kill quite a few as well and from the looks of it she never left her place in the clearing; a perfect circle of dead monsters surrounded her.

Nellie was grateful that she'd remembered the display of weapons she saw once outside a shop in Athinia. She knew Val weapons were often dipped in the blood of a *Drogosterra*, and if it was good enough for the Val, then it had to be good enough for them. It was instinctual, to have Faria dip her weapons in her blood. It proved a theory she had—that she didn't just change her appearance when she shifted, but wholly transformed.

It was shortly before dawn. Bloodthirsty as she felt as a dragon, Nellie was relieved that the fight didn't last long. She felt like she had endless energy but her clan was in no shape to fight off those hell beasts.

The good feeling passed when she realized how few of the Earth Clan survived. Their numbers were insufficient to begin with, and each loss was felt tenfold. Off to the side, Garrett and Tommy tied up a few shifters from the Air Clan, ready to question them. Good.

It took a while for her to get used to the new vision she had as a *Drogosterra* now that the threat of battle was over. It felt as though she were looking through a crystal; each person and object had a series of colors flowing outward from them. Even the dead beasts had a tinge of black surrounding them. It was as if she could see people's energies or auras. She had no idea what the different colors meant and there was no one she could ask, but she made a mental note to pay attention to it if she ever had need to turn into a *Drogosterra* again.

Nellie watched Faria collect her arrows and clean the tainted weapons on the grass. Her queen glowed faintly with the lightest blue aura, different from the shifters who were gathering the injured and dead. The light around Faria pulsated like a heartbeat, and Nellie had the strangest feeling the light itself was alive. It was different than the soft green light coming from Tommy, or the yellow glow emanating from his mate, Samantha. No one else's light shifted the way Faria's did.

Seeing no reason to stay as a dragon now that the danger had passed, Nellie made the painful change back into her human form. Spots appeared before her eyes as they readjusted to being human, and she stretched her limbs, getting used to the lighter weight and density of her body. Once her vision cleared, she was shocked to see the glow still emanating from Faria.

"Hey," Nellie said, covering her nose as she walked over to Faria. Before she could say anything else, her stomach rolled and she vomited all the blood and guts of the monsters she'd eaten as a dragon. Retching over and over again, she leaned against the nearest tree, knees shaking, trying to get the incessant mouth sweats under control.

A water bottle landed at her feet. "Rinse your mouth out," Tommy said, then went away to check on his other clan members. It seemed as good a peace offering as any. Perhaps they could work themselves up to being at least friendly. At any rate, the surviving members of the Earth Clan no longer sneered at her or eyed her suspiciously. They could be allies, anyways.

Not that it mattered. Now that they were no longer in danger, it was time to grab Faria and get back to the search for Ander.

Nellie swished her mouth out then walked back over to where Faria stood beside a campfire. "That was seriously disgusting," she said as she sidled up to Faria's shoulder. "Never, ever, get that stuff in your mouth."

Faria gave her a sweeping glance and once she seemed to assess that Nellie was fine, turned on her heel. "Let's go find that horrible former clan leader of yours. Garret!"

Garrett lurked on the other side of the fire. "If you're expecting a thank you—"

"We're not." Faria held up her hand. "You will take us to whomever you managed to capture."

"Wait, what?" Nellie asked. There was no reason to prolong their time with the clan, whether they were still weakened or not. "What are you talking about? We need to leave."

"I will do no such thing," Garrett said, ignoring Nellie altogether. "This is a clan matter and as you and *her*," he glanced at Nellie, "are not one of us, you have no business—"

Faria turned her nose and walked away from him. Nellie almost laughed at the shock on Garrett's face, but she couldn't wrap her mind around Faria wanting to stay any longer than they had to. She followed Faria to the prisoner who was trussed up against a tree, black and green blood stained across his body. The carcass of one of the rabid wolf beasts sat festering next to him. The stench overwhelmed Nellie, upsetting her already fragile stomach. She could only imagine what Faria dealt with her enhanced senses, but the queen's face was stoic as ever.

"What are we doing, Faria?" Nellie whispered. "Why do you care what he has to say? Garrett was right, this really isn't our business."

Faria glared at her but Nellie didn't dare look away. The Earth Clan wasn't their problem anymore.

"Don't you think those foul creatures were a little odd?"

"Of course," Nellie said. "But from what Callie said, weird things have been happening on Earth. For all we know, this is what the wasting disease looks like. Monster zombies." A horrifying realization struck her. "Oh my *gods* I ate them! They have the sickness and I ate them and now I'm going to get sick and this is the end of me."

"No," Faria said. "This wasn't the wasting disease. They only died by your bite and my weapons which were enhanced by your blood. Evil creatures who could only die by magic? Sound familiar to you?"

"How dare you walk away from me," Garrett said as he caught up with them. Nellie moved to block him.

"You," Faria addressed the man tied to the tree while caressing one of her daggers at her hip. "Who is your leader? Where did these beasts come from?"

The man narrowed his eyes when his gaze fell upon Faria's ears, and for a moment it looked as though he wouldn't answer. Nellie stepped closer, experiencing a sense of satisfaction when the man blanched and backed away as far as the ropes would allow.

"I lead the Air Clan." he said, lowering his eyes. "You seem familiar."

"Why are you attacking us?" Nellie demanded, ignoring him.

"It was a retaliation for refusal to comply."

Faria crossed her arms. "Comply with what?"

"That's enough!" Garrett said. "You'll not be getting information from him. He's a traitor to his kind and a liar."

"I will hear his answer," Faria said, moving closer to the prisoner. Nellie wondered when this animosity between the clans had begun. Before she was banished, there was a peace treaty of sorts. She didn't know the specifics, just that it kept each clan in their own territory, but demanded that they work together to defend their lands from any threat. When had that changed?

"You cannot hide from him," the prisoner said, his gaze fixed on Garrett. "He is going to come for you."

"Who is he?" Faria asked him, getting in his line of sight. "Was he tall, darker skin with purple eyes? Or did he have red eyes, claws for hands?"

Nellie gasped, unable to believe she hadn't put it together. Their attackers had sounded like what they heard in Anestra before she forced Faria through the Gate of All Realms. So much had happened since then that she didn't even stop to consider Darroc might be behind this attack, too. Garett put his hands in his pockets and took a step back.

The guy on the tree coughed, blood spurting out of his mouth onto Faria's tunic, though she didn't move or act as if she cared. Nellie hoped he really didn't have the wasting disease, because that was totally disgusting.

The shifter continued, "He wore a wooden mask. Both him and his partner. All I know is the beasts are his. They are completing their mission to get what he needs." His breathing turned ragged and if he weren't tied up, his body would have sunk to the ground. "He will come for you."

A smile turned up his bloodied lips as his eyes glassed over. He was dead.

NINE

HUNTER

Carnage.

The dying screams from humans and monsters alike reverberated through the air, and reeking, pus-filled bodies and carcasses littered the blood-soaked ground. The fields where they normally had such bountiful harvests, where they planted and grew enough food for all Anestra, were now ruined.

Hunter struck an enchanted blade he'd stolen off a dead warlock straight through the heart of a giant werewolf. He was lucky to have found that dagger; it appeared that only magically enhanced weapons seemed to work against the rabid animals. Humans were dying all around him, and the warlocks that remained didn't have enough magic to be useful.

Even King Dennison struggled. He could not manipulate the elements the way his wife and Faria were able to, but he did have the ability to predict what someone would do before they did it, and an unerring sense of accuracy which seemed to be the only thing that kept him ahead of the game. The Elven Royal Guard seemed to be okay; each of them possessed their own abilities that enhanced their superior skills.

A tugging on his pant leg caught Hunter's attention and he looked down to feel a bloodied hand grip him.

Faline stared up at him, blood gushing from her mouth. Her breathing was labored, and she had the graying look of someone soon about to enter the Beyond. Dismayed, Hunter knelt beside her and grasped both of her hands, cold dampness seeping onto his knees from the ground. She tried to speak but he shook his head.

"Hush now," he said, placing his hand on her forehead. "It's okay to go on." His heart broke a bit at this loss; he really liked Faline and knew Nellie would be crushed to hear of her Fading. "I will look after Nellie."

She nodded, relief in her eyes. Just then, someone fell down next to them, smattering mud over Faline's fragile body. Hunter instinctively grabbed for his weapon.

It was Endo. The young warlock held his gore-splattered hands over Faline's abdomen.

"What the hell do you think you're doing?" Hunter violently pushed him back. "Haven't you caused enough damage?"

Endo flinched but his stare was unwavering as he moved to put his hands on Faline again. "I'm trying to heal her, asshole," he said.

Hunter clenched his teeth. "Not a chance. You deserve to be imprisoned for the part you played in this." He started to lunge toward

Endo but Faline's gurgled cough stayed his hand. He couldn't believe he was fighting over a dead body.

"Let me try before it's too late!" Endo shouted. "You can punish me all you want after."

Hunter let out a grunt of frustration. He couldn't very well let Faline die over his stubbornness, especially if something could be done to prevent it. "If you kill her, I will murder you with a fucking smile on my face, understand?"

Endo wasted no time as he hovered his hands over Faline, a light blue glow radiating from them as he closed his eyes and concentrated. Hunter watched both in fascination and confusion. The bleeding slowed, but it didn't seem like that would be enough. Hunter wasn't even sure why Endo was here helping Faline when he had been on the wrong side for the past year, fighting for Darroc. If it was the Fate's design to have her Fade, then it would occur no matter what Endo did.

Even still, Hunter placed his hand gently on Endo's arm. He didn't think his power would come through—The Elders had seen to that—but perhaps the Fates would interfere with that as well.

The sun rose over the Forest of the Dawn, its rays spreading across the field like a sick joke; such light on so much death, as if they were supposed to admire its beauty. Even still, Hunter felt as though Endo's power grew stronger, with the increasing light. Either that, or the Fates really did not wish Faline to Fade just yet.

The quiet across the field was unnerving after hours of screeching, howling, and yelling. Around them, the monsters were dead, and the elves were gathering their own who had perished. They would do a memorial as soon as they could; some to pyres, others into the ocean. Especially with these brutal murders, their passing would be celebrated with the sacredness it deserved.

King Dennison caught Hunter's eye and signaled him over, leaning wearily on his broadsword. Hunter gave one last look at Endo, whose forehead had broken out in a sweat, his hands shaking with exertion. Faline's color seemed to be returning. He left Endo, but kept him in his line of sight as he went to stand next to the king.

"This cannot be called a victory though we have prevailed this night," the king said to those who had gathered around him. "Darroc will not stop until we perish or bow to his will." He took a moment and looked each person in the eye as he spoke.

"We have lost Queen Amira tonight, as she bravely fought for a chance for my daughter to escape. Our new queen Faria is on a mission to put an end to Darroc. We must be prepared for if she succeeds or fails. Let us gather the dead, attend to the wounded, and then sleep. We will honor those who have passed on tonight and then tomorrow we will plan."

Elves and surviving humans scrambled follow his orders, while a group of warlocks hung back, unsure of what to do. Hunter almost felt sorry for them. Though not all warlocks were on the side of evil, he was sure they felt like they didn't have a place where they fully belonged. He knew the Agostonna family would put an end to those thoughts.

The King of Anestra looked at them and smiled, and despite the exhaustion and heartache of the night, his voice filled with warmth. "You are not to blame for what your brethren have done. There is much more to the story than I think either you or I know, but what is certain is that you are still citizens of Anestra. You are of this land, and as such, you will mourn with us, you will dine with us, and you will fight with us again—if you wish."

Hunter's admiration for the king had grown exponentially over the years, precisely in moments like these. The warlocks looked relieved, though he was certain the guilt they felt would not go away, not after seeing so many of their friends killed.

He knew exactly what that felt like.

King Dennison turned away to address the Royal Guard. "Wil and Reed will go into Athinia to check the city, see what repairs, if any, need to be done. Anyone who needs shelter or help is welcome to *Mentage*. There will be plenty of room. Enis, do a recon mission, see if any warlocks will turn back to our side. Johanna, after you sleep and eat, go to the outer borders. See if there is anything worth mentioning. Bring a team, report back as soon as possible."

"My king," Hunter said, putting one arm over his chest and giving a quick bow. "May I have a private word with you?"

Though he was absolutely starving and reeked of rancid guts and blood, Hunter had to share with the king what he knew.

"Can it wait, Hunter?" the king asked wearily.

"No, it cannot."

The king wiped his sword on his pants and sheathed it. Though they stood in a pile of blood and gore, he indicated Hunter should say his piece.

"I am…not human, but a protector of sorts," he said, not wanting to reveal that he was Val. It had been a secret for a thousand years. That he could not die, except through one particular spell was dangerous knowledge. He couldn't risk Darroc finding out. His powers, that he was controlled by the Elders…The Fates would punish him if he ever told anyone the truth of his heritage, and it would put him and the Agostonna line at risk if the wrong people found out the true way to end him.

"I have been protecting the Elven Royal Bloodline for many years, always from a distance, until Faria was old enough to train." He took a steadying breath, the butterflies in his stomach distracting him. He swallowed the nausea he felt at speaking to his lover's father at a time like this, but he had to rip off the bandage. "I don't know if you knew but I am the father of her child."

The king's nostrils flared but he remained silent.

Hunter rubbed the back of his neck. "I was sent to the human realm to find out information regarding Darroc. There was reason to believe he spent time there. After questioning another type of Protector to the humans, I found out that these creatures are not only allies with Darroc but his own personal creations. He made them centuries ago, so many that he dumped them on Earth, and they eventually evolved into the shapeshifters we know today. These, however, are not the evolved beings, and there are so many more than what he sent here. I know that Darroc is after something, and he seems to think my son can help him achieve it. Though I have not voiced my suspicions to my superiors, I believe he will use the child to gain access to a weapon that would ensure he takes over this land. We must not let that happen."

The king stared off in the distance. "I know you are holding back more information but believe you told me all I needed to know. For now. My wife trusted you beyond any doubt, and because of that, my faith remains steady in you as well."

Hunter bit his tongue and nodded. He knew it wasn't the time, nor the place to go into more detail. Not until they could properly hash it out and then come up with a plan.

"Judging by that mark on your forehead, I'm guessing you and Faria have something more profound than a secret tryst."

Hunter furrowed his eyebrows. How the king could see anything under the mud and gore was impressive. He remembered what Jacobi had said. Something about a mate mark.

"Are you sure?" Hunter asked. "I look human, and if there is a mark, as you say, it certainly wouldn't show up while I'm in this form."

"Yes, but you are not a human, and I am not just any elf. I am king for a reason." He winked at Hunter and patted him on the shoulder. "Get some rest. We have much to discuss in the coming hours and days."

King Dennison was right. Hunter was on the verge of passing out. It had been just a few hours ago that his body repaired itself from death, and with all that had happened in between, he needed to lie down.

"One last thing," he said. The king turned back to him with a raised brow. "Endo is here. Faline was gravely injured and he claimed he could save her. I am happy to take care of him for you."

"What?" The king's eyes grew with worry as he looked over to where Hunter indicated then back at him. "Do not harm him. Look at how she is breathing easier. We'll discuss it more tomorrow."

Hunter felt a pang of regret but nodded. He wouldn't refuse the king's order. He watched Endo and Faline for a few minutes more, waiting to see if Endo might have a change of heart. It wasn't until Wil and Reed stood watch over her that he summoned the last of his strength to help move any bodies that lay between him and his own rooms beyond the barracks.

SUNLIGHT FILTERED THROUGH THE OPEN window, and the autumn breeze brought with it the stench of the battle. Hunter sat up, stretching his muscles like a cat after a long nap, and descended upon the tray of food left for him.

It had been tradition for him to gorge on meats and greasy food after going through a death cycle—a common human cure for a hangover, as that was what it felt like after coming to life again. Today's meal, however, consisted of hot oats, fresh fruit and spiced nuts. He wasn't complaining, though. It was hearty, full of protein, and successfully filled him up—even if he did still crave salty fries.

His cottage was simple, as were much of the huts that were part of the barracks. It was one large room with a bed in the corner, a table with two chairs in front of the fireplace, and a series of mirrors hanging along the walls. They were a gift from the warlocks long ago, enchanted for quick communication between the queen and her army. The queen normally carried a small mirror on herself and had her own set hidden throughout *Mentage*.

He walked into the bathing chamber attached to the main room. He was lucky enough to have one as a weapons master. It was a higher station, not that the elves really followed such things, but he commanded more respect than others. Because of that, Queen Amira had expanded the cottage on the edge of the barracks where the Royal

Guard and other soldiers usually stayed.

He stepped down into the inground pool, the steaming water soothing his aching muscles. There was no window in here. Instead, lit torches presented a cozy light. If he hadn't just rested, he would have fallen asleep again. He'd barely had time to rinse his hands and face last night before collapsing into bed.

Now, as he worked to scrub caked blood off his skin and hair, he wondered idly how much time had passed on Earth. There was no set algorithm so he couldn't be sure. When he was last on Earth, he was there for one day but ten months had passed on Anestra. The time before that, he was on Earth for two weeks and hardly a day had passed in this realm. He knew Faria would be okay, but he still worried for her. If Darroc were to appear on Earth where she had no access to her powers, he didn't know how she would survive.

And his son. He cursed the Elders for not allowing him to find his son. He knew it was crucial he stayed in Anestra, that his skills were needed there, but this was his child. A Val! They were the only two in existence and he needed protection almost more than anyone else.

He climbed out of the water and dried himself. Wiping off the looking glass hanging on the wall, he observed his reflection. He looked the same as he always did as a human. Exceptionally ordinary. Muted green eyes, and golden skin, as if he spent an abnormal amount of time in the sun. His brown hair was longer, and he noticed a shadow of a beard starting to come in. Despite his mundane appearance, he could just make out white lines across his forehead. He dared to believe it was the mating symbol that would let others know that not only was he taken, but he had acquired more powers—usually those of his mate. It made him a leader, a formidable opponent, and well-respected.

Mated couples were few and far between. Elves used to always be part of a mated pair but over time their numbers dwindled as it became harder to procreate. In this part of Anestra, it could sometimes be half a century before a pregnancy successfully came into fruition. More children who survived were mixed in some way with either human or warlock. The same could be said about the other races. Not to mention, he'd never known a Val to mate with an elf, but of course he didn't have much to refer to in that area.

Hunter grabbed a fresh tunic and pants and strapped on his boots. He loaded up as many weapons as he could fit on his person, and stepped out into the sun.

He shielded his eyes as he looked past the barracks out onto the blood-spattered and reeking field. What would it be like once people found out he was Val, and mated to an elf, and had already sired another Val? He wondered if it were the turn of the tides all their people needed. If it meant they would win whatever war this was.

A triage had been set up near the gardens and healers bent over bodies, their poultices and potions lined up on makeshift tables. Volunteers with stretchers carried bodies, some dead, some alive, to their assigned places.

As Hunter approached, he saw a familiar shape lying on the edge of the triage area. Endo lay across a bloodied body, his face pale and fast asleep. Sweat soaked his clothes.

"He hasn't left my side," Faline whispered. "I was ready to go. Thought it was my time to Fade. Then this one shows up." She smiled down at the body lying across her. "Nellie was so fond of him. Nice to see she is an excellent judge of character."

Hunter grunted. "I am very happy you are alive," he said, not willing to comment on his distrust of the warlock. "We need you, still. Your knowledge, your guidance. It's appreciated now more than ever. Plus, Nellie would have murdered me if you died."

Faline's eyes narrowed at that. "What news have you?"

He slashed his head to the side. "Nothing."

Faline stared at him with a look that said she knew he was lying.

"I don't know what you know…but there are things I cannot say. I know that they are in the human realm. The last thing I…discovered was that they were fighting a pack of the same monsters as us, but fewer of them. I know they are with Nellie's former clan."

Her eyebrows knitted at the news. "But they will kill her," she said, worried.

"Faria would never let that happen, though this does mean that this war Darroc is bringing to our door is much larger than we thought. It's bigger than just us. If he's starting battles in the human realm as well who's to say he isn't doing the same in other realms? We should do what we can to prepare."

Faline nodded then winced, holding her hand to her head. "And… your son?"

Hunter was surprised she knew and wondered who else did, too. "I do not know. I have a suspicion…but I hesitate to voice it. I worry he won't be recognizable to us. He is still with Darroc, but for what purpose I am unsure. I don't think I will be allowed to find out."

Faline reached out a shaky hand and grasped his own. "Faria will find him. She will do everything in her power and beyond to save him. And then she will return to us."

Hunter mimicked the nod he just received from her.

"What are you going to do about him?" she asked, pointing her chin at the sleeping warlock.

"It isn't up to me to decide if he should be punished. Though I don't believe he will be. Endo was always beloved. He will have a place here. Plus, he might have information that can help us, and I am more than willing to do what it takes to extract it from him."

Faline pursed her lips at him but chose not to reply as Endo stirred, his eyes blinking slowly. A healer was at his side in a moment, giving him water and what Hunter suspected was a concoction for energy, like the human's caffeine. She left a plate of elven bread and grapes and walked away again.

Endo drank deeply and bit into the bread before he realized Hunter stood just beyond his periphery. If Endo had been at full health, he would have known where Hunter was even if he were blind; one of his warlock abilities was to sense what was unseen—feelings, people, things of that nature. Hunter tried to hold his anger at bay. Just a year ago Endo had been his second in command. Trusted beyond measure. His friend.

Perhaps that was what made his betrayal so difficult.

"Hunter," Endo said in a rush, his voice coming out in a scratchy whisper. "I was wrong. I thought I knew what I was doing. I believed him when he said the queen stole our power. It made sense why this land prospered while my home festered. It made sense why children survived here, and crops thrived, while my people grew old and sick, infected by the smallest thing the way humans are. I just wanted to see my people live. I was the last child to be born, over twenty years ago. I just…I wanted to see children again."

Endo's eyes implored Hunter to side with him. Hunter would not, because the result was the kidnapping of his son, their people dead at the hands of a deranged warlock, the foundations of their home shattered. Though, if it were the Val race at stake, if there were a way to bring them back or save them, would he have done the same? It didn't matter. His people were never coming back.

Hunter tried to swallow back his anger, not wanting to cause a scene in front of so many sick and injured people in the triage area, but the more he tried, the more he felt a darkness inside him seep through the cracks in his control. For a moment he pictured exacting his revenge on Endo, on blaming him for every terrible thing that happened in the past year. "It isn't me you must explain things to. It is the king. He is a benevolent one, even if what you sided with resulted in the death of our queen and put our new queen in untold danger."

Endo flinched at his words, but pressed on, begging Hunter to listen to him. "I have information. I don't know how much of it is useful. It's not as though I was in an inner circle or anything. But maybe, it could help." His voice raised with conviction. "I'm not sorry for doing what I thought was best for my people, but I am sorry for what happened as a result of it."

"But it doesn't change what happened, does it?"

They were quiet a moment, Faline's labored breath and the moaning from the injured the only sounds around them.

"Rest well, Faline," Hunter said, turning away. "I'll check on you later." He glared at Endo. "You. Come with me."

"Wait," Endo said, running his fingers through his dirty hair. "I have to know. Where is Nellie? I looked for her everywhere, before I came upon Faline. I have to see her. I just have the strangest feeling that something isn't quite right."

Hunter and Faline shared a look, unsure of how to respond. He wasn't sure how much Endo knew—about Darroc, about Ander.

Faline smiled at Endo. "She is with Queen Faria, on a special mission. One that will determine the winner of this war."

Endo nodded. "So, she's not in danger?"

"Undoubtedly she is getting herself into trouble. But I'm sure she will be fine."

Endo stood up, ready to accompany Hunter to request an audience with the king.

The two of them traveled in stony silence across the field, over a small stone bridge leading to one of the many gardens. The scent of jasmine flowed around him and a desperation for his mate consumed him. His attempt to suppress the feeling only made him burn further for what he lost. He needed to clear his head, needed to focus on the things he could control. He was stuck in Anestra, and *Mentage* was what required his attention.

The sprawling estate where the Royal Elves had lived for centuries was slowly coming back to life after the previous night's battle, but a somber feeling hung over the land. *Mentage* was always a haven, open to all who needed it. It looked quite modest from the outside, no larger than a luxurious log cabin humans might rent on a lake-side vacation. But once visitors crossed the threshold through the front gate, something else was revealed entirely.

A huge stone wall with parapets surrounding it for protection, a large inner courtyard, sprawling gardens and the seemingly innocuous estate turned into a stronghold akin to a mansion. Inside was a labyrinth of never-ending hallways, secret passages, and more rooms than anyone knew what to do with. It rivaled the best of castles, and its unassuming appearance helped maintain the open, friendly, equal quality that the Royal Elves prided themselves on.

Subdued murmurs permeated the air rather than the usual laughter and songs. The previous year, Darroc had left a dark stain on the land—a wasting spell that had destroyed much of the available farmland. Now, he was sending armies of rabid beasts. How much more would they have to endure before finally ridding the world of him?

Hunter blamed himself. The warlocks had been a problem a thousand years ago and he never followed through to make sure the threat was eradicated. Instead, he'd protected the Agostonna line, taking down potential enemies to the throne, doing whatever the Elders told him to. He longed to help the farmers and other volunteers around *Mentage* with cleaning up and rebuilding, but first he needed to speak to the king.

Hunter and Endo entered through the huge oak double doors and were greeted immediately by the scent of fire and spice. The familiarity when everything was so different struck a chord in him. Last time he had entered these halls, the queen was alive and Faria was safe.

Two wooden staircases on either side of the entryway curved up and met in the middle, hallways just barely peeking through on either side. Hunter knew those to lead to various activity halls, guest rooms and infirmary stations. Straight ahead across from the main doorway was a vast fireplace, the smoke from its flames shooting straight up through the chimney. Carved in stone making up the chute were Fae, elves, warlocks, humans, shapeshifters, mers, dwarves, and a lone phoenix. It was beautiful, the way they were all intertwined.

Normally there were guards situated every so often along the halls, but anyone that could be spared was undoubtedly attending to whoever needed them most. A lone guard stood next to the door to the Council Chamber, and he nodded his head in greeting at Hunter and Endo as they entered. King Dennison was hunched over the table, mapping out his plan for the next few days and undoubtedly awaiting intel.

Endo had walked with determined purpose throughout *Mentage*, silently challenging anyone to say something to him, but seemed to shrink once they were in the Council Chamber. Hunter pushed Endo further into the room, taking care not to notice the significant absence of Queen Amira. Though they were never friends, they'd had a sort of alliance and it was strange to be in this room without her. He instead focused on papers that were scattered over the table and maps that were pinned on the wall, both of Wendorre and Anestra, along with what looked to be the United States on Earth. Markers were set up around each of the maps, most of which were placed on Earth. A series of lines drawn between pinned areas stretched across each map, with the words "Gate," "Boat," "Fly?" next to them.

The king looked up from the map and stood at attention when he saw Endo. Hunter had to give the warlock credit; the king's steely blue eyes stared him down and he didn't flinch, though he was paler than usual.

"Endo believes he has information that may prove useful to our cause," Hunter said.

"Is that right?" said the king. "You know that I do not possess the extraordinary gifts my queen did, including how to tell where there is deceit…how do I know you are not here under his command?"

Endo cleared his throat. "I've watched my brethren struggle and die for years, and when he said it was the queen who took our power and that he simply wanted it back…I never thought it would lead to something like this. He promised it would all be friendly. An exchange." He swallowed, but kept his eyes firmly on the king's. "I know that what I have done, that what I have taken part in meant the killing of the queen, meant Faria's child in danger, and the lives of our people. I humbly ask for your forgiveness and will accept any punishment you wish."

So, Endo knew the baby was in dangerous hands. When had he learned of such a thing? It seemed he had been battling just as much as everyone else when Darroc disappeared.

King Dennison's face remained dispassionately blank, but Hunter knew Endo would be forgiven, or at least have a chance at forgiveness. Having grown up right in *Mentage* along with most of the Guard, the king knew Endo's character. It was part of the reason everyone had wanted Nellie to reach out to him last year on her secret recon missions.

"I do not have the luxury of turning down people who are on our side," the king finally responded. "But that does not mean you are forgiven. Every person at this stronghold knows where you have been and what you took part in. It will be up to more than just me to forgive you."

Endo nodded. "I understand."

"King Dennison," Hunter said with contempt. "The fact that he thought a foreign being, whom he'd never met, could invade our land and take 'power' away from our queen without any repercussions or casualties is bullshit! He was an active part of the rebellion. He rightfully shares the blame for everything leading up to that battle last night and what is yet to come. He deserves punishment."

Endo stiffened, but the king shook his head. "It isn't that simple, Hunter. Nellie trusted him. Amira trusted him. We received good information from him several times in the last year, which greatly helped steer our course. Part of war is knowing who your enemies are. Endo isn't the problem, nor is he the one we need to focus our vengeance on. It isn't black and white."

"He shouldn't be allowed to roam free," Hunter spat. "He shouldn't be privy to any of this." He indicated the maps around the room. "We don't know what he will do with that information."

"And I still don't know *your* history, who you take orders from, and what information you will share, and yet I am still putting my trust in you. I am the king, I am running Anestra right now and I will decide who is worthy of punishment or not. Understood?"

Hunter stared at Dennison, the darkness inside him shrieking at the lack of vengeance. He tamped down on the feeling. His thirst for punishment occupied his mind more than usual.

"Good. What is this information?" The king turned back to Endo, effectively ending the argument. "Perhaps it will be of use while we use this reprieve to restock on weapons and rebuild what we can of the land."

"I don't know how much time you thought you might have had," Endo said, "But it isn't nearly as much as you think it is. Thousands of Darroc's army will be here in a few months' time with the arrival of the new year."

Hunter whipped his head at Endo's declaration. Thousands? There weren't enough weapons imbued with magic to take on an army of that size, and a few months wouldn't be enough time to make much more. Not to mention, Anestra was not a large country and wasn't very heavily populated. The cities had some people, sure, but most of the land was filled with farms and small villages. Who could they call for aid? The Forbidden Continent? That seemed unlikely.

"More of his creations," Endo continued. "And other things. He has recruited some shapeshifters. Warlocks from back home. Rumor of darker beings he met on his journey through the realms."

That peaked Hunter's interest. *Realms?*

"How many thousands?" the king asked.

"I don't know. More than what you have, I am certain."

"That's not hard to do," Enis, one of the Elven Royal Guard, said as she entered the Council Chamber. She looked ragged, though her small frame was still held upright. Hunter doubted she slept at all, but she still looked ready to go at a moment's notice. "There are only one thousand of us that are able to fight, if that, if we stretch it to the very ends of our borders. And that's not nearly enough to defend our perimeter, let alone *Mentage* or Athinia."

"And with half those being human," Hunter said, "that means half of our people don't have magic or special abilities to help us."

"Still, we will send a group to leave at once and gather all who can be outfitted with armor and weapons. We need every person capable of fighting, magic or no."

"There's more," Endo said. "He has had centuries to perfect dark magic. I don't know how he is capable of it. Warlocks aren't inherently good with anything dark. We grow plants, we heal. We typically don't do damage. The things he must have learned…I cannot fathom it. I do know where he had been hiding for the past few decades. And I believe he has a secret library there that houses the Book of the Dead."

"What is that?" the king asked.

"Rumors, something warlock children were told when we were bad. That our parents would get out 'the Book' and show us unspeakable terrors. Only once was I in the same room as him, and he'd said he had the book to thank for his friends on Earth, and that he kept it safe so no harm would come to them. I believe there is a spell of unmaking there. One that can reverse and kill off what he had done."

Hunter shivered inwardly. He had been too close to his own spell of unmaking and didn't like the idea of Darroc having one, whether it would work on him or not. He would rather not find out, but as soon as Darroc realizes that Hunter was alive, he would put together what Hunter really was and possibly even test it out.

The king turned to Hunter. "Is there anyone we can call on us to help?"

He knew what the king was asking. He knew the king wanted to know if there were more like him, whatever he was, or if those in charge of him would send aid. Unfortunately, Hunter knew the Elders wouldn't help, and was quite sure they couldn't anyway. Who was there to call?

"There is no one else." The finality of that rang through the room as they all realized how alone and unprepared they were.

"Darroc's armies will destroy everything," Endo said.

"But we have a thousand," said the king. "And we still have magic at our disposal, and some of the most ingenious inventors of our time. We can create special weapons, special potions. And we have you," the king added, giving Hunter a meaningful look.

Hunter barely managed to not roll his eyes. "I cannot do much like this."

"You are still our most skilled fighter," the king said. "And now we have you, too." He looked at Endo. "The pair of you are formidable together. We can be strategic about this."

Hunter scoffed. "I am not partnering with him for anything. He doesn't deserve to be here."

"It still won't be enough," Enis cut in, giving Hunter an annoyed look. "We still don't have enough information. Will he send others through the sea? Through the mountains? Maybe we can get the dwarves to side with us, though we all know they keep to themselves. We need a miracle."

"What we need are the Fae," Hunter said. The others fell silent. He inwardly cringed at himself. He didn't mean to let the knowledge slip that the Fae were still alive. He didn't want to answer any questions on why he would know such a thing. Too many questions would mean they would eventually figure out what he really was. Not to mention, the Elders were likely to punish him all over again for sharing knowledge that they had sworn him to secrecy over.

The fire crackled as they all looked at Hunter as if he'd spoken another language. He sighed, knowing he had to finish his thought since he'd already spat it out. "They have numbers that almost rival those on Earth."

"You're talking about billions of people. You are saying there are *billions* of Fae?" Enis asked, disbelieving.

"They do not die, not easily anyway. And they were always rumored to procreate quite easily. The last anyone knew of them, they were in the hundreds of thousands. It stands to reason they have larger numbers now."

This time it was Endo's turn to scoff. "No one has seen or heard of a Fae in centuries. They didn't come to our aid in the Great War. We have no idea how to contact them, especially not in the next few months. There simply isn't enough time, even if we could ask them. If they even still exist."

"They do," the king said. "Faria is Fae-blessed. My beloved queen never told me how, but we can assume that in the past eighteen years there was at least one Fae in Anestra. At least one that knew the importance Faria would have in the future. And this entire land is soaked in their magic. We would no longer have their protective magic on this home if they were no longer in existence. The Gate is a Fae creation. It, too, would no longer be around if the Fae were not."

"So we're in agreement that the Fae are alive then?" Endo said. Everyone nodded their heads at the king's logic. "But do we believe we know a way to contact them? And if we do, will they come?"

Hunter had a feeling he knew the Elders would be able to contact the Fae, but he also knew asking them would be hopeless.

"Endo saved Faline," Hunter said, thinking out loud. "She was dying last night, and he used his magic to heal her enough for our healers to do the rest."

"We should thank you," the king said. "Faline, as you know, means a great deal to us."

"She does to me, as well," Endo said. "I had to do what I could."

"I didn't know you could heal people," Enis said, suspicion in her voice.

"Neither did I, but I had to try."

"What this means," Hunter continued as they seemed to be slow to catch on, "is that we have someone with a connection to the Secret Keepers still alive, and on our grounds. If anyone would have any information on how to save us, such as how to contact a race thought to be extinct, it would be her."

The king finally seemed pleased with some scrap of news. He put down his quill and stretched. "Good," he said, popping a piece of fruit in his mouth. "You can work with her on that. I daresay you have some skills she might need." He looked meaningfully at him.

"Don't you need me available to train those who come? To make sure we have enough weapons?"

"Yes. You will help with that as well." The king made his way out the door.

"Where are you going, my king?" Enis asked, ready to follow him.

"Those I had assigned tasks to are still gone. I need you to sleep for a few hours, then come find me." He grabbed onto Endo and pulled him toward the door. "Endo and I will be out in the fields, overseeing the rest of the clean-up."

"Surely someone else can do that?" Enis asked.

"Of course someone else can do that. But a leader is as good as his weakest person. I cannot expect others to do tasks that I myself would not do. It's good for morale. Remember that, should you ever wish to lead."

Hunter waited for the king and Endo to leave the Council Room before turning to Enis. "Listen, there was something I didn't want to say in front of Endo."

"Does the king know this information?" she asked.

"Yes. Faria and Nellie have their work cut out for them on Earth. They were fighting Darroc's beasts last night in the human realm, just as we were here."

"With no magic? And did they survive?"

"I did not see the outcome, though Faria looked formidable as always. And Nellie took the form of a *Drogosterra*."

"You're kidding me!" Enis' smile widened until it engulfed her whole face. "I cannot believe I missed that."

"I don't know how exactly. They disappeared around the same time as the Val, right when they performed their sacrifice. I think when Nellie returns, we might have the slightest of chances."

"Slight is better than none."

Though Hunter wanted the females back as soon as possible, if he knew Faria, she would demand to take care of those shifters if it were possible. It would be better strategically, especially if she had reason to believe that Darroc would return there with Ander.

He nodded to Enis before leaving for the infirmary. *Mentage* was a bustle of activity, though Hunter could still hear the moans and screams of the injured. Faline sat up as he approached her bed.

"I suspect you have some questions for me," she said, her face pale and sweaty.

"As you have for me, undoubtedly. Are you sure you are well?"

She waved a hand, brushing him off. "Actually, I've known about you for a while, I think, and I've suspected even longer. The queen and I had our suspicions and our hopes."

"I have failed her. I failed them both."

"No, you haven't. You have done exactly what the Fates had in store."

Hunter looked around and noticed they were alone and lowered his voice. "The Fae are still in existence, are they not?"

"I should think so. They were rumored to be wicked creatures, weren't they? They love having their fingers stirring all the pots."

"Is there a way for us to contact them? Can they aid us?"

"The last known Fae interference was nearly nineteen years ago, with Faria," Faline said, confirming what the king had told them. "We tried contacting them, the queen and I—about a year ago, based on information I received from the Secret Keepers. There was no response. There is much speculation about whether the Fates interfere with the Fae. Others believe the Fates *are* the Fae. Whatever it is, it will require more research and time than what we have. Do you not remember what happened to them? Considering you were there for their disappearance." She turned a sharp glance on him.

He shook his head. "My memories over the past thousand years are spotty at best. I remember certain missions I did, certain acts I had to perform, but when it comes to the end of the war…I remember nothing besides sacrificing my magic. I remember the pain I felt as it ripped through me, but then I blacked out. I assumed I was dead until…I simply wasn't." He felt the echo of that pain even now. "I don't think I gave up my magic, though I cannot use all of it. I don't know what happened. It's like that part of me is locked away."

"I don't suppose you'll tell me who it is that revived you?"

"I don't know what I can say without repercussion. They are as old as I am, or older. That much I can tell you."

Faline nodded slowly, considering him. She had a sharp mind. She would figure it out eventually, if she hadn't already. He couldn't help but feel a nagging sensation in his own mind, as though there were something so obvious that he couldn't remember.

Hunter sat back, sighing. It was no use trying to remember the ghost of who he used to be when he had real problems to focus on. He hoped that if the Elders wouldn't help, that the Fates at least had them on the winning end of this thing. He hoped Faria and Nellie would make it back safely.

He hoped beyond anything he ever dared, that help would come.

TEN

FARIA

He will come for you.

The hostage's words repeated in her head, solidifying the exact thoughts she'd had since they arrived in the human realm. It had to be Darroc. There just wasn't another option. But why would Darroc grip his claws so heavily into a shifter civil war, and how could he do it with a baby? Did the order to attack the Earth Clan take place before he'd stolen Ander?

Her heart broke. She had held him a few minutes before he was taken from her. Her breasts ached with the milk that she had not been able to develop and though her wounds had long since healed thanks to her abilities, she still felt a pain deep in her belly, as if a phantom pregnancy still haunted her, mocking her for her failures.

He will come for you.

"What did he mean by that?" Faria rounded on Garrett. "Tell me what you know!"

He sneered. "I don't need to tell you anything."

Before she could react, Nellie clenched Garrett's throat with a clawed hand and fire in her eyes. Faria knew she was a rare shapeshifter. She knew almost nothing about them but did know that they shouldn't be able to change into whatever they wanted the way Nellie did. She had realized how formidable Nellie was as a whole animal, but seeing the fiery spirit in the human part of her was impressive as well. She just needed to learn to control her emotions better. Goddess knows Faria had needed to learn the same thing, once upon a time.

"You will not speak to my queen like that."

Faria placed her hand on Nellie's arm, indicating that she should release him.

"You're no better than a trained dog," Garrett taunted Nellie, smirking at her quick compliance to Faria's order.

Quicker than blinking, Faria whipped a dagger to his neck, another at his gut, and though she knew her elemental magic did not work on Earth, she still felt a flash of ice in her veins and thought the grass around her withered a little.

"Show some respect," Faria said with her own cruel smile on her lips. "Nellie is no dog, as you say, but she can swallow you whole and she does not need my permission to do so."

He looked at her with contempt but before he could say anything, Faria added, "One swipe and your insides will fall out faster than the blood at your jugular."

Thomas interrupted them, exhaustion etched on his face. He raised his hands in the air to show he wasn't a threat. "Garrett, you should answer. This is getting to be too much of a coincidence. Callie arriving a few days ago asking where Nellie is, then Nellie returning, bringing with her an elven queen. Now the Air Clan is attacking us and it seems as though Nellie and Faria are familiar with who could have created these monsters."

"It sounds like these two are the ones who need questioning," Garrett spat. He seemed to notice that the surviving members of the Earth Clan were listening closely and hesitated. Maybe he was swayed by their dwindling numbers and felt a surge of protection for them, but Faria rather thought he was worried they would all turn on him if he still refused to answer. She stepped back, daggers still raised.

"It was a few years ago," said Garrett. "He arrived out of nowhere. The clan leaders all received notice to meet, to discuss the peace treaty, or so we thought. He was there. In a wooden mask and frayed looking robes. He told us he was our creator. That we came from him and he demanded our service. He promised us things in return. More territory to roam around, endless numbers. We'd never have to worry about the humans taking over our lands or risk persecution by anyone who was afraid of us. He said he could provide for us, in another place, but he needed our help when the time came."

He paused for a moment to catch his breath, sweat trickling down his brow.

"Each of the clan leaders agreed to it, at first. But then one by one they refused or decided they could not help a stranger who wouldn't even reveal himself to them. Who was he to say he created us? It divided us. We were split, those who would follow and help this mysterious leader, and those too afraid." For the first time, real fear shone in his eyes. Faria understood what that felt like, to be completely at the mercy of a psychotic murderer. "Somehow he knew those who were too afraid. And he disposed of them."

"Disposed?" Thomas growled. "What do you mean?"

"I mean they don't exist anymore."

"The wasting disease?" Faria asked. "Is that what you're saying?"

Shocked exclamations rippled through the Earth Clan. Faria wondered how many people had died because of the monster she married.

"Who is left?" Nellie asked, getting the conversation back on track.

"It all got messed up somehow. He showed up again and saw that there were only two of us left and that even we were hesitant. He was pissed. His partner questioned us. He could tell who was lying somehow. He let the leader know which of us didn't intend to follow him anymore. It took me a while, but I realized that accepting his terms when he first came was a mistake." He swallowed and looked around at his clan, his eyes begging their forgiveness. "You have to believe me, I tried to keep us safe."

Garrett raised his shirt, revealing a band of symbols blistered onto his stomach. Faria had never seen such markings before. It looked as though it were branded on his skin, and the wound seemed fresh. "His partner did this to me, and I believe I am not the first to receive such a mark."

"How long ago was this?" Faria asked.

"A month ago."

No. Panic flowed through her as she started to put it together. *It can't be.* Faria gave Nellie a horrified glance to see if she realized what this meant, but Nellie was too busy staring at Garrett with utter disgust. "What did the partner look like?"

"A carved wooden mask covered his face. Tall. Muscular. Teen, maybe. Piercing green eyes shone through the mask. I don't know anything else."

The world closed in around Faria. Her breathing was erratic and shallow as she was slammed with the realization. The difference in time between realms. The hours she thought her baby was taken away from her were really years. Her heart threatened to crack as it shattered all over again.

She'd missed his first words, his first steps, the first time he beheld something beautiful in his eyes. The sleepless nights, the way he would have clung to her for comfort, the way she would have held him tightly each morning as he snuggled into her.

Everything about him was stolen from her, and it wasn't just time, but her influence, too. What kind of monster did Darroc train him to be in all that time?

What kind of male did Ander become?

A gentle brush against her shoulder brought her focus back to Garrett and the rest of the Earth Clan as she forced herself to take calming breaths before she was lost to the panic. Nellie leaned up against her in a quiet form of support, and as Faria made eye contact with her, she saw for just a second that Nellie had the same realization before putting on an unreadable expression.

A wailing cry broke out.

Cursing herself for not staying vigilant, Faria searched the sky for more danger, but she soon realized it was the sound of someone sobbing. She had failed so miserably at so many things. At protecting her people, at being a mother, at saving Ander from the grips of a monster. She was desperate for something—anything—she could do to help. Without thinking, Faria ran over to a woman huddled over a bloodied shape on the ground. It was a child, no more than twelve years old, her breath ragged.

It was wrong. All the suffering. All the death. Especially that of someone so young lying in a puddle of blood that did not belong to her, alongside monstrous bodies that should not exist.

Tears threatened to flow at the thought of another child leaving right in front of her, especially when she could not help but blame herself that any of them were in this situation. She swallowed hard and knelt on the ground, closing her eyes. She looked for a calm place in her mind, away from the terror and exhaustion, and focused on it until she felt as though her limbs were controlled by someone else.

A sense of peace overcame her grief, and as if on instinct, Faria opened her eyes and sliced open her palm. She trailed her hands in the bloodied dirt, then spread it across the girl's clammy forehead and the other on her belly. She rested her brow against the girl's as if it were the most natural thing to do, and prayed to all the Fates and goddesses above that whatever instinct took over would save the girl's life.

ELEVEN

NELLIE

The past twenty-four hours had felt like one long nightmare to Nellie. The crises never ceased. Finding Faria in the woods, Darroc destroying everything—killing Hunter, stealing Ander—being forced to decide between protecting the people of Anestra or going through the Gate. Then once they'd arrived on Earth, they were surrounded by shifters, taken for questioning, attacked by vicious monsters, and she found out her former clan leader was in cahoots with Darroc for months or possibly even *years*. And now, judging from the screams that broke through the night, something else had been added to the mix.

Nellie wasn't sure when she'd last eaten, but she knew for a fact both her and Faria hadn't slept. That's what they needed—to consume before they perish. She didn't want to find out how well she'd function as a ghost.

But the wailing cry only persisted so Nellie followed when Faria took off at a run, musing about Garrett as she went. She'd always known something was off with him. She'd been banished by him, of course, after he accused her of murder. Nellie could barely remember that night…the horror of finding her mother with her throat torn out lay deep in her subconscious. She'd spent months learning how to bury that image and everything that followed deep in the recesses of her mind. And now, hearing about his duplicity set off an alarm in her head. There was something she felt like she was on the cusp of figuring out, but she just couldn't place it.

Something else did intrigue her, though. The symbol that was etched onto Garrett's stomach looked like the reverse of an old healing mark, one the Ancient Originals had used when they walked the land. Nellie had learned of them when she went through Faline's cache of special documents in search of the true prophecy last year.

A healing mark revealed itself when one of the Originals, and then later, the Fae, healed those who were meant to die. It could also show up on those who were Fae-blessed, as they were "healed" or cleansed in a sense. The only Fae-blessed person Nellie knew was Faria, though she had never seen a symbol like that on her before. The mark on Garrett, however, was completely inverted of what she recognized. It looked crude, evil.

The person who had done the marking interested her as well. The partner of the masked male, a boy approaching manhood with piercing green eyes. She knew based on Faria's impending freak-out that she suspected it was Ander. It just seemed impossible to her that so much time had passed between realms, given that they'd passed through the Gate no more than three or four hours apart. Unless, of course, they were in other realms before Earth…

A woman lay on the ground, her wailing reaching new heights. Nellie would be annoyed if they weren't surrounded by carnage. It wasn't that she lacked sympathy, but the onslaught of problems was frustrating. Her stress level was at a high, her adrenaline still flowed through her veins, and they had way more questions than answers. She just didn't have it in her to comfort anyone on their loss, sad though it may be.

But it wasn't her who needed to do the comforting. Faria dropped to her knees next to the woman and gently pushed her away. On the ground was a girl of no more than twelve or thirteen, her abdomen ripped open. Her ragged breaths echoed in the sudden silence. All around them, heads dropped in mourning, honoring this girl though she was not yet lost to them. That pissed Nellie off even more, that they gave up on one of their own so soon, though Nellie didn't blame them. It wasn't like shifters had the ability to heal from mortal wounds. She was surprised the girl was still breathing.

Faria gently guided the woman to the waiting arms of another clan member. Nellie recognized her as Tommy's new mate, Samantha. She wondered who the girl was to them. Faria then knelt in front of the child and whispered to her in another language, one Nellie didn't recognize, before she slashed open her palms and placed them onto the girl.

This was twice now that Nellie had witnessed Faria use blood magic, something she thought only warlocks did. She seemed as though she were in some sort of trance. Hadn't Faria lost touch with her powers when they arrived in the human realm?

Everything around them was silent. Samantha's moaning turned to soundless sobs, and the birds stopped their chatter. Even the wood from the fire seemed to no longer crackle. The painful chorus of the dying diminished.

Faria gently hummed a soothing tune, and the blue aura that poured from her brightened.

The morning sun crested over the distant mountains, its first rays breaking through the trees as a breeze picked up between Faria and the girl on the ground, the pair of them glowing from their combined light. Nellie felt her own brand of magic stir—whatever it was that made her a shapeshifter. It was as if her spirit, the core of who she was, awoke from an endless sleep. She knew she was witnessing something legendary, something so profoundly special that it brought tears to her eyes.

Faria shifted away at last, revealing a swirling blue symbol shining brightly on the child's brow before becoming a white mark on pale skin. The mark of the healed. Of a Fae-blessed.

The same symbol glowed on Faria's brow and faded, quickly followed by another, darker mark. Nellie wasn't well-versed in ancient magical symbols, especially those that stayed as if tattooed on the body, but she was certain the second one was the mate mark of the Fae. The elves had adopted the mark long ago, when the Fae and elven bloodlines began to mix. Once the descendants of the gods and goddesses started fading, new mating bonds occurred between races. Most races in Anestra didn't mate for life, but those with the special mating bond were said to have extra powers between them until one Faded into the beyond.

Wait, did Faria just mate with that child? Nellie thought. *That would be…weird.*

But no, this mark was a series of intricate whirls that banded across Faria's forehead, settling deeply under her skin. They were luminescent and moved as if alive, traveling back and forth along the width of her.

They reminded Nellie of symbols she'd seen on the tapestry of the Val that hung over the entrance to the secret corridor in *Mentage*. The gears in her mind turned. She had often stood in front of it wondering why they had all died out. It wasn't too long ago that she had even wondered if they would come to save them, like in ancient times…

All stared open mouthed at Faria as she stood up, but Nellie was the first to realize what happened. Not just that she somehow healed another being, but that she did it on Earth, that she, a Fae-blessed elf, just Fae-blessed another. Years spent roaming around *Mentage's* endless hallways, studying its tapestries, drinking up whatever knowledge she could on the history of Anestra. She knew what it all meant.

Nellie dropped to her knees and bowed low, resting her forehead to the ground at Faria's feet. One by one, she felt others doing the same. It was not because she was a queen, nor even because she somehow had this extraordinary healing ability that allowed her to return a child from the brink of death.

It was because she was a Fae-blessed healer.

It was because she was a creator and avenger.

It was because she was a punisher and protector.

Faria Agostonna, Queen of Anestra, Destroyer of Flame, Healer of Death, was somehow, miraculously, a Val.

TWELVE

FARIA

Blood pounded in Faria's ears. For just a second, while the world was dim and her bones hummed with magic, she thought she smelled earth and spice and everything good in the world, thought she could hear the echo of Hunter's voice calling her name, his touch against her skin. And then it faded and she opened her eyes to see a mortally wounded child before her.

The young teen smiled up at Faria despite the pain she must have been in, revealing a sweet gap in her teeth. Faria took in her frizzy red hair, piercing blue eyes, and the smattering of freckles across her cheeks. Her eyes shone with tears as she grasped Faria's hand, surprisingly warm under her own cold fingers.

"That you, my queen?" she whispered.

"What is your name?"

"Moira."

Faria sensed something elementally different about the girl. Though she looked human, she wasn't entirely. She didn't seem to be a shapeshifter, either.

Faria leaned closer to the girl, instinct taking over as a language she had never spoken before, the native language of the warlocks, poured from her. "What are you?"

The girl simply smiled. The sun had risen and the clearing was filled with blood and the scent of foul things. And yet, Faria was distracted by the memory of Hunter, by the wonder of the echo of magic in her blood, by the way this girl was familiar and yet not. Not to mention, she had just spoken a language she didn't know, and Moira understood. Her life was bordering on insanity and for the first time in a long while she wished she had a moment alone to process.

Grief, she thought. *Grief had a funny way of settling in.*

Movement caught her eye, and she turned around, filled with shock; everyone was bowing down to her, on their knees, in such reverence as she had never seen before. All except Garrett—which she was happy to see that he was nothing, if not consistent.

Embarrassed, she cleared her throat and hissed at Nellie. "What are you doing? Stand up."

"Queen Agostonna," Nellie said, the awe in her voice causing it to tremble. "How are—do you—do you understand what you have done?"

Faria reached down to pull Nellie up and murmured in her ear. "Queen Agostonna? Who am I, my great-great-grandmother? Stop that."

"I can't…I just…we really need to talk about what just happened. About something I think I just realized."

Holding back a sigh of frustration, Faria lowered her voice. "Later, Nellie. I really don't think now is the time for any more revelations." She glanced meaningfully at the Earth Clan still staring slack jawed at her.

But she couldn't help but think about what she'd just done. What it felt like in her veins. Like sunshine and comfort had poured through her and into the child. It was then that she remembered something her mother had said the last time Faria saw her. That she was Fae-blessed. Was this what that meant? That she could then somehow bless others?

Even so, it wasn't something she could worry about now, not when she had a grown and possibly evil son to look for.

Faria desperately wanted to talk to someone, to anyone who could give her answers. She looked at Garrett, frustrated that he had no more information to share. "There has to be more to this," she said. "More to that man in the mask. More to the child that was with him."

"There is nothing more to say," he replied, before he turned on his heel and walked away.

She made a move to follow him but a hand at her shoulder stayed her. For a moment she was affronted that someone should wish to touch her, from a male that she did not choose, but then she remembered that things were different, now.

Thomas looked into her eyes. "We are calling a trial for his punishment. Any further information, if there is any, will be found out then."

Faria bit her tongue. She didn't have time to wait for a trial. She could feel the *innulum*, the bond between an elf and her child, stronger than ever, telling her that Ander was somewhere on Earth. Another tugging feeling, one she felt deep to her soul, beckoned her back to Anestra. Her heart ached. She was so torn about returning to her people but she could not give up on her child. Her last remaining connection to Hunter. Her flesh and blood. Unsure if it was her intuition or something more, she felt more eager than ever to find Ander and get him to safety.

"My queen," Nellie said. "We must stay for the trial. At least so we have answers and closure. Plus, he's an ass. I'd love to see what his punishment ends up being." She smiled a twisted, evil smile that Faria's newfound bloodthirsty side appreciated.

"We don't have much time. He is near, I know he is," Faria murmured not wanting the others to know about the *innulum*. Now that the immediate danger was gone, she wanted nothing more than to leave. But she was just craving a moment alone. It might not be the worst idea to rest, if only for a bit.

"It will happen in a few hours while they get everyone together. Let's eat and maybe catch a bit of sleep."

Faria noticed Nellie giving her the side-eye and wondered why she was acting so strange. Yes, she had healed a girl from the brink of death in a land where her magic didn't—shouldn't—work, but that didn't mean she needed to be treated differently.

Even so, Nellie's words seeped into her and Faria finally felt how tired she was. The last time she slept was before she gave birth, ran away, fought for her life, landed on Earth, fought for her life again, then healed a child. Sleep sounded like a great idea. She would have to find the time to question Nellie after they both rested.

Nellie led her away to a clearing to the north, one where the entire camp was in their line of sight and allowed them to defend themselves if necessary. The thought of sleeping in the woods, of having no control over her consciousness, put her on edge and hardened a piece of her heart.

She used to be carefree. She used to be dedicated and happy and ready to give her love to her people and those she didn't know.

The abandonment she felt when she was pregnant and then again when the people she loved most left her in such a cruel way burrowed deep within her. Suddenly, she wasn't so sure that sleeping was a good idea. If it would keep her old nightmares at bay.

"I'll keep watch while you sleep," Nellie said.

Faria lay on the ground, unsheathing a dagger. She placed her bow above her head and used her quiver as a makeshift pillow. As the quiet before sleep settled in, grief washed over her again, and she fell into a restless sleep.

THERE WAS NOTHING. DARKNESS, FLOATING, and nothing. She wondered if somehow she had landed in the Beyond. If the simple act of sleeping had drained the last piece of her until she was nothing, anymore.

A pinprick of light shone in the distance. She walked, or maybe floated toward it. No matter how she moved, it never seemed to get bigger.

She stayed her motion, thinking that if this were the Beyond, it was likely to drive her insane.

A humming rang out, echoing around the darkness. Voices vibrated deep within her, hissing in her ear, whispering words she could not quite understand, until finally, one called out.

"Faria Agostonna, apparent Queen to Anestra, daughter of the late Amira Agostonna, former Queen of Anestra, it is nearly time."

Time for what? She wanted to yell. She didn't seem to have a mouth to yell from.

"Time for your trials. To show whether you are capable and accept your position to be Queen."

I cannot do the trials, she thought at the voices. It can't be time. There is so much to do. I am needed on Earth. I must find my son.

"Once you learn of all he has done, you may not wish to return so quickly to the human realm. You may not wish to return anywhere, at all. You will be given that choice, just once. You cannot change your mind once you decide."

What are you talking about? She yelled into the void. Put me back, please. I cannot do the trial until I am finished with my task. I must save my people.

A flurry of hisses echoed around the dark chamber. They were displeased.

"You are as insolent as your mother was. We have changed your Fate once. We can do it again, and the result this time may not be something you like."

Was I supposed to like Hunter dying? Was I supposed to like the murder of my mother? The abduction of my son?

"Not all is as you believe, and not all that is true is as it seems. Be warned, Princess of Anestra, your trials will begin soon.

Faria gasped, awakening from her dream, or vision, whatever it was. The Fates would take her. Would it be hours? Days? Would people look for her? Would she miss another battle? Perhaps start another war?

She stretched her neck, working out a sore muscle as she glanced to the sky. It would be impossible to sleep now, thinking she might be whisked away at any moment.

Nellie stared at her, or rather through her. If the glazed look in her eyes were any indication, she was not properly seeing anything. The poor girl looked as tired as Faria felt, and she probably was even more so, with all the shifting she had done.

Faria considered telling Nellie about the vision, but decided to keep it to herself for now. There was nothing that could be done about it, anyway.

Faria turned over and watched as Samantha clutched onto Moira. She didn't fail to notice that she didn't get a thank you for saving the girl's life. Moira was another mystery added to the pile of things she didn't want to have to think about. Why did the girl refer to her as her queen? How did she know the language Faria spoke to her? More than that, why did Faria feel so fundamentally different after saving her life?

Her thoughts spun in her mind and she felt herself start to unravel. She breathed deeply, holding her breath for four seconds before releasing it for six, a technique she learned when she was younger to encourage her heart to calm down. She watched the camp around her, saw fires being built, breakfasts being made, and wondered where the strength came from to carry on when the world was falling apart so thoroughly.

The thought sent her into a fitful, dreamless sleep.

THIRTEEN

NELLIE

"**M**iss Nellie, wake up," a quiet voice whispered. Nellie shooed it away, unwilling to acknowledge it.

"Please, wake up!" it said again, shaking her this time. Grumbling, Nellie opened her eyes, grogginess blurring the trees and activities around her. She looked over at Faria, still sleeping on the ground, then down at the small girl staring up at her. Bright blue eyes met her own and a wide gap-toothed smile spread across her face.

"What? Are you hurt? What is it?" Nellie asked, taking quick stock of the girl, thinking perhaps her injuries had returned. Rather than answer her, the girl put a finger to her lips, then put her other hand against Nellie's face.

Nellie felt a heated, tingling sensation spread from her cheek down her neck. It felt as if she were drinking a steaming cup of hot chocolate, its warmth relaxing into all the nooks and crannies of her body. Before long, a series of images flashed in her mind, one after another, as though someone were flipping through the channels on TV.

A male of royal blood with purple eyes, and an elderly couple on a farm. A bare cottage, worn with age and love. A girl hiding under a table as body parts rained down the walls around her. A fire.

The cottage was familiar to Nellie; she went there, once, on one of her assigned recon missions. She recalled an overgrown farm and a house that had burnt to the ground. She'd slept on the edge of that farm with Johanna, one of the other members of the Royal Guard. Johanna said it reeked of evil magic.

"What the heck was that?" Nellie asked, breathless from the onslaught. "Who are you?"

"A chosen," the girl whispered back.

Nellie nearly snorted. "Another chosen?"

"We are all chosen. You, me, Queen Faria, the Val prince."

"What do you mean?"

The girl got up, dusting stray leaves and pine needles off her pants. For someone who had nearly kissed death an hour ago, she seemed quite agile to Nellie. The girl walked away, grabbing a waiting Samantha's hand. She cast a sly, secret smile behind her while Samantha scoffed in Nellie's direction.

Tommy walked over to Nellie with fresh water and a plate of eggs, bacon, and potatoes.

"Thought you might be hungry," he said.

Nellie nodded her thanks and swallowed a few scalding mouthfuls. "Hey, Tommy, who is that girl that Faria healed?"

He shrugged. "We don't know, really. She was found about a year ago. She barely knew English, didn't seem to have any family around here. She spoke in strange languages and the words we did understand didn't make sense. We thought she was disturbed, to be honest, until we realized she must have traveled through the Gate at some point. Samantha took a liking to her and sort of adopted her as her own."

The girl must be a seer of some sort, one that…what? Predicted the past? "What's her name?"

"Moira. We never figured out where exactly she was from. She kept saying something like, 'everywhere, all times.' Once she picked up English better, she tried warning us we were in trouble but again, we didn't think much of it. Just that it was part of whatever ailed her. Maybe she heard voices or whatever, I don't know." He shuffled his feet. "Although, with Faria healing her and you guys showing up…I don't know. Maybe she isn't as disturbed as we thought."

Nellie nodded. She knew the girl was from Anestra based on what she saw, but to warn her clan that danger was coming…how could she possibly have known that?

"She didn't…show you something?"

Tommy gave her an assessing glance. "She didn't have any belongings with her if that's what you mean. She smelt like fire and her hair was wind-whipped. She was hardly clothed properly, and definitely didn't have any pockets to store anything."

Nellie finished the last of her potatoes, barely eating the bacon; she had gone so long without meat and it just didn't settle well anymore. Tommy appeared lost in thought while staring at Faria. Normally this would be the time where Nellie admired him, and his strong features, the way his skin seemed to soak in the morning sun as if it belonged there, but she stopped herself from traveling down that lonely road.

"What did she show you?" he asked quietly.

Ha, so he did know what I meant. "Nothing. She just wanted to say thank you." She decided to play dumb, see what other information she could dig out of him. "What do you mean show me?"

"She can do this thing…I don't know. I didn't really believe Samantha and it never happened again, but she was convinced that Moira can somehow show you her memories. She did that to you just now, didn't she?"

Nellie turned her attention to Faria as she tossed in her sleep again. "We need to find the kid," she said, changing the topic. "We have to leave soon. Today, if we can manage."

Tommy seemed as though he wanted to say something, then shook his head as if changing his mind. "We can give you some supplies, but you'll probably want to give it a few days to prepare. You both need human clothes and things to hide your queen's appearance. And money."

Nellie's heart sank. She'd forgotten about money. Her mother had left her some after she passed away, but she hadn't accessed her bank account in years and no longer had any ID. She groaned.

"And," he continued, "we need you here for the tribunal. The new leader will want to figure out what to do with you."

"What to do with me?" she asked, her screeching voice sending squirrels skittering away. "What, like I'm a prisoner? I'm no longer yours, how many times must I say it? No one decides what to do with me except my queen."

"We don't know the danger you pose to any of us Nellie. Turning into that dragon—"

"Saved your asses out there!" she interrupted. "I protected you!"

"Still, your loyalty is not to us. Who's to say you won't turn against us?" He walked away, leaving Nellie sputtering in his absence.

That stubborn a-hole, she thought. *As if I would harm the only other family I knew? Did he forget everything we shared together?*

Grumbling to herself, Nellie settled back in against the mossy tree behind her. She couldn't help but think that she was forgetting some piece of vital information. It tickled the back of her mind, dancing across a recent memory. It was something she had come across in the many documents she and Faline had scoured in the past year. Something that would determine their chances of not only success, but their survival.

FOURTEEN

FARIA

Animals chittering their morning song blended with the sounds of the breakfast rush throughout the camp. Not for the first time, Faria wondered if this was some type of holding ground or if this was how these people lived—in tents and broken-down cabins, doing what they could to survive.

She kept her breathing even so as not to alert Nellie that she was awake, feeling her anger rise the longer she heard her talk to this Thomas Selwyk. How dare Nellie just decide that they would leave? They had hardly had any time to discuss what happened between them, let alone what they should do, and they hadn't spoken at all since all the new information had come to light. If they had, Nellie would know that Faria didn't want to leave. She didn't care about anyone else's apocalypse, but she knew Ander would show up. She knew Darroc would return to finish what he started on Earth, because there was only one thing he could possibly want.

To unite the clans and use them in the war against Anestra.

But Darroc had messed up, which wasn't a surprise. His ego was too big. He assumed others would just follow him blindly, and while he did get a few, the result was something he couldn't have expected. That there would be a significant number of people who wanted nothing to do with him, who would not go to war for him.

But he brought war and death to their doorstep anyway, and that left them with only one choice. Faria had to help unite the clans. She had to help them fight and win against Darroc on Earth. And then perhaps see if they would return the favor.

It was a long shot, but suspecting that Ander was no longer a defenseless baby changed things. She wondered if now he was a teenaged Val, or perhaps he was an elf...*by the Fates,* she didn't even know what race he was. She shook her head in disgust. Either way, what if he was on the cusp of the Change—the two-year process when magical abilities manifested and settled in as an elf approached their eighteenth year— something she was still on the verge of completing herself, with her own twentieth birthday approaching.

Decidedly angry enough to not pretend to sleep anymore, Faria sat up, gazing intently on Nellie. She didn't think she could get used to seeing this version of her. For five years Nellie had been her light haired, thirteen-year-old little sister. Now she was formidable enough to be an enemy at worst, acquaintance at best.

Thomas returned with a plate of food for Faria. She was pleasantly surprised to see he left off the meat. Her plate was filled with cooked potatoes, fresh fruit and what looked to be almonds, though they were much saltier than what she was used to.

"Almonds don't grow around here," Nellie said, as Faria's mouth puckered at the taste of one. "They probably bought a jar from a grocery store or something. Same with the fruit. They don't quite live off the land like you're used to."

Faria didn't say anything, wanting to enjoy her food in silence. She found herself willing her stomach to not turn the raspberries sour in her belly.

Nellie cleared her throat. "Listen, I wanted to tell you last night, but my friend Callie mentioned something she saw in the south."

"I don't really care to hear about others' problems. We have enough of our own."

"It has to do with this disease. And Darroc." She contained her huff of indignance as Nellie continued anyway. "Perhaps he started it and it mutated to affect the humans."

"None of this is interesting to me."

"And if it wasn't him that started the disease? If it was perhaps his partner who accidentally infected someone while torturing them for not complying with Darroc's orders?"

Faria sat up straighter, the potatoes sticking in her throat. She forced herself to swallow. It would be her worst nightmare if what Nellie was saying were true. If Ander not only took after the evil influence he grew up under, but was spreading such a devastating virus, too. It was unfathomable to think he could be the cause of thousands of deaths.

"There is one other thing we should consider," Nellie went on biting her lip. Faria narrowed her eyes at her the longer Nellie took to say whatever was on her mind.

"Spit it out."

"Well…how do you feel?"

How did she feel? Physically? Emotionally? Mentally? Breaking. Everything was breaking. What kind of question was that? "Want to be a little more specific?"

"I mean…well, after you healed Moira, did you feel different?"

"The only thing I feel is annoyed at this line of questioning. We have more important things to discuss than my feelings. Like what we're going to do with the clans."

Hurt shadowed Nellie's eyes before she blinked it away. Faria should have felt badly and maybe a part of her did, but so what if she felt differently after healing Moira? She couldn't put words to describe the way she felt different, nor was she going to question why the Fates saw it fit to give her an ability to heal the girl, either.

"You used blood magic to heal her," Nellie pressed on, and from the forcefulness of her voice, Faria could tell Nellie was trying to rein in her temper. "Only the warlocks use blood magic, who, according to documents I read in Faline's cache, were taught to use by the Val, who also were said to use blood magic in dire circumstances."

"What are you saying? That Darroc did something to me? I tried telling my mother he planted a seed of darkness in me, not that anyone cared what I had to say in the past ten months. Is that what you're saying? He gave me some innate ability to use blood magic?"

"No…" Nellie trailed off, staring at her as if waiting for her to put the pieces together, but Faria had no idea what she was on about. "You used blood magic another time, when you doused the black fire consuming the Forest of the Dawn."

Faria scrunched her eyebrows, trying to remember that day. Had she? She remembered being in the zone, remembered finding that well of fire magic within her and coaxing it out. She remembered slashing her palm and holding it to the ground, as if it were a natural instinct to do so, but that was months before ever meeting Darroc.

"I need to find Thomas." Faria stood up, brushing dirt and pine needles off her pants. Though the air was crisp, the sun started to heat up the forest and she was sweltering under the layers of clothing she wore.

"Did you ever consider that perhaps you aren't an elf? That maybe with your Change coming to a close, you're turning into something else?"

Faria paused. "Impossible." She waved the unsettling thought away. She didn't want to have this conversation now, anyway. The pull of the *innulum* felt stronger than it had since arriving in the human realm and she didn't want to risk weakening the connection by putting her task off any longer. "We will remain here, where Darroc is sure to return. It wouldn't pass by him that his monsters were destroyed by magic. And in the meantime we will help unite the clans. Teach them to fight. If anything was clear, with irrefutable proof, it is that these people have no idea how to properly fight or defend themselves. They have no discipline. No bravery. You and I were trained by—" her throat stuck as she almost said the name— "the best. We were both trained by the best. We can show them. We *will* show them."

The stony silence that followed let Faria know that Nellie was unhappy with that plan, and likely that she didn't agree. But as Nellie repeatedly told anyone who approached her, *she* was the queen.

"You don't care how I feel about anything, do you?" Nellie asked quietly, tearing a stick she held in her hands into pieces. "You don't care that being around him physically pains me? You don't care how much I'm hurting over him moving on, while I had to remain a child, unable to pursue anyone I might have been interested in, with constant reminders of him echoing all around Anestra. For five years I had to hold in my loneliness, do nothing, smile, follow orders, be someone else because I feared for my life, and now I'm back here witnessing how thoroughly he moved on. Can you begin to imagine having to suffer through that pain, while being surrounded by the very people who sent me to my death?"

If Faria had any feeling left, if she had been her old self, she would have been devastated. She would have understood Nellie's plight. She would have wanted to protect her, make things easier for her.

But that wasn't who she was anymore.

"Did you hear what I said?" Nellie continued when Faria gave no response. "Garrett called the order, but it was voted on. The same tribunal that is about to happen to him had happened to me. Except then he lied about me murdering my own *mother*. And they all agreed, with no proof. No one tried to save my life. And now you want me to remain here, train them, save *their* lives?"

The tension between them thickened. "We all need to do things we don't want to do. It's how we survive. You'll be stronger for it. We stay."

Faria grabbed her bag and walked away from Nellie, settling behind a copse of trees out of direct sight from the camp. She rummaged through her belongings if only for something to do, and her fingers passed over the cool glass bottle of the Elixir of Life. Her heart clutched at the memory of her mother shoving it into her bag after giving it to Ander. She shook her head, dispelling the memory.

Her fingers snagged on something thin and papery she hadn't noticed before. A sealed envelope.

Faria searched her mind, thinking back to when her mother had put it into the bag in their hurry to escape.

"Take the boy, go straight into the Forest. Are you healed enough now?"

Faria nodded. She was sore and exhausted beyond belief, but no longer torn. Her adrenaline spiked, realizing what her mother asked of her.

The queen lay the baby down in his crib. Faria watched as her mother prepared a bag filled with linen and food, along with a sealed envelope. She picked up the baby again and turned back to Faria.

"Take him and run, quickly. Do not stop until you get to the meadow. You will not see me again."

Faria gasped as she came out of the memory. It was the last she had seen her mother alive. The last time she had spoken to her.

She cracked her neck and steeled her nerves before tearing the envelope open. A bracelet fell out in her haste, along with a folded piece of parchment. She picked up the jewelry, her jaw dropping. Tendrils of the most wonderful colors reflected off the morning sun, encased in a long, thin, crescent moon-shaped piece of glass. The colors swirled as if they were flame one minute and smoke the next. It was mesmerizing, watching the purple, green, blue, and silver wind their way around each other, as if they were suspended in some form of thick liquid. The entire glass piece was circled by what seemed to be silver, though it was much lighter and far sturdier. Faria recognized it immediately as the bracelet Darroc had sought, the one he swore was stolen from his own mother. She placed it on her wrist, taking care to cover it with her sleeve. A heated vibration hummed against her skin and she felt as though the bracelet were melting into her.

Faria turned her attention to the parchment, her fingers shaking slightly as she opened it. The words blurred on the page as she recognized her mother's beautifully delicate writing, all sweeps and brush strokes. She read through it three times before she fully understood the words, her heart pounding in her chest.

My dearest Faria,

You know in the human books, where someone receives a letter and it starts off with, "If you are reading this, then I am dead..." Well, I'm sure you know the rest. Yes, I'm sure you are shocked that I know what human books contain. I have been alive for decades and find great entertainment in them. I'm sure you're equally as surprised to hear me jest, when it seemed for so long that I was incapable. The timing is not quite right, I'll admit, but I couldn't resist.

My darling girl, there are so many things I wish I could have told you, and even more I wish I could change. Truthfully, I'm not quite sure where to begin, so I shall start at the beginning.

Your father and I had a hard time conceiving you. I lost three babies before the age of twenty, and then after that, I was unable to conceive at all because of the dreadful curse. We had worried, of course, that the Agostonna line would be finished after that. I never had siblings, but there were distant cousins, and even more concerning, elves and other races who did not live in Anestra who were rumored to want my throne. We spent years—decades, really—planning for the worst. If war would come to our doors again.

Fifty years went by and still, I did not come with child. I knew you would come, of course, because the Fates had told me as much, just as I knew war would come, but I didn't have the specifics, then. I didn't realize the hardship that would grow, the loneliness that would bore into my soul, over not having you.

Your father and I had just come to terms with it, and we were perfectly happy just being the two of us. We had considered adoption, as well, though I still held onto the hope that you would finally come.

And then, after my hundredth year, I was with child. Oh, how I prayed to the Goddesses above and the gods below that it would stick.

It did not.

Your father and I still held onto our purpose, however. Anestra was our child and our mother. We established new trade routes, we welcomed and trained new races, we upheld the Treaty, we had even started a school for the orphan children right at Mentage.

Just when we had completely given up hope, you arrived.

The night I gave birth I was visited by two strangers. The first was a woman I hadn't recognized. She had the strangest green eyes, freckles all across her face, and the wildest hair I had ever seen. I asked how she had gotten past my guards, how she came to be in the birthing room at all as I recovered. I was frightened that night. My powers didn't seem to work on her, or rather, I didn't detect any sort of deception or lies from her. She was rather comforting, if I'm being honest, and I felt the strangest connection to her.

She told me she was from another time and place, and came to give my darling girl her blessing. Of course I wanted to refuse, though something stopped me. She handed me a piece of jewelry, and told me a truly unbelievable tale, that it was the magic of her people. She said she was no longer fit to rule, that the person who loved her could not let her go, and turned her into something else. She said she worried for Anestra, and that my darling girl would bear the brunt of it. I knew there was some truth to it, as the Fates had shown me that very thing when I had my trials.

She kissed your forehead and spoke in an old language, one from the time of the Ancient Originals, if I had to guess. She said I must not let her son find the magic, that he would corrupt it and it would become a fate worse than death for not only her people, but for everyone.

I asked her what I was to do with it, and she said to give it to you when the time was right. This, I believe, is that time.

You remember when Darroc first visited and I allowed him to see what I held on my wrist? It was to see if he really was the person we had to look out for. The second the spark of recognition hit his eyes, I just knew.

The woman left shortly after, and said it was time for her to be something else for a while. I never did see her again.

Not long after, another visited me. This one was a Fae. She said something similar, that she was there to give you a blessing. To say I was speechless is an understatement. A Fae! Her features were so alien to me, something out of a tale. Her limbs were elongated, her eyes so round, and she had shimmering runes that writhed under her skin. She told me an ancient sort of magic that would help protect you for as long as you stayed in Anestra, or until I had Faded. It was why we never let you travel through the Gate to visit other realms. I'll not deny that I was paranoid enough to keep you close to me at all times. You should have been safe anywhere in our land, but I needed you near. I couldn't bear to think that anything would happen to you, not after I waited a human lifetime and a half to have you.

It may have seemed like I put you directly in harm's way, or that I used you 'as a battle strategy' as you once said, but I promise you my darling, I would have given every possession I owned, every jewel I had, every secret I housed, if I knew I had a chance to save you.

The Fates are cruel, unforgiving, and absolute. There is no way around Them, which you will find out shortly if you haven't already. I am so, so sorry for the heartache I have caused. I am so sorry I didn't see the truth in things. I'm sorry I didn't see how badly you were hurting, and most of all, I am sorry that I failed so heavily at being a proper mother to you. I knew my end would come and I did what I could to keep you at a distance, to make the pain less, and here I am—hours away from when I am to Fade, and I fear I have done the type of damage that is irreversible.

You will be a fairer queen than I, my darling. You will rule each of your lands with love in your heart, and will prosper because of that love. Your inquisitive nature, your thirst for adventure, and your need to satisfy your people will all serve you well in your role. You will be everything that I could not, and I have never been prouder of who you are.

Please, don't lose that part of yourself. Give yourself time to grieve and ache over the things I could not prevent, but come back from it my darling. Come back from that dark edge you will find yourself on. Pick yourself up, and choose life. Choose love. Choose the adventure.

I love you, more than the words in this letter could ever convey. You are *the foundation of all I am. You are my most precious gift, the greatest ever presented by the Fates.*

I will greet you in the next life with arms wide open, but until then, lead with honor, purpose, and love.

Yours always,

Memi

Faria swallowed a lump in her throat and wiped her sweating hands against her pants. She felt the prickle of tears threaten as she focused on her breathing, rather than the cyclone of emotion building inside of her. If she had her magic, she would have summoned a rain of fire to burn away the pain she felt at reading those words. At learning how much her mother had loved her. At the shame she felt at defying her mother at every turn. At the immense loss she felt with her gone.

She read and reread the letter more times than she could count. A never-ending list of questions built up. Who was the woman who gave her mother the bracelet? What magic did the Fae teach her mother? Would more Fae show up? What did she mean when she said she would "rule each of her lands" with love…what lands, besides Anestra, was she supposed to rule?

Faria folded the parchment carefully, making sure to fold the creases exactly as they were before tucking the letter gently into the bottom of her bag. She would have time to sort through her emotions later, but not now. She had a trial to attend, clans to unite.

Most importantly, she had a friendship to mend. She shouldn't have been so harsh with Nellie. She did know what it was like to lose someone she loved. She couldn't imagine what it would be like to see Hunter again, especially if he had moved on with someone else. She wasn't mated to him, though, so she didn't know the full extent of the ache Nellie felt.

Was it better to lose your lover forever, or to know they were alive but unreachable?

A GREAT BOOM OF DRUMS started at sun down, its steady thump engulfing the forest. Tiny pebbles vibrated on the ground in time to the beat.

Faria joined the masses walking toward the trial. Some of the shifters smiled at her, others bowed. It was unnerving, being around so many creatures that her people had persecuted not long ago. There would be no way for them to know that, but she felt guilty, nonetheless.

They entered a wide clearing, the buzzing of the Gate of All Realms alive around them. No one else seemed affected by it, but she could feel its magic deep in her bones, as if it were part of the blood she was made from. It was even more disturbing with the sound of the drumbeats heightening in intensity as the shifters poured in. She was pleased to see even the children came. It was important for them to learn the customs of their people, no matter what their laws were.

Thomas entered the clearing from the opposite side with Garrett trussed up behind him. He sneered at everyone, as if he didn't care that his life was on the line.

The tribunal started by Thomas announcing the accusations to the clan, that Garrett knowingly and willingly aided an unnamed male claiming to be their creator that ultimately resulted in the death of two clan leaders and numerous other clan members. Then Thomas asked for witnesses. Faria edged closer to the front so she could have a better view. She was used to the mundane happenings of court. She had sat through so many proceedings in her own home, though none were as interesting or as meaningful to her as this one.

After several other witnesses, who all corroborated each other's stories—that Garrett had left for many hours at a time over the course of several months—Nellie was finally called up to give her account. Faria was proud of Nellie for standing against them. For looking them in the eye. For daring to live, and daring them to do something about it. She felt a tinge of regret as Nellie strode to the middle of the enclave, her head held high as she stared defiantly at those around her.

Jeers and hisses echoed among the circle, though they weren't as enthusiastic as when they first arrived. There were a few shouts calling her a liar, that she couldn't be trusted, though the words she spoke were as much the same as everyone else. It felt cruel to let the taunts go on, but Faria was interested to see how Nellie would defend herself.

"I wasn't a liar five years ago, and I'm not now." Nellie's eyes shone with a fierce gleam. "Everything I said has been corroborated by those before me, that much is evident. What should also be evident is that I was falsely accused of murdering my own *mother*—sent to death—by all of you, because you chose to believe a liar. He put you and your people in danger, as he had been doing for years since before I was banished, and it was my queen and I who saved you. Imagine where you would be if we were not here? If I were not alive. So *you're welcome*, though you are too proud to say thank you. *You're welcome* for ensuring your survival. I expect you to speak to my queen with more respect than you did to me, or you will soon see how I really feel about being back among you."

There was a shuffle and whispers. Someone must have said something Faria couldn't hear because Nellie said, "I agree. I am not one of you anymore. I belong to Anestra. I follow their laws, not yours. I don't need to stand here, I don't need to defend myself, my queen does not need to remain here, and if we remain it is because she feels much kinder to you than I do."

Then Nellie walked away, the crowd parting for her. Finally, Thomas called Faria up to say her piece and as one, the shifters turned toward her and bowed their head in reverence. Faria lifted a brow.

"I think Nellie said all that needed to be said. She is correct. I do not take kindly to the disrespect you show her, because that means you are also disrespecting me. You actually owe me nothing and her everything. She is correct, we remain here due to my kindness." She paused, looking at them each in turn. "I will extend you another kindness and say that that man does not deserve to live." She pointed to Garrett, disdain dripping from her. "He led you all to your deaths. Prince Darroc L'Azare is a warlock skilled in dark and forbidden magic. He will kill you once he is done with you even if you side with him. You do not know his brand of evil. You do not understand the monstrosities he is capable of. Those creatures he created are nowhere near the worst of his sins. So, as Nellie said, you are welcome for the help. There is nothing more to say."

Faria saw Nellie's relief in the way she slightly relaxed her stance. Faria might not be well practiced as a queen, but she knew not to let her feelings for Nellie personally stand in the way of them professionally. They were loyal to each other. They protected each other. They would always show a united front, no matter their differences. That, at least, would not change if she could help it.

Thomas looked at Garrett, his face drawn in a frown. "Is there anything you wish to say in your defense?"

Garrett looked Thomas up and down, Faria delighted in his discomfort. A sheen of sweat dappled on his forehead. "I already admitted to having knowledge that *someone* who may or may not be a warlock, was our creator. I had knowledge that he wanted us to do whatever it was he said. I saw myself how evil he and his partner were. I tried to get out of it."

"And because you failed, because you kept it to yourself, you have brought ruin to us all." Thomas shook his head then faced the crowd.

The drums beat again, slowly, before rapidly building in cadence. Faria's stomach turned sour. He had to be wrong. If it was Ander with Darroc, she refused to accept his labeling as evil, even if she had the same thoughts. Faria watched as Thomas and a group of others convened off to the side, trying to figure out what the punishment would be. If they were in Anestra it would be death, but nothing like this could happen in Anestra because of the Blood Contract. Of course, they did still have an uprising.

No matter how advanced or behind a culture might be, there would still be those who wished to bring it down.

Once the drums reached their frenzy, Thomas yelled to the crowd, "You have caused the deaths of countless others, both past and untold amounts of the future. You will then bear the weight of what you have done. You have been banished."

Faria observed the reactions of the clan members. They were battered, these people. Broken. Defeated. She knew what that was like because it was how she felt inside. It was a good decision to stay and help them, especially for when Darroc returned. She couldn't leave more people unprotected, the way she left her friends and family. She couldn't have more death on her hands. Soon, Nellie would see that.

Until then, they had much to prepare for. Weapons, practicing, food, tallies of everything.

Garrett screamed, begging for his life. As one, the group started walking in the direction of the humming, and with great concern she realized they were walking toward the Gate.

"Wait," Nellie yelled next to them, trying to be heard above the commotion. "He could survive! I am proof of that!"

"It is what we do," Thomas said. "We do not change our ways. This is still the ultimate punishment. The likelihood of him surviving is slim, and of him returning even less so. If he does return, we decide what to do then."

He gave her a pointed look, as if reminding her that they still needed to figure out what to do with her, but Faria took a step to block Nellie from his view.

"She is mine," Faria said.

Thomas held her gaze for a moment, then turned and ushered Garrett through the Gate. His howling and begging echoed in the woods until it broke off in a gasp. He was sent through to whatever unknown hell he deserved.

Thomas's expression was unreadable as he waited for his clan members to quiet down. "We must elect a new leader. We cannot go on as we are, not when there is still a threat to our people and our territory. It is nearly dark, should we wait until—" His voice died down as one by one the clan put their arms across their chest and bowed to him.

Faria thought it was a positive sign, that at least they were all united in this. She had to agree with them. No one else had stepped up the way he had, and he seemed to have a commanding way about him, judging from the way they all listened to him before the battle with the animals. Not to mention, he was the strongest mated male. She believed the clans put much stock in the strength of their men rather than their women.

Thomas nodded, his eyes misting, though he seemed to be expecting it. His back straightened and he readjusted the bow he held loosely in his hand.

Faria's own approval of him cooled when he next addressed the crowd. "Now we must vote on what to do with Nellie Glazer."

A small noise escaped Nellie's mouth, her face a mixture of both fear and indignation. Though Nellie's head remained high, her face immediately paled. Nellie clenched her fists and then relaxed them over again, as though she were picturing strangling Thomas. The thought amused Faria.

There was some murmuring among the clan, looking both at Nellie then at Faria. She raised her brow at them, daring them to say something that would result in nothing but bloodshed. She knew they respected her, thought of her as something more than mortal because of the way she healed Moira.

Faria cleared her throat and the whisperings ceased. "As a sign of peace, I am prepared to offer you our guidance in the form of protection.

We are willing to train those of who you remain. Nellie and I both learned under Anestra's weapons master, the most skilled fighter our land had seen in centuries. We are both well capable of teaching you what we know, in the short time we have here, so you will be better prepared for when Darroc returns."

Thomas looked at his clan. Their bruised, broken faces lit up with hope. "I agree if they agree. But if you do so," he turned to face the clan head on, "you must treat Queen Agostonna with the utmost respect. And Nellie. They saved us and are likely to do so again." As one they put their hands across their chests and bowed their heads, this time at Faria and Nellie, a sign that they agreed and appreciated Faria's offer.

A throat cleared angrily beside her. Faria knew she had backed Nellie into a corner, but regardless of Nellie's disapproval, these people needed her knowledge and she knew that she needed to stay. At least for a few days, a week. She couldn't be sure how much time passed in Anestra, but she hoped they could risk it.

The clan started to disperse and Faria approached Thomas, who watched them grimly. "You will have to send word to the Air Clan. Let them know their leader is dead." He nodded. "This would be a good time to have a formal meeting. Try to redo that peace treaty."

He looked at her. "I know you are a queen in your land, but you are not in mine. I am the leader here. I will make the decisions."

"A wise leader listens to those who are willing to work with them and considers all angles. A wise leader knows that they do not know everything and accepts help when it is offered."

"Really?" He said pointing his chin over at Nellie. "Is that what you did? Listen to her when she made it clear she couldn't be here? That there was something else happening worth investigating that likely has to do with who you are looking for?"

She gave him a blank stare. "Tell them I will train them as well," she said, as she walked away.

FIFTEEN

HUNTER

Pyres surrounded the fields of *Mentage*, well away from the Forest of the Dawn. The smoke curled and drifted, undoubtedly to be seen for miles. The scent of ash and sweet incense permeated the air as hundreds of mourners ushered their loved ones into the Beyond in the glow of twilight.

Some said prayers in the old language, some asked the three goddesses for protection, and some prayed to a single god, asking for forgiveness of their loved one's sins so they might enter into Heaven.

Hunter didn't know what sort of afterlife to believe in, but he hoped that wherever these spirits went, they were at peace.

King Dennison walked from group to group offering his condolences, flanked by the Queen's Royal Guard and others. He refused to wear armor, much to the Guard's annoyance, but he had weapons along his belt all the same. The king didn't think they would be attacked again so soon, and Hunter was inclined to agree. If they could trust Endo's information, they still had some time to prepare for the next onslaught.

Warring emotions raged inside Hunter. Anger, at all this loss. Sadness, that the king offered his condolences but refused to accept anyone else's, insisting that the queen's loss was everyone's loss. Rage, at the Elders for withholding information from him, for not allowing him the use of his powers, for daring to keep a Val as their slave. The colors of twilight melted into the horizon as yellows, pinks, and purples bled together. Hunter's eyes watered, threatening to spill down his face. The incense was too spicy, too heavy in the air.

"Are you okay?" a voice murmured beside him. Hunter counted to ten before turning to the warlock. He didn't entirely blame Endo for his naivete, but in this moment, it was nearly impossible not to lash out on him for choosing to blindly follow Darroc, for falling in with the likes of Crispin and Smyth. And, he couldn't deny, he blamed himself for not spotting the signs. He had trained Endo himself and chose him personally to be his second, grooming him to take over command someday. He was the closest thing to a friend Hunter had had in a long time.

"Yes," he finally answered. "I am perfectly fine."

"You know I can feel others' emotions and you feel, well, murderous."

Hunter slowly turned his head as Endo took a slight step backward. He felt murderous? Of course he did. What else could he feel when hundreds were dead because of his failure to protect Faria? Because of the parts they both played, no matter how large or small.

"Do you understand why I feel murderous?" he asked, his voice low. "Do you fully grasp what has happened?"

Endo swallowed. "I think so."

"I used to consider you a friend, Endo. At least as much as I could have. I trusted you. We shared things—nights out, females a few times—and you knew there was something different about me but never pressed me for answers that you knew I couldn't give. And now you come back here and expect us to be as we were before? Do you really think I want to sit here and share my feelings?"

"Hunter, if it was your people that you had a chance of saving, you know you—"

"That was my son who was taken away from me. My fucking son, Endo. My friends are dead. My queen is dead. Faria is gone and I have no way to help her. I cannot access my powers and all I see is destruction and the part I—*we*—played in it. Yes. I am feeling murderous."

Endo's eyes widened at the mention of Hunter's son, but he didn't ask for further explanation. "What can I do?"

A silence stretched between them, interrupted only by the occasional moaning of a nearby mourner.

"You are going to bring me to Crispin."

"Are you—do you really think he would hang around after all this?"

"No doubt about it." Hunter chuckled darkly. "He probably assumed those beasts would best *Mentage*, especially with Faria and Queen Amira out of the picture. Not to mention, he is such a narcissist, there is no way he wouldn't have stuck around to see the damage he inflicted."

"You're probably right about that, but how should I know where he is now?"

"You spent the past year following him around. Are you telling me you really have no idea where to start looking?"

The seconds ticked by as Hunter stared down Endo, waiting for his admission.

Endo paled. "He can kill me, Hunter."

"So can I."

The cold declaration rang with truth. He'd left his compassion on the beach with the Elders. He no longer cared what it took to get the answers he needed. Whether that made him a villain, when he had been a protector for so long, he didn't know. It was no longer of consequence.

There was the Blood Contract to think about, but if the warlocks and Darroc got around it, then so could he. With the king's approval, he was sure they could figure out a way around harming another. Not that he truly wanted to kill Endo.

Crispin, on the other hand…

"I will do what I can to help, Hunter, you know that. But can I trust that you'll be on my side when it comes down to it? If Crispin decides to retaliate against me, can I count on you?"

He wanted to say no. Desperately, with every fiber of his being, he wanted to tell Endo that he would do whatever it took to get his revenge against anyone he could, regardless of who got in the way. The thought was unsettling. That sliver of darkness he held at bay inside him pressed against him, but he kept a firm lock on it. He might have left his compassion on the beach, but he didn't leave his humanity. "You can count on me to get the job done."

"WHAT IS IT YOU MEAN to do?" King Dennison asked later that night as he stared at Hunter, Endo, and Wil over his maps lying on the table in the Council Chamber.

The funerals were long since over, the food was eaten, and tasks were picked up again to sort out *Mentage*. Citizens of Anestra worked in shifts so they each helped with clean-up on the grounds, nursing in the makeshift medical tents, and cooking and caring for orphaned children.

Hunter and Endo had run into Wil on his way to give his report to the king. They had spread the word to Mercy Bay and beyond, looking for volunteers to fight and protect the borders. Wil, normally friendly and easy going, had stared daggers at Endo, and it was only through Hunter's intervention that no harm came to the warlock. He quickly told Wil what he had in mind, but Wil didn't think it was a good idea. Still, it was up to the king now to decide how to handle enemies to the Agostonna crown.

"I want to find Crispin. And Smyth, if I can."

"And do what?" The king stressed each syllable, as if he couldn't believe what Hunter was suggesting.

"Get information."

"Through what means?"

"Torture, specifically." Hunter's statement hung in the air, as if the walls themselves couldn't believe such a remark was made.

The king's pale face turned a dark shade of red. "That. Is. Not. Us."

"It used to be. The queen's ancestors would employ my kind to do more than just protect them. We would do whatever was necessary to keep everyone safe."

"And you are saying…what? You tortured and murdered people?"

Hunter clenched his jaw. The truth was, he only remembered bits and pieces of his past. It was as if his memories were locked in a cage, forgotten in the dark caverns of his mind. He had no idea what happened to him to make that so. "I am saying, I did whatever it took to protect the Agostonna bloodline."

He squared his shoulders and looked the king in the eye. It was no use denying what he used to do, whether he remembered all the details or not. The Val were fierce, deadly protectors. They didn't always play fair. They weren't heroes in armor for others to pant over and worship. They were warriors chosen by the gods, and as Prince of the Val, he was the one who led their army against the warlocks one thousand years ago. He was the one who had to make the decision to sacrifice their people in order to do as the goddesses commanded.

Nothing got in the way of protecting what was his.

Except the Elders.

"I cannot have the two of you traipsing around this country looking for enemies to the Agostonna crown." King Dennison took a deep breath before continuing. "You need to remain here and help train our people. We cannot risk you leaving at such a pivotal time."

"Then send someone else to find him and bring him to me." Hunter was unwilling to let it go. He knew what it took to make a person break. He used to do it so often before. The darkness took over him with a swiftness that made him dizzy, heady with the feeling of having a person's life or death so delicately in his hands. He hadn't felt that way since over a year ago when he questioned a human named Anwyn, who helped start the fires at the rebel warlocks' request. The darkness had been satiated then, for a long while.

Until now. He needed to get his hands on Crispin. He needed to shake off this urge before the rage ate at him so completely that he hardly recognized himself.

"No one is dispensable enough to send away for any period of time on a witch hunt. The answer is no." The king looked at each of them in turn. "If anyone happens across him by Fate's design, then we can broach the topic again. Until then, we help our people heal. We collect our harvest. We stock up on potions and healing agents. We train newcomers to *Mentage*. We create magical weapons. We have more than enough to do and not enough time to do it all."

"Your majesty," Endo said. "What about the Book I told you about? The one that has the spell of unmaking. If we get our hands on that, then we could avoid another battle."

"The war has already begun, Endo," the king sighed. "Just because you know the last known location of the Book doesn't mean it's still there. We know the last known location of the Eternal Flame and the Crystal of Light, both of which would tip the Fates in our favor, but that doesn't mean they're attainable. What we need are more people. More magic. And stronger defenses."

"Of course, your majesty." Endo bowed then excused himself from the room. Hunter followed, leaving Wil to give his report to the king.

He was being foolish, he knew, with how quickly he wanted to act. The skill of torturing took time and the removal of feelings, neither of which he had. He knew the king was right; there was too much work to be done, especially without Queen Amira.

The king was right about something else, as well. The Eternal Flame and Crystal of Light were both artifacts created by the gods and goddesses who ruled the land long before the elves did. The Eternal Flame was said to be in a different realm, hiding in a volcano. The Crystal of Light, however, was rumored to be in a part of Anestra that had not been explored for centuries.

In the city of Farrah, through the Caranek Peaks, was a temple under which it was said that the Goddess Farrah had been laid to eternal rest. Rumor had it that within that temple lay the Crystal of Light—the physical manifestation of Farrah's remaining power before she slumbered. Those who harnessed the Crystal had the power of the gods, or so the story went. As far as Hunter knew, it was just rumors and no one had ever laid eyes on such a thing.

In fact, no one had ever gotten through to the other side of the Caranek Peaks for as long as he was alive. It was as if they were a sealed gate, not allowing any passage until one worthy enough presented themselves.

He did know someone who had attempted just a year ago, however.

Hunter followed Endo, keeping to the fingers of shadows splayed across the grounds. He didn't want Endo to catch on that he was close behind. Though Endo never became an official member of the Guard, the king had allowed him to move back to his old quarters. And, it meant there would constantly be eyes on him.

He took another step before his vision blacked out and for a brief moment, wondered if the Elders were snatching him away against his will again, until he saw another forest, with another set of beings in front of him. The image was distorted, as though he were looking at it through a foggy window. He was rooted to the spot, unable to turn around, until a voice reached his ears and turned his insides molten.

"You didn't…animal side…felt threatened…"

He felt his heart beat in his throat as his body unlocked, allowing him to face his mate for the first time. "Faria?"

The image in front of him sharpened as his gaze zeroed in on her. She looked good, all things considered. She still wore the mucked-up clothing from her fight, so he had to assume not much time had passed since he saw the vision of her. Her long black hair was tied back and she wore a frown on her face. She looked exhausted, the light in her eyes had gone out. Hunter searched her for any signs of injury but found none. His gaze snagged on two symbols etched along her forehead. Both were thin and white, filled with swirling designs, but were distinct. His eyebrows shot up as he recognized one as a healer's mark. He had only seen those on the Fae-blessed or other Val. The other made his breath catch in his chest as his heart forgot to beat. The mate mark.

So it was true.

"Can you see me, Princess?" he asked, moving closer to her. He waved his hand in front of her face but she kept her gaze forward, steadily looking through him. He huffed out a breath. "I'm still here," he said, desperate.

A flash of light blinded him as he found himself back in Anestra, standing outside of Endo's door. *For the Fates' sake.* Did they really have to taunt him like that? He was happy to see the bond was trying to work, and more than relieved to see that she was still alive and well, but to have mere seconds just wasn't enough. It would never be enough.

He tried to stomp down his bitterness toward the Fates and kept his cursing of the Elders to a minimum as he pounded on Endo's door. He still had work to do on his end and couldn't risk the distraction the rush of feelings presented him with.

"I don't need a constant watch," Endo grumbled as he opened the door. "I've been trying to make my amends. I'm not going to do anything against Anestra now."

Hunter forced his way past Endo into the small, one-room cabin. It was tiny, about half the size of his, but these cabins were made for members of the Guard who didn't spend much time in their room anyway. Endo hastily put on a tunic over his shirtless body.

"You know I've seen you nude before, right?" Hunter asked with his eyebrow raised. "In several different situations. You don't need to feign modesty."

"Well, you don't need to see me now," Endo muttered with his back turned.

"Why are you trying to hide from me?"

"I don't know what you're talking about." Endo turned fully around and stared Hunter down. "What are you doing here?"

He narrowed his eyes. Endo's behavior was strange, but he didn't need to push it just yet. "Nellie reported to us last year that you spent some time trying to get through the Caranek Peaks."

"We camped out there for a while."

"For what purpose?"

Endo shifted on his feet. "It was orders that were relayed to Crispin.

He had me go with him, along with a few warlocks who lived out there, to find a way through the mountains. If we did find a way, we were to do nothing but tell Darroc how to do it."

"He didn't want you making the trek through the Peaks if you found a way?"

"No, but it didn't matter because there isn't a way through. Smyth was supposed to find a way around them. He took a small crew and had a mind to sail through Widow's Passageway, but by the time they found a ship, Darroc called them off. That was shortly before the bonding ceremony."

"And you have no idea why he wanted to get through the mountains, knowing that no one is known to survive the travel? Knowing that the Crystal of Light is supposedly on the other side?"

"I really couldn't tell you what he wished to gain from the knowledge."

Hunter clenched his teeth. "And at what point in time did you decide to stop blindly following orders?"

Endo bristled. "About the same time that I realized who and what Nellie was. And just so you know, I did work extra hard trying to find out more information to relay to her, but there just never was any information to give. He gave orders. He disappeared. He didn't answer questions."

"And then what?" Hunter bit out harshly. "You just happened to leave without him knowing? Do you really think he won't come back to punish you?"

"My motives were always pure, whether you agree with them or not. You're just angry because I pulled one over on you and you're hurt that your friend betrayed you. Well, I'm back now, I apologized, and I'm doing what I can to make it right."

Hunter felt the runes under his skin writhe. If he were in his true form, he knew by now his ire would have turned their normally silvery color almost black and his gold skin would have brightened. His magic, if he had it, would have been right at his fingertips to exact justice where it was needed. He could admit that he was not pure of heart. If he were, he would never have kept Faria so close to him, never have been tempted by her in the first place. He didn't want to worry about that, however. He felt enough guilt about who he was to last him another five lifetimes.

"If he didn't find a way to the Crystal, then it's possible he's going after the Flame."

"Do you mean the Eternal Flame that is in a volcano in the fire realm, protected by dragons and other dangerous beasts? You think he would rather risk his life going there?" Endo looked doubtful. "There is no way he would survive, even with all his dark magic. What makes you think he can do it?"

"Because now he has something that has not been seen for more than one thousand years. Another thing that was prophesized long ago."

"What is that?"

"My son."

SIXTEEN

FARIA

The forest, already packed with what was left of Nellie's former clan, seemed even smaller once the other clans arrived the next day.

The rest of the Air Clan and the Water Clan from the west arrived first, bringing with them maybe just under a hundred shifters at most. They arrived wearing heavy coats and fur-lined gloves though it was only cold at night; the sun still burned them during the day and the warmth lasted until it was fully dark. They greeted each other cautiously, showing each other things on small metal boxes no larger than their hands.

"Those are called cell phones," Nellie confirmed as the pair of them watched the visiting clans from among the tree lines. "They allow you to reach anyone at a moment's notice."

"Is it magic?" Faria asked, thinking how useful that would be in Anestra.

"No, it's something called technology. There's a lot of science behind it and cell towers and satellites and stuff."

She didn't know what all that meant, but Faria was quite sure it was the human's version of magic.

"It won't work in Anestra because the realm, I think, is in a different dimension or something. There's no way for us to connect to what Earth has done, just as they cannot reach the magic there."

"Do you know these people?" Faria asked, changing the subject. She was aware of the plethora of eavesdroppers and she really wasn't interested in having strangers learn more about her land than they needed to.

"No, not really. Some are familiar but I was really only just accepted to the Earth Clan shortly before I was banished. There weren't many opportunities to meet the others."

Faria nodded, understanding that. The land they were on seemed much bigger than Anestra and filled with so many more people than hers.

As the day wore on, Faria and Nellie took stock of what weapons were available and made notes of who turned into what type of animal so they could strategize. It was grim. There were a handful of bows, adequately made, but not as many arrows as she would have liked to see. They would need to make more immediately, and dip them in more *Drogosterra* blood to avoid another massive loss of innocent life. There were a few daggers, some thin blades, a couple wooden staffs, and a huge cache of some sort of metallic weaponry. Nellie told her they were called guns and started naming the different types.

"No," Faria said. "No guns."

"They can probably kill those beasts and it would help the others that haven't shifted yet or aren't strong fighters in their animal form."

"They are cold and cruel. There is no honor in using them. No warmth. They are a coward's weapon. Not to mention, they aren't magical. They won't stop the beasts."

"You just don't understand them. You don't respect what they could do."

"I respect all weapons, but a machine that can kill someone without you ever needing to be near them, without hearing their last breaths, without feeling their struggle as they fight to survive is cowardly. That is where the honor is. That is where the respect for life comes in. Those weapons stop enemies because they fear death, not because they respect the weapon. Fear and respect are not the same thing."

Nellie looked as if she wanted to argue about it but she let it go. Undoubtedly it would come up again, but if they were going to fight in Anestra, Faria wanted nothing about those weapons on her land.

Thomas signaled to Faria, Nellie following close behind like a shadow. She appreciated Nellie taking her duty to protect her seriously but it was starting to irritate her.

"When do we begin?" Faria asked as she approached Thomas.

"After the last of the stragglers are here. I want the same information passed to everyone at the same time."

Faria nodded her head at an extra surly group. "They aren't wondering where their clan leader is?"

"They know he's dead. They felt their connection to him sever when he died. There are others from the Air Clan missing as well. Only about twenty of them are here, so I think they have an idea of what happened."

Faria wondered what it was like to have a connection to their clan mates like that. She imagined being connected to every elf, or every person on her land. She only had a connection to Ander, and it didn't seem like there was room for any more than that.

"We are low on weapons," she said. "We need arrows immediately. I don't know what some of those blades are, but I am familiar with the rest. We will not be using guns."

"That's a mistake," Thomas said. "Everyone should know how to shoot one at least for their protection."

"No."

"They are Earth's weapon. We are fighting on Earth. We have to assume they will be needed."

"If that's the case, why did no one successfully use one last night?"

He stared at her, unable to provide an adequate answer.

"I understand it's the weapon of choice here, but it won't matter against Darroc. He could just as easily have you turn it against yourselves. I know him. Murder by gun is something he wouldn't tolerate."

A fight broke out between one from Thomas' own clan and one from the Air Clan. He sighed. "We'll discuss this later," he said as he went to break up the fight.

"Such brutes," Nellie huffed. "Those who can change into predators are contesting each other to see who is more alpha. There will be more fights soon, I'm sure."

"You mean like werewolves?" Faria's interest peaked as she recalled a series of books she'd found in her room one day after she complained to Faline about wanting something with more spice.

"Well, I guess in a sense. I mean, shifters aren't exactly animals, just as they aren't exactly humans. Their animal halves can fight for control over their human halves sometimes, especially when they feel threatened, which they probably do in a situation like this."

"Your animal side didn't seem to fight against your human side when you felt threatened when we first got here."

"I suppose because I can change into anything I want. I didn't feel anything other than the need to protect you and to get out of there. I suppose the human's version of fight or flight response took over."

Faria having two warring halves inside of her, though hers weren't animalistic. Each of her halves were torn between a past she couldn't change and a future she couldn't control. Now, even though she stood in the middle of a foreign land, surrounded by so many unknown beings, she couldn't help but get lost in the memory of the scent of Hunter's skin, the way his confidence shook everything in her.

Tears prickled her eyes at the thought of Hunter disappearing after she'd given herself completely to him. At how he didn't save her, probably because the *Fates* had forbidden it, though he knew she was hurting and in trouble. At how he ultimately died for her.

A breeze lifted the hair off Faria's neck, like fingers caressing her skin. Faria thought she felt warm breath on her face as a voice whispered, *"I'm still here."*

She shut down that line of thought. Her heart was already in a million pieces, why add the stabbing agony to it?

At long last, hours after everyone had been fed, the sun colored the twilight in oranges and purples as it sunk behind the trees. Fires popped up around her. She felt almost as if she were back home, surrounded by her people. The tension in the air was palpable, but she also felt the tremors of excitement throughout the clans. They had never met under these circumstances, and it seemed as though they were ready for the tides to change.

Faria scoped out who she thought were the leaders of the other clans, evident by the way they each had a large group of people hounding over them as pups to their master. One was a woman with beautiful inked images covering her tanned skin. Long black hair with streaks of magenta and several piercings gave her a dangerous vibe, and her sharp features and proud stance let Faria know she was a fierce leader. Faria immediately took a liking to her.

The other was a tall man with blond hair and a scruffy beard. He wore a torn plaid shirt and pants that looked well-worn. He seemed like a leader who wasn't afraid to get dirty, which appealed to Faria, though whether he was effective remained to be seen.

The rest of the stragglers arrived just as they were finishing their dinner of grilled meats and potatoes. Thomas had explained to her over dinner that the stragglers were those without a clan or were more nomadic in nature. They seemed to be much more friendly than the Air and Water Clans, and their positivity warmed her. She couldn't tell what it was, exactly, but she knew the group of stragglers would be more receptive to what she wanted.

Thomas stood on top of a jagged tree stump in front of the gathered clans, dressed in a button-down shirt and freshly pressed pants. His hair was slicked back, allowing for the jagged scar sticking out from his collar to be on full display. He waited, and Faria felt a subtle push against her skin.

"He's trying to assert his alpha nature over everyone," Nellie whispered. "To prove his status and attempt their compliancy before he begins speaking." The clans' murmuring died down immediately.

"Thank you all for coming on such short notice. I know there is a lot of distrust between our clans, and the rivalry has set us against each other for years, but I bear very grave news that affects us all. First, I must report a crime against shifters."

The clans raised their voices in question, accusing one another of causing the crime, though Thomas had not yet told them what it was. Faria shifted on her feet and tried desperately not to roll her eyes. If she was to help Thomas and the others, she had to look committed to them. And she was. They both needed this.

"If you have noticed, our numbers have been greatly reduced. We were attacked last night by enemies. Among them were members of the Air Clan. Including their leader."

Shouts came out from everyone except the Air Clan, who remained silent. Their stricken faces told Faria they were ashamed, or surprised. Either way, she felt sure that none who were there were had taken part in the attempted coup.

"Their leader is dead. Before he died, he admitted that all the clan leaders met with a male who knew magic who hid his face behind a wooden mask. He told them that we are his creations and he is calling on us to help. Does anyone know what I am referring to?"

"Our leader disappeared a few months ago." The woman with the tattoos Faria had been admiring spoke out. "I was elected recently to lead the Water Clan. There had been no indication of anything amiss."

"Why didn't you tell anyone?" the blond man from the Air Clan said. "Seems strange to not warn others or have someone look into it."

"And what would you have done?" she spat. "Your clan wanted nothing to do with ours. We relied on the Fire Clan until they were wiped out by this disease. We didn't need you."

A young boy stood, but kept his eyes averted from Thomas. "Where is the proof of what you say?"

"Monsters attacked us. Do you wish to see their bodies? Shall I take you to our gravely injured?"

"You broke our peace treaty by killing our leader," an older woman shouted out. "How do we know you aren't lying?"

A chorus of agreement echoed at that. Faria thought how silly it was, these humans arguing over things that could be answered with critical thinking and trust. If they couldn't believe each other when they said they were viciously attacked, they were in worse shape than she thought.

Thomas had difficulty getting the crowd back under control, even with the press of his alpha power radiating from him.

A shrill whistle sounded within the group and at once, the shouting ceased. Heads whipped in Nellie's direction. She looked at each person in turn, allowing the silence to build. Another, more demanding pressure forced itself against her skin, attempting to mold her to another's command. Shifters from the other clans stepped back or bent their heads, except for a few whose faces looked strained as if they were attempting to resist its power. Nellie's hazel eyes brightened. Faria realized she was feeling Nellie's alpha power for the first time, so much stronger than anyone else's there.

"Do you really think we would call you all here to lie to you? Look around you. The broken trees, the blood and pus still spattered on the leaves. That just appeared of its own accord, did it?" She looked down at them all, fierce as any leader Faria had seen. This Nellie was so different from the one she was used to, but the same fire still burned in her.

"Would so many of you have come here if you thought we would trick you? Would we have first provided you food, a place for you to sleep, offer you our *weapons* if we would do something nefarious?"

She shook her head at them while staring down her nose. Faria thought it rivaled what her mother used to do to her. Bitterness and regret poured through her. So much wasted time. So many missed opportunities, and for what?

Nellie glared at the boy who had spoken out. "Your leader led an army of monsters here. Many of both clans died." Her voice carried out over the hundred or so shifters sitting in front of her. "Your leaders betrayed you. We called you here because we would like to negotiate a new peace treaty. One signed in blood. One that means we will call on each other when we are in trouble. We will help out in times of need. We will provide a haven to each other when the need arises. We will go to war with each other. We will fight with each other. We will learn from each other. We will be as *one* clan. We are prepared to offer you this. Will you accept?"

One by one people from the various clans stood and put their hand over their chests, nodding at Nellie. Faria was impressed by her leadership, by the conviction in her voice. That she would put aside the feelings she had toward her old clan, that she would put the need of her queen before her own needs, sent a surge of loyalty through Faria.

There were still a few who did not move. A voice in the back yelled out, "And who are you that we should be swearing the lives of our clans to you?"

There was something about the gruff voice that irritated Faria. Whether it was the ego dripping from it or the absurd way he thought to question Nellie, it grated on her nerves. Somewhere in the back of her mind, she was reminded of someone else who had irritated her so thoroughly in a past life.

In one swift movement, Faria stepped next to Nellie and said, "She is my second."

"And who are you?" The owner of the voice stepped closer to the fire. He was a man with a scruff of a beard and his eyes glinted with an amused spark as though he were laughing at Faria. She immediately recognized him as one of the alphas of the group, the one she believed to lead the Air Clan, now. She felt the press of power slide along her skin as if he thought to challenge her. As if he actually could.

She removed her hood to fully reveal herself. "I am Lady Faria, daughter of Amira Agostonna, Queen of Anestra. This is Nellie Glazer, my second."

A fury of whispers echoed within the clearing. Faria remained with her head held high, waiting for their excitement to die down.

"An elf queen?"

"She bares the mark of a healer."

"They really exist?"

"Wasn't she the one who was banished?"

"But they're so young."

Faria was used to the whispers surrounding her, but she did feel weird about them knowing so much about her when she knew almost nothing about them. She thought Nellie had said that people in the human realm didn't know about hers, but that couldn't be as true as she had thought. They all knew about the Gate of All Realms, so they had some indication of what lay beyond.

The male who addressed her no longer looked as if he were mocking her, but his face turned quite serious, that sparkle in his eye dimming. He walked slowly to the front, and just as slowly, Nellie stepped in front of Faria to shield her. She wasn't the only one. Many from the Earth Clan stepped closer, surrounding her. Her heart warmed at these strangers' allegiance to her.

The male took note but did not stop his advance until he was within a few feet of her. She noted his rugged clothes, the way he carried himself. He did drip with ego, but there was also the quality of a warrior within him. He held no weapons, nor did he give off a hostile vibe. Faria pushed aside a young girl in front of her with a smile and moved herself closer to the stranger, intent on meeting his challenge. Nellie shifted with her, ever the proper shadow.

"What is your name?" Faria asked. She stared him down, daring him to answer, wishing he would provoke her for an excuse to show her own dominance. Perhaps being surrounded by so many shifters was starting to affect her, too. She would show no sign of weakness, no sign that she was anything less than the queen she was.

The breeze shifted and his scent hit her, a mixture of snow and wind, sweet like melted sugar, smoky as a fire. The cool spice played with Faria's fire, and she felt her heart thump in a way it hadn't in a long time. Her throat dried and mixed emotions nearly brought her to her knees.

"Jameson Young," he said, extending his hand. Faria recognized this as a custom of Earth, and held out hers as well. A pulse of electricity went through her at his touch. An irrational surge of anger spread through her because her body called to his. Because his scent played with hers. Because his presence occupied every inch of shadow she cast and suddenly she wanted to know what it would be like melt into him and share his space.

Bile crept up her throat. Hunter was dead for a day and a half—mere hours—and she reacted so strongly to another already? It sickened her.

"What skills could you possibly have that we do not? What do you think we can learn from you?" His voice was a slow rumble of thunder rolling through her.

She tried not to appreciate his candor, his annoying tone, the way his mouth quirked to the side. It spurred her fury and further stoked the fire she had come to embrace.

Faria cocked her head to the side and gave Jamison a half smile. Then she moved with her elven quickness, snatching his leg, using his body as leverage to flip him over her shoulder. The air whooshed out of him as surprise sparked in his eyes. Before she could celebrate her win, he wrapped his legs around her waist and flipped her over, rendering her limbs useless. His smug face blurred as she slammed her forehead against his, a dark chuckle escaping as he reeled back.

She took advantage of his temporary release on her and slid one leg up around his neck and used the momentum to pin him again. Her body weight rested on his chest as they both panted from the movement. It took him a moment to realize she had slid a dagger from one of her holsters and rested it against his throat. She bent low over him, their breath mingling, yet instead of the surprise or disdain she expected to see, his face was alight with amusement.

A laugh broke out behind her, and another male approached, this one larger with a much friendlier disposition than the one she had pinned. He clapped his hands and laughed again.

"No one, and I mean no one, has been able to pin Jamie down like that. I'll learn whatever it is you have to teach us," he said, chuckling. Others approached them with interest as well. It seemed as though she had picked the right person to challenge.

The man reached out his hand to help Faria up. She accepted, feeling the callouses beneath his fingers. At least these two seemed to appreciate hard work.

"My name is Jim, but my friends call me Luck. It's a pleasure to meet you, ma'am."

Nellie stepped in between them. "She's not old enough to be a ma'am," she scoffed. "You can call her Lady Agostonna, or Queen if it suits you." Faria almost laughed.

"Faria is fine for now," she said, shaking her head. She looked down at Jamison and his face crinkled in a smile as he nodded up at her. She smiled back at him, the fluttering feeling in her belly returning as she helped him up. He stood inches away, looking down on her, and it struck her again how his energy interacted with hers. It was warm. It was comforting. It felt something akin to home.

Guilt wracked her as she stepped back and pushed her way through the crowd surrounding them, seeking a moment away from everyone. And to get away from him, a stranger who seemed capable of providing enough distraction to make her forget for a moment how thoroughly wrecked she was.

And she needed to get away from a hard truth she wasn't prepared to face.

Her dead, cold heart slowly beating back to life.

SEVENTEEN

NELLIE

Nellie didn't think this was a great idea, if she were being honest. Training the clans. Uniting them. She would much rather have let the clans fester as they would, a product of their own mistakes. However, there was more than just the livelihood of the clans at stake. thousands of innocent humans could be lost, thanks to Darroc, and she would never let that happen.

No, she had agreed to this meeting of the clans, to their training, because she knew Faria would never have left them to die, which they undoubtedly would without them. She had taken it upon herself to make sure their outcome was a positive one. Nellie hoped Faria was right in thinking Darroc would return, and that luck would be on their side when he did. Hadn't Moira mentioned that they were all chosen ones, or something?

Nellie walked back toward the tent she shared with Faria, thinking of the B.A.E.—Big Awkward Event—that had occurred between Faria and Jamison. Nellie had stood back, watching the two pin each other to the ground and she had to admit—it was…hot. The chemistry between Jamison and Faria bounced off each other and influenced those surrounding them. She could see the members of each clan wrestle with their inner beast, as if it were the start of mating season.

Of course, Faria was an alpha in her own way, most dominant of anyone there besides Nellie, but she was still surprised to see how much her power could influence the shifters without trying. Some had bowed their heads in submission, and the more alpha of those around seemed to double or triple in size, their animals calling to the frenzy in front of them.

It had lasted no longer than a minute but Nellie's own heart beat as if she were the one that fought. She had found it hard to resist looking at the others, searching for who she found attractive or wanted to challenge to a fight. She swallowed down the pheromones suffocating the crowd.

She was surprised, shocked in fact, because even Hunter and Faria hadn't had that effect when they were together. Although, she did only witness them when Hunter was in his muted, human form. Perhaps they were just as powerful together. Or, perhaps it was just the power behind shifter energy.

"That was…interesting," Tommy had murmured next to her. Nellie shivered, still feeling the attraction in the air. She took a step back, careful not to look at him.

"Sure was. At least now everyone recognizes the dominance of who is in charge here," Nellie said. "I'm gonna go check on her."

So that was how Nellie found herself just outside of their shared tent, feeling suddenly awkward and unsure whether she should enter or leave Faria alone. Her old self would have just run in, unannounced, but now there were walls where there weren't before.

"Faria?" Nellie called, deciding to stay. "Can I come in?"

She heard Faria's ragged breathing but no response. She entered with a flourish, tossing the tent flap open dramatically. If she wanted things to go back to normal, then she might as well start acting as her normal self.

"So…that was hot." *Smooth, Nellie.*

Faria let out a bark of sardonic laughter, shaking her head. "He has only been dead for, what? Barely two days? Hours…and already my body betrays my heart."

"If it makes you feel better, we all felt the same as you did."

"No, that makes me infinitely more annoyed. And ashamed. And guilty." She looked down as she twisted the sheet from her cot in her hands.

"Attraction is a physical quality. We can't choose who we are attracted to, or when that attraction pops up." Nellie shifted. "Humans generally can be shyer about their sexual attraction to each other, but shifters are very open about it. It's all chemistry and how our pheromones interact with each other. It doesn't equate to love."

"I don't need the reminder that the Fates have been so cruel to me."

"I know…we don't have to talk about it if you don't want to…" Nellie didn't know what else to say. She didn't know what territory to avoid when it came to Faria and her experiences, but she couldn't help but wish Faria would take control of her own Fate and tell everyone to fluff off.

They were quiet for a while, each of them in their own thoughts, until Faria finally said, "I never wanted this life."

Nellie's eyes flew to her friend. She still played with the sheet and her mouth was drawn in a tight line. Nellie, hoping that the admission was a stepping stone to rebuilding what was broken between them, waited for her to continue.

"I didn't want to be queen, not yet. I didn't want to lead my people until I had time to live, experience things. I wanted to learn more. I wanted to make my own decisions, ones that were good for me, not my people. I wanted to be selfish. I wanted to fall in love when I was ready, have a child when I was ready. And now here I am, married to the harbinger of the apocalypse, a mother for mere hours and already lost the child, the cause of my lover's death—someone I had once desperately wished would be my life-mate. I abandoned my people and got dumped here."

Faria took a deep breath. "And now I'm in a strange land, surrounded by beings I never knew existed. The only person I know has lied to me and abandoned me for months, and now…I feel an inappropriate reaction to a male I never met before, an attraction that activated something in me that was dead for so long, from the moment Hunter abandoned me after my bonding ceremony. What am I supposed to do with that?"

Nellie was stung by her words, taking offense to her accusations, true as they were. "Well, perhaps it's just a reaction to the stress you're under." Nellie knew what she felt out there was not a reaction to stress, but rather a true physical attraction, but that wouldn't help matters. She knew the truth of what she felt as well. It gnawed at her. "Actually, no. It's time you take control of what the Fates have given you. It's time to live your life, experience what you can of it, and stay true to the mission at hand. We rescue Ander. We go home and defend Anestra. We kill the baddie. Whatever else you might experience between all that…it's okay. I say go for it."

Faria dropped the crumpled sheet and raised her brows. After a moment, she said, "I've had a thought. After we fight to defend them, I want to ask them if they'll come fight for us."

Disappointment filled her at the sudden change in subject. She really didn't want to ruin the open dialogue they were finally having, but she had to be a voice of reason. Nellie shook her head. "How would we transport them all? We'll be lucky if *we* make it back to Anestra through the Gate, let alone hundreds of shifters. Not to mention, I really don't want them to come with us."

"It isn't about what you want, it's about what's good for Anestra. We have our abilities there, but think of all the humans who are defenseless. Anestra is what Darroc wants. He's going to bring most of his army there. We need to bring back whoever we can to help us."

"Assuming that Darroc hasn't taken over already," Nellie said.

"He hasn't. He didn't attack the Earth Clan as a distraction, he attacked as punishment for Garrett not following his orders. That means there are still orders that need to be followed. Plus, I feel like there's still something he needs to do here."

"Speaking of which, I think we should try to get some more information. Maybe a few of those shifters that don't belong to a clan have information or can lead us to someone who might know more about the disease and who caused it? Maybe your new healing powers can reverse it."

Faria shook her head. "I've felt the *innulum* strong here. Darroc needs Ander for something, and they will return here to get the last of his army before he heads back to Anestra."

"But if we go, we might be able to take back Ander before Darroc has what he needs. We could put a huge wrench in his plan, which means victory for us. It's a win-win."

"And do you think Darroc will just accept that? He punished Garrett and the Fire Clan because they changed their mind about having, what, thirty shifters to add to his ranks? Imagine what will happen when we take back my son. How many will he punish for that?"

"You are being complacent, Faria. It's time to go on the offense. We need to get Ander back and go home."

The tension lay heavy between them, thickening the underlying animosity and Nellie thought for a moment she had crossed a line. Perhaps telling Faria she wasn't doing enough was too much. She was doing everything in her power, wasn't she? Defending the shifters, preparing them to fight for her. She was still acting as a queen. Why was Nellie so eager to send them away?

"Maybe you are okay with abandoning these people, but I am not. I'm done having others sacrifice themselves for me. I will do what is necessary not just for my people but for all people. We stay."

Nellie's frustration built and she made to leave the tent, needing space from both Faria and the words floating between them. She was emotional, Nellie understood, but she didn't understand the urgency and she knew they weren't going to get anywhere tonight.

A hand appeared around the tent flap, followed by the ever-smiling face of Moira, who was dressed in thick pajamas, ready for the chill of the night.

"I'd like to be alone, Moira," Faria said. "We can talk in the morning."

"Why so glum? Was it because of what happened with McHottie out there?" Moira asked.

The question was so similar to what Nellie used to ask Faria, Nellie felt her heart pang from hearing it. She looked quickly at Faria whose bemused expression lightened the air, if only for a moment.

"You are too young for me to speak about any hotties," Faria said, smiling at her. She sobered quickly, though. "Really, I need to lie down and think. Please let me rest." Faria folded back the covers on her cot but Moira stopped her.

"There is something you both must see," she said.

Nellie inched closer to the girl, shocked when her freezing hand cupped Nellie's cheek. The other hand stretched out toward Faria before she shut her eyes.

Pictures passed through Nellie's mind, as if an artist were flicking through a sketchbook, until it landed on a single image. A tall, elegant male stood in a forest clearing, broad-shouldered with angular, elven-looking features. His skin seemed to glow a golden color, his iridescent green eyes shimmering as a look of rage shot across his face. He looked dangerous and beautiful, the way Nellie imagined the avenging angels of heaven would look. Wearing faded jeans, black biker boots and a Henley that fit his muscular shape, Nellie would put him somewhere in his mid to late teens. He held a black crossbow in his hands and seemed to be waiting for someone.

Wow, talk about hottie.

Distantly, Nellie could hear Faria gasp, its sound seeming to echo within the clearing. For a moment it seemed as though the male heard it as well. He closed his eyes and listened, eyebrows furrowed. When he opened them again he seemed troubled, less angry, and more confused.

The connection was quickly severed and Nellie and Faria were both back in the tent. In the dim light, Faria's face glistened with tears.

"Who was that?" Faria asked, trembling voice filled with hope and desperation.

"I think you know who that was," Moira said.

"How?" The question was forced out like a command.

"I do not have all the answers. Those who would know are hidden from you."

"Why? Who?" Nellie asked, looking around as if whoever had the answers were standing invisible in the tent. "Where are they?"

"Elsewhere."

"Moira," Faria said, trying to keep her voice calm, "You are extremely infuriating right now and I am feeling volatile. Speak. Plainly."

"He has been through many realms," the girl answered in her whimsical voice. "He has spent many years searching for something, at the evil warlock's request. You must get to him before he finds it."

"He grew up?" Faria asked. "He grew up without me? With Darroc as his parent?"

Moira nodded. "This does not mean he is evil. He merely follows Darroc's request because he does not know any different. He is of you, my queen, and the Val Prince. He has good in him, but it is hidden." Moira put her hand on Faria's knee, attempting to comfort her. "No matter what he has done so far, he can be redeemed."

"What the *fluff!*" Nellie exclaimed, realizing that they just saw a full-grown Ander. An icky feeling trickled through her. Ander was practically her nephew, and she thought he was hot. *Seriously gross.*

She needed to keep her focus because if she fell down the rabbit hole of time theory, she would start to bug out. How could they have missed, what, sixteen, seventeen, years of his life? How had so much time passed between whatever realms he had seen? He was nearly as old as Faria, now. Freaking. Weird. "What does Darroc need?"

At that, Moira's face twisted into a half smile, her grin evil enough to fill Nellie with unease. The contrast between the meanness of her face and the laughter in her voice was the stuff of nightmares.

"A flame."

PART II

EIGHTEEN

NELLIE

The days passed much the same way. They woke up with the sun, they ate breakfast, they trained. Nellie's main objective was to help train the shifters in their animal form. With her unique ability to shift into anything she wanted, she was able to teach the others different tactical formations and where to attack enemies most effectively. Tensions were still high between the clans, but slowly, they began to share their campfires and exchange a few jokes among each other.

Callie chose to stay, though she didn't say why. Every now and then she said something about the disease and how they needed to find a way to take care of it, and Nellie suspected she stayed close because her visions and guides told her it was important. Whatever the reason, Nellie was grateful to have another friend nearby.

It only took a few days before someone broke out bottles of alcohol and drinking games were played. Nellie played a few games with everyone, but she was careful about her intake. No one knew when Darroc might show up and she thought everyone needed to be cautious, but it was nice to see them become more comfortable with each other.

One of their first nights, the leader of the Water Clan named Marisa joined Nellie, Faria and Callie around one of the campfires with a bottle of vodka and they played Never Have I Ever. Faria lost, because she had never done many things in the human realm, but it seemed the vodka didn't faze her. The rapid way her body transformed from the Change concerned Nellie, but Faria didn't seem to fuss about it.

Now, their group sat around a large fire apart from the others. Luck and Jamison joined them after they ate dinner with their clan, and they all sat together laughing about when Luck had tripped backwards over a log while attempting to shift into his hawk form.

"Hey," Luck said, laughing with the rest, "you try shifting when a giant tiger is inches away from your face. I was distracted by her teeth!"

Indeed, Nellie had spooked him with a tiger form, and it was freaking awesome.

"Shame on you, Luck," Faria chided. "You can't afford to be distracted, especially not by a few sharp teeth."

"I'm willing to try again. Lady Faria, Queen of Everything, will you do me the honor of a wrestling match?" Luck waggled his eyebrows at Faria across the fire.

Faria smiled widely before shaking her head. "I would never wish to embarrass you, Luck. I think you've suffered enough for one night."

"You didn't worry about embarrassing Jamie."

Nellie chuckled at Luck's dejected tone. "You pinned him again?" she asked Faria.

"Hardly," Jamison scoffed. "We were competing to see who could hit the most targets. I was the obvious winner."

"Ha!" Luck rolled his eyes. "Is that why she hit every single target with arrows, hatchets, daggers, and even a set of darts someone had on them?"

"I did the same!" Jamison answered. "We're evenly matched."

"Actually," Marisa chimed in, "you missed seven targets. Faria missed none."

"Dude," Nellie said. "You know you were competing with the Chosen One, right? She doesn't miss targets. It's like, her thing."

"He needed to be put in his place." Faria shrugged as Luck let out a bark of laughter. Jamison brushed his shoulder against Faria's, who smiled back at him. Nellie thought it was nice to see Faria make friends. She seemed to thrive no matter what situation she was put in, and she was grateful to Jamison. He seemed to be one of the only ones to bring out her spark lately.

"What about you, babe?" Luck turned to Marisa. "Care to try me?"

"First, don't call me babe," Marisa said, flicking her hair over her shoulder. "Secondly, no. You'll cheat like you always do and fly away because you're too scared I'm going to beat you."

"Don't be a hater just because you haven't been able to train in your shifter form," Luck said. "I'll take any advantage I can get."

"Oh, I'm a hater?" Marisa asked. "Let's see how well you do against my other form in the water."

Nellie actually would love to see that. She had heard rumors of what the Water Clan members turned into, but she hadn't seen any proof. Because they'd fight on land, they were training with Faria on land techniques.

The fire crackled and popped during a lull in conversation, a chill autumn breeze drifted between them, and an owl hooted in the distance. It was a surprisingly pleasant evening, and Nellie felt a sense of contentment sitting around the fire with new friends. At least, she thought she might be able to call these three friends one day.

"What is your other form?" Jamison asked after a while. "What do any of you turn into?"

Marisa snapped her teeth at him. "You really don't want to know."

Jamison chuckled uncomfortably as Luck shifted closer to her. "I think I really do want to know, babe." Nellie and Faria snorted at his boldness.

Marisa shoved him off the log but smiled anyway. Callie, who had been sitting quietly off to the side, sucked in a breath and stared off into the distance. Everyone trained their eyes on her, recognizing that she was having a vision, and waited for her to speak.

"Oh wow," Callie said, breathless and sweating. She had explained to Nellie once that the more detailed the vision, the more it felt as though she had just run a marathon. "Wow, Marisa. Your other form is terrifyingly beautiful."

Faria perked up at that. "You saw her shifted? When does it happen?"

"I don't know," Callie shook her head. "It didn't make sense. There was an ocean but it was unlike any I had seen before. The coral and fish that swam in the waters glowed bright colors. The water itself was blue and green with currents of purple running through it. It was beautiful." Cassie looked over at Marisa. "You were leading quite a few toward the shoreline in the distance. Many more than the numbers we have here."

"More of what?" Luck asked, still sprawled on the ground. "What are you?"

Marisa lowered her eyes. "What do you mean more than we have here? This is my entire clan. We don't have more numbers."

Callie shrugged, but something nagged at Nellie. "The ocean you saw, you said it was multiple colors?"

"Yes, it was quite beautiful and vast. There was a body of land in the distance, but all I saw was Marisa and her other mers."

"You turn into merpeople?" Faria asked excitedly. "I didn't know any existed in the human realm! Nellie, why didn't you tell me?"

"We never really talked about shifters, did we?" Nellie asked. "Anyways, I thought you were all sirens?"

"Sirens?" Jamison perked up. "How come we never knew that? We assumed you guys just turn into fish or sharks or something."

"You didn't know," Marisa said, "because we didn't want you to know. We didn't anticipate a situation where you needed to know. Imagine if the humans got word there were sirens or mermaids or whatever around them? They freak out enough over Bigfoot. We didn't need fanatics trying to hunt us down."

"I wonder where you were," Faria mused. "The only ocean I'd seen was the Sea of Aurelia on a trip to Mercy Bay when I was younger."

"Actually," Nellie said. "I passed through Mercy Bay with Johanna a few months ago. We were trying to see how far Darroc's reach was and recruit more people to go up to *Mentage*," she explained at Faria's questioning look. "When the sun sets on the ocean the whole thing lights up in beautiful fluorescent colors. It's quite remarkable to see."

"I'm sure it is," Faria murmured.

Marisa looked between the two then pulled out a bottle of rum from under her sweater. "Okay," she said into the awkward silence. "Who wants to play Kings?"

"I'll go grab the cards!" Luck said as he scrambled off the ground.

The rest of the night was spent playing drinking games, but Nellie wasn't into it, and she could tell Faria wasn't either. She wondered if Callie's vision had anything to do with Anestra, and if so, why would Marisa lead a group of mers anywhere? Nellie was desperate to get Faria alone so they could discuss what Callie said, and so she could properly address her theory of being Val, but it never seemed like the right time. She tried to speak to her when they went to bed, but Faria turned her back to her as soon as they entered the tent. They desperately needed to resolve their issues. Each day that they continued to ignore what had happened between them, the less likely it seemed they would ever get back to where they were.

The next morning, before the sun rose, Nellie ate her breakfast of cold oats and tried to keep her frustrations down. She'd have plenty of opportunity to let out her aggression in that day's training. She resolved to speak to Faria that night. If she could live amongst the people who accused her of her mother's murder and banished her from the only family she ever knew, then certainly she could talk to her friend about what was on her mind.

"Hey," Tommy interrupted her thoughts. "Can I talk to you?"

"What's up?" Nellie asked, wondering what he needed. They only spoke when they needed to about the clan. Nellie felt out of place talking to this older version of who she once thought she'd spend her life with, especially when she hadn't changed at all.

He was dressed in thick sweatpants and a hoodie, his hair mussed from sleep. Tommy cocked his head to the side, indicating she should follow him. She glanced at Faria, who had just emerged from their tent, to make sure she was fine, but Faria quickly shooed her away.

It was strange to walk, just the two of them, though to Nellie's happy surprise, no memories rushed back to her. It was just two shifters, walking a path along the trails within the campsite. Of course, it would be nicer if it were Endo with her. She hoped Endo was alright, because if she returned to hear of his downfall, she was going to lose her shit.

"So," Nellie said, clearing her throat. "What did you want to talk about?"

"I overheard you yesterday talking to Marisa and Luck about needing to purchase clothes and stuff."

"Yeah, there are only so many spare clothes to go around," Nellie replied, glancing down at the clothes Marisa had lent her, "and I figured we should get a few items since we can't keep taking trips out to the laundromat, which costs money. I need to figure out if my bank account is still active and then how to get the money."

Tommy nodded. "I thought that might be a problem."

The rustling of leaves and the occasional skittering of critters through the underbrush flittered in between her thoughts. Should she say something more? Was he expecting her to ask him for money? Because there was *no* way in heck she was going to do that. Before she could think of something else to say, Tommy veered off the path and into the early morning darkness of the surrounding wood.

Nellie had perfected how to shift individual body parts, and her eyes stretched and contracted as they turned into those of an owl. At once, the woods around her brightened as the outlines of critters in the brush became clear. She zeroed in on where Tommy had disappeared and caught up to him, following closely behind. Why was he so eager to get her alone?

"After you were gone," Tommy started, "I was a wreck. It was as if someone had yanked a cord, a piece of fabric of who I was, a part of my soul, out of me. I felt it unravel for hours until all that was left was an ache that took months to subside."

Nellie said nothing, allowing his moment of vulnerability. She was surprised that losing her had hurt him as much as it did her. Her gaze snagged on his eyes, filled with something like regret. They looked so similar to Endo's. Perhaps that was why Nellie had always seemed to have a crush on him.

"We were only seventeen. You had just lost Maggie, and you know I never really fit in anywhere. It seemed like we belonged."

Her throat closed at the mention of her mother. She tried not to remember the place where she was murdered, not a few miles away from the campsite. Tommy had been there for her, but no one else was. She was taken in out of obligation, because their numbers were already dwindling, nothing else. She was with them for barely a summer before she was banished.

"I made a grave for you."

Nellie choked. "I'm sorry, a what?"

"After you left. I still had your things. No one else wanted anything to do with your belongings. It helped me finally say goodbye to you."

Tommy stopped front of a tree, and she saw NG carved into its trunk. Her initials.

Tommy reached into a hollow portion of the trunk and removed a small box.

Her hands trembled as she took hold of it. She glanced up at him once. Swallowed. Then lifted the lid.

Inside, she found a few keepsakes. A movie ticket stub, a necklace her mother had given her as a child, a photobooth strip of her and Tommy when they'd taken a trip to the pier just a few days before she was banished. Underneath it all she found—

"My license?" She laughed, scaring an owl out of a tree nearby. It hooted indignantly which only made her laugh more. "My license, from six years ago, is sitting in this box, and it hasn't expired yet?!"

Tommy chuckled beside her. "We renew them every seven years. I remembered it was in here. I figured you could use it, especially since you look the same. Maybe you could still access the money in your bank account."

"This is incredible, thank you."

"There's something else I want to say." He rubbed the back of his neck, suddenly uncomfortable. "I didn't know I would find another mate so soon, especially not one within the same pack. I didn't look for someone else."

"I know," Nellie sighed. As angry and hurt as she was, she knew none of them had control over when their inner beasts found their match. "It was just…a shock. To be home, to see everyone had aged without me, to see you."

"The clan was wrong in banishing you. We both know that you never murdered anyone, and for them to try to pin your own mother's death on you just because of what you are—"

She didn't need the reminder of how different she was, and how she would never fit in with anyone. It wasn't like she'd asked to be the only shifter in history that could turn into whatever she wanted. "They feared what they did not understand. They wouldn't be the first to do so."

"It isn't an excuse," Tommy said. "I'm the leader of this clan now. I am offering you my formal apology, on behalf of the clan, and myself."

"Tommy, you were just a teen. You were the only one on my side, and you tried defending your mate. No one faults you for that, and I certainly don't blame you for the way everyone else reacted."

"Still," he mumbled as he turned back around the way they came. "I don't know that we will ever see each other again after all this and I can't stand the thought of you thinking me a monster."

She brushed her arm against his. "I never thought that."

He offered her a small smile then put his arm around her shoulders and kissed her temple. It was a nice feeling, thinking that the bandage she put on her heart when she arrived no longer needed to be there. She didn't feel jealous, or insecure. He gave her a sense of closure that she had been missing for almost six years.

They walked along in silence back to the campsite, both lost in their thoughts, when something occurred to her.

"Tommy," she said. "You remember when we…found my mother?"

"I could never forget," he said darkly.

"Do you suppose Darroc did it?"

His eyebrows knitted and he rubbed his neck as he considered it. "Well, if you asked me this a few weeks ago, I would never believe it but, it's possible."

"What would he want with her?" Nellie wondered. "We were nobody, just a mother and daughter traveling the country for most of my childhood. She always said it was best never to stay in one place too long. That the past catches up to you if you do that."

"Are you saying she knew him?" Tommy asked. "That she was running away from him?"

"I don't know," Nellie said. "I am finding more and more that nothing is what it seems."

"What has your queen said about it?"

"We haven't exactly had time to talk, just the two of us. It isn't something I want others overhearing. The last thing I need is for anyone else to think I need to be banished again."

"Nellie Glazer, you have saved our asses more than enough times for you to never be banished again." His teasing took on a more serious tone. "But it might mean something. You should talk to Faria about it."

"Yeah," Nellie said, though she had no idea how she would bring it up. "Soon."

NINETEEN

FARIA

Sanity leaked away from her, widening the cracks and fissures she attempted to keep glued together, to maintain the front that she was a strong, capable queen.

But this voice seeped into her, and every time she felt herself drowning in her grief, she heard it say, *"I'm still here, Princess,"* in that taunting way that made her ache. *"Come back to me."*

Faria knew it was grief that was forcing her to hear his voice, to remember his scent as she felt it on a breeze. It was also guilt, she knew, that forced her to remember who she'd lost, while her body longed to get closer to someone else.

Hate consumed what broken shards were left of her. Disgust. How could her heart and her mind tell her one thing, but her body does the opposite? Except that she knew why. Because when she was with Jamison, she didn't feel as gutted. She didn't hallucinate. She didn't drown in the never-ending darkness. His laughter was infectious, his leadership was unmatched, and most of all, he didn't treat her like a fairy tale come to life. He didn't bow to her. He didn't revere her like the other shifters. He didn't fear her.

He treated Faria as an equal and it was so gods-damned refreshing. He was like a salve she used to help keep her demons at bay. She knew it would only be temporary, but she needed it. She craved it. And after the dream she had last night, the one where Hunter told her he was alive and waiting for her in Anestra, she needed her fix badly. It was all she could do to resist the temptation.

She dressed slowly, still getting used to the feel of jeans on her skin. They were tighter than she was used to, and the pockets were useless, but it was better for her to blend in. She put on a black sweater that zipped up the middle over a plain white t-shirt and stuck on some sneakers. Marisa let her borrow some clothes since they were most similar in size, and for once Faria was happy to be wearing them.

Today, after several weeks of training, they were going on a mission. Well, part one of their mission. Nellie called it: Operation Get That Dough. Faria didn't know what it meant, other than they were heading into town for human currency; they were finally doing something other than living amongst the trees.

It was excellent timing, too, because Faria couldn't stand the sight of the campground any longer. She walked miles daily, still did her workouts and her meditations, and the training with the clans was proving fruitful, but she longed to find answers. She felt the *innulum* so strongly every night, now. She knew Ander couldn't be far.

Time was running short. They needed to stop Darroc from getting the Eternal Flame, which Faria had learned would allow him immortality and his lands to be prosperous. It was an alleged secret of the Val, gifted to them by the gods, and she suspected he needed Ander because only a Val could retrieve it.

Lucky for them, a week after the clans united, one of the straggler shifters named Mo approached her, Nellie, Marisa, and Jamison as they all sat around the fire. They'd been discussing what to do about the illness, wondering if Faria could heal a sick shifter but they were wary about finding one and risking themselves to exposure.

"I beg your pardon, ma'am," Mo had said once he stood in front of them. "I, uh, I think I might have, um—"

"Spit it out, Mo!" Luck laughed at him. "What is it?"

Mo's cheeks pinkened as he looked down at the ground. "It's just that I heard you talking about the shifter illness, and I know someone who is sick right now."

"What!" Nellie said. "Someone here?!" She reached in her pocket for some gel that she quickly rubbed on her hands. Faria and Marisa shared a look.

"No, not here," Mo said. "Out in the Blue Plains area. Her name is Stacey, she owns a special shop. One of the ones that sells crystals and stones and stuff like that."

"How do you know her?" Faria asked. She didn't know why a store would sell rocks, but she'd be willing to see. If she could read the signature of illness, she might be able to find out where exactly it came from and perhaps she could help, like she did with Moira. Fortunately for her, she was accustomed to what Darroc's dark magic felt like, so she should be able to figure out if it was he who caused the illness or Ander. And if it was Ander…well, she would deal with that if it came to it.

"I met her a few years ago, when I first left my pack. She'd never been part of a clan and spent some time teaching me how to live without one. Anyways, she sent me a text when I was on my way here, telling me not to visit her for a while because she has whatever is going around. That was two weeks ago and I haven't heard from her since."

"Blue Plains is a few hours away by train," Jamison mused, scratching his beard. "But it's also a big city. It would be a full day trip, maybe longer. Is that something you're up for?"

Faria nodded. If it meant finding a lead on Ander or at the very least, potentially a cure for the disease, she was willing to go.

But first: Operation Get that Dough had to be completed.

THE VILLAGE HAD TOO MANY flashing lights: on big metal stands, on poles in the middle of the street, and even on top of speeding vehicles. The huge boxes of machinery were terrifying. Thousands of pounds of crushing metal raced down the road toward each other, next to buildings, next to people walking beside the street. And everyone was just expected to trust the drivers of such vehicles to follow and operate the machinery correctly. The horrible rotten smell of the exhaust filled her lungs, made her feel as though the chemicals were killing every inch of what kept her alive.

She huddled in the back seat of the car, eyes shut, covering her ears to try to escape the incessant noise. She thought she would love Earth. She thought she wanted to embrace everything humans had to offer, but this was too much.

"Good thing we didn't take her into the city," Marisa said, trying to hold back her laughter.

The shifter from the Water Clan was as arrogant as they came, but she also didn't take any guff. Faria had taken a liking to her, but she didn't feel so friendly now.

"Piss off," Faria said, using the new phrase Marisa had taught her earlier that day. "You do not have the senses I do. You cannot possibly understand how this feels."

"Hey," Luck said from the front seat. "Shifters have heightened senses, too." He stuffed his face with popcorn, its sickly-sweet scent clanging against Faria's teeth.

"Not like an elf, and certainly not like me, I can guarantee you. I could hear this village from the first night I arrived in this realm all the way from the Gate. Can you hear that far?"

They both shook their heads, impressed by Faria's abilities. More than once she'd cursed her gifts, and today was no exception. Her head pounded from all the stimulation.

Nellie had run into the building she called a bank to try to convince them to give her money. She said she had an account there, and now that she had her identification card, she hoped to get as much as she could to help them on their trip to the city tomorrow.

"Here," Marisa said, pulling a bottle from her bag. "Take this." She handed two pills over to Faria.

Faria sniffed at the small tablets. The smell of plastic emanated from them. "What is it?"

"Aspirin. You'll feel better in no time," Marisa said.

Faria tossed the pills back with a sip of water and waited. "I don't feel different."

"It'll take some time. We don't have magic concoctions here, you know."

"Ha, dummy, you just told her it would take no time." Luck tossed another piece of popcorn into his mouth while Marisa gave him a rude gesture. "Nellie's coming back."

Nellie crossed the street, her jeans hugging her curves, her sweater tucked neatly into her pants. She looked completely at ease here, leaving Faria to wonder if Nellie missed Earth, if she perhaps would not want to return to Anestra when all was said and done.

Nellie opened up the passenger door and jumped in, warming her hands on the heater. "Well, I could still access my account." She showed off a fan of the paper currency. "Got about a thousand bucks, which is sweet. Should be more than enough for our trip tomorrow."

Faria still hadn't had a chance to talk to Nellie alone. They'd been busy formulating their plan with their new cadre. Ever since Moira showed them the vision of Ander a few weeks prior, Faria agreed that they had to either find Ander, find information on the Flame, or get to the bottom of the virus. They were hardly ever alone, and besides, Faria didn't really know what to say to Nellie.

"Let's head back and finalize tomorrow's plan," Faria said, eager to get back to the quiet of the forest. They were missing the bulk of the day's training session, but she felt confident that they could at least successfully hold the line of fighting without chaos ensuing.

"Hang on, there's something I want to do first," Nellie said. She directed Luck to a nearby shop that had delicious doughy scents coming from it.

Nellie put a cloth mask over her face and ran into the restaurant, returning a few minutes later with a box filled with the most tantalizing scents Faria had ever smelled.

"Pizza," Nellie said, picking up a slice and holding it reverently. "It took me years to stop craving this."

Faria watched as Nellie closed her eyes and took a huge bite before offering the box to the rest of them. Faria selected a slice without any meat and tried a bite. The gooey cheese melted perfectly with the sauce and the veggies on top added just enough to be satisfying.

"Why haven't the humans made this in Anestra?" Faria wondered. "Surely they miss this."

"Undoubtedly," Nellie said. "But the produce in Anestra doesn't taste anything like it does in the human realm. It is probably impossible to replicate it and no one wants to be caught selling shoddy 'za."

Faria marveled at it. She hadn't realized the taste of food was so different between the human realm and Anestra. She couldn't believe no one had opened a pizza shop in Athinia, the capital city. She could understand not wanting to mess it up, though. It would make the homesickness worse to have only the ghost of something that was once beloved.

Who wanted to settle for something that was second best? Better to be without it rather than always knowing you could have had something more.

They spent the rest of the car ride answering Luck and Marisa's questions about Anestra's cuisine. She was so thoroughly enjoying the conversation she almost didn't realize her headache was gone.

Human medicine was its own magic, Faria thought.

They parked in a wooded area about five miles away from the campground and walked the remaining way. It was a cold, drizzly day. Almost three weeks had passed since they had entered this realm and the weather seemed to turn from seasonably pleasant to almost miserable. Nellie said it was the mark of a true northern fall. Faria didn't like it.

Dusk was upon them by the time they returned. They were due to set out at dawn, and while she wanted to get an early night, Faria was determined to get a small practice session in. Discipline was one of the only things keeping her sane.

She waved goodbye to the group and changed into looser clothing then grabbed her weapons that she kept stashed away in her tent.

Walking through the trees to a secluded area reminded her of the countless walks she'd taken in the Forest of the Dawn, both as a child and later when she would meet Hunter for their private practices. It felt wrong here, though. The colors were muted, the smells were off. She missed the golden leaves of the Forest of the Dawn, and yearned to be surrounded by the gilded petals, rather than the crunchy brown reminder of dead things. She missed her home and everything that went along with it.

A few miles away, when the chatter of a hundred shifters finally softened to a dull murmur and there was nothing but her and nature,

Faria began her warmup. Taking deep breaths and relaxing her stance, she allowed her body to melt into a series of stretches, increasing the tempo a little at a time. She loosened all her limbs, her muscles appreciating the movement after sitting for longer than usual that day. Her heartbeat increased and soon she was sweating in the cold night.

She selected her daggers, chose the tree she would use as a target, then centered herself, allowing her body and the weapon to become as one. Dagger after dagger blurred as she aimed for the tree again and again. All were buried after a moment, all directly on target.

Hunter once told Faria that the prophesized Chosen One would never be able to miss her target once she chose it, and it seemed to prove true even on Earth where she couldn't access her usual abilities. The familiar pang of her heart breaking sent her into a flurry of activity as she selected new weapons, and new targets, anything to distract her. She needed to stay focused on the present, not the past. It didn't help, of course, that everything she did, every choice she made, reminded her of him. Of how he broke her heart. Of how he came back. Of how he died.

She reached for her bow, felt its familiar grip, the wood smooth against her calloused fingers. It was the one thing that never changed. It had been a gift from Hunter, or maybe he let her borrow it but never asked for it back. She couldn't remember now. It was not elven-made, the carving too exquisite, the craftsmanship even more precise than that of elves. He never mentioned where it came from but she felt it must be a Val weapon, now that she knew Val were still in existence. Or were they? Was he the last one? He had never told her his history.

There was so much she didn't know and now, never would.

Tears threatened to leave her eyes but she refused to let them fall. She shook her head and repositioned herself. She thought she could smell ocean and spice; thought she could chase the memories the scent suffocated her with until they led her to him. She imagined his fingers brush down her cheek, and the rumble of his voice in her ear.

"*Looking good, Princess,*" it whispered on the wind. And then, "*I'm still here.*" The words drifted through the leaves, rustling in the breeze.

She waited for the last of her hallucinations to die down. She cursed herself for allowing her grief to play with her head again. The fire in her blood that tried every day in vain to make its appearance fueled her anger at succumbing to the longing, even for the barest of moments. She nocked an arrow and drew the string back as far as it would go, relishing the pain it left in her fingers, and let it fly. Then another. And another. She closed her eyes and felt for the trees, the different targets she chose, and let the arrows loose until there were none left.

She opened her eyes and saw that all her arrows had hit exactly where they were supposed to. At least one thing in her life remained perfectly predictable.

The power from the Gate called to her own as it hummed through her body, and though it was still at least a mile away, she opted to take the long way back to camp.

Faria grew lost in her thoughts as she walked deeper into the forest. She reached out for the *innulum,* the bond so strong in that moment, almost as if he were waiting for her to find him. She took comfort that she had that link to him, and even though they were strangers to each other, that they had a bridge that would hold them together for both of their lives.

The sudden stillness enveloped her, the quiet so complete she wondered if perhaps something had happened to her senses. Gooseflesh prickled along her skin.

Something was watching her.

It was too dark to make out more than the shapes of trees, but there, just a few feet away, the darkness was heavier, denser. It shifted slightly though there was no wind, and Faria could tell she was looking at a person.

Faria scoffed to herself. It was probably Samantha. She had spent her time stirring up trouble with the clans, trying to convince them not to trust Faria and Nellie. Of course, no one would listen to her, as she was not as dominant as the two of them, but she tried all the same. Faria wouldn't be surprised if she were spying on her, waiting to discover some sort of weakness to report back to the others.

But there was no weakness to be found.

Faria crept closer to the figure, but it didn't move, as if afraid to startle her. She almost laughed to herself. Hardly anything startled her anymore.

She stopped when she was less than a foot away from the body of darkness and she sensed it again, the familiarity of it. Perhaps it was the buzzing of the Gate's magic humming through her now that she was so close to it, but she felt that she knew this person. Knew they waited for her to claim them.

The breeze shifted and again she smelled it, the scent of earth and spice and sea breeze and sunshine and for a moment her heart flipped. It couldn't be.

"Hunter?" Faria whispered.

Like a deer startled by sudden noise, the figure shot off through the trees, fast enough to appear as if he were flying. Faria chased after him, quicker than she had ever gone, attempting to catch up to him. Why would Hunter run away from her?

Was it a trap?

She had the realization that they were heading for the Gate, and she called out to him, "Wait! Stop!" because she was not ready to go through that portal, not without her son.

They entered the clearing, the moonlight casting thin beams through the trees so she could finally see him. Finally see who had been spying on her. Finally see that it was not her dead lover that haunted her that evening.

She laid her eyes on her son for the first time since he was born.

It had only been a few weeks for her since she gave birth to him, but standing in front of her was a male on the cusp of full-grown adulthood. He stood with his back to the Gate, a white bow slung across his back, a crossbow in his hands. He didn't raise it to her, but his face was carefully blank. Faria didn't know what his intentions were, and he was so close to the Gate, so close to disappearing again.

"I have sensed you before," Faria whispered, not wanting to push him too far.

He shook his head, unable to form the words.

"Please don't go," she said, reaching for him. "I have been looking for you everywhere."

"Who are you?" he asked, his deep, melodic voice filled with confusion and hurt. He knew she was someone to him but didn't know who.

"I am your mother," she said, the words flying out of her mouth. "You were stolen from me, and I have been trying to find you."

"Why do we look the same age?" he asked.

"I don't know how you aged so quickly. Time is different between realms." She searched for what to say, for a way to keep him there. "Are you well?"

Are you well? Really, Faria. Idiot.

Of course he was fine physically, but it was his emotional and mental state she was worried about. What she really wanted to know was whether he was evil because of Darroc or good because of who his parents were.

"You can't be her," he said, his features changing into something sharper, more predatory in the darkness. He seemed to suck in the shadows around him, masking himself from her. "She's dead. You killed her."

"What?" Faria gasped. "No, I haven't killed anyone."

"He told me you killed her, that's why I feel called to you. To avenge her."

"Does he know you're here?" Faria said, more urgency in her voice.

He shook his head. "He wants you dead. He wants me to do it, but I couldn't until I knew the truth."

"I am your mother," she said. "That is the truth."

"No, you aren't." He leaped into the Gate, disappearing almost as quickly as he had appeared.

"Ander!" she yelled, not caring who heard them now.

But it was too late. He was gone before she could take a step to follow.

Her breathing quickened, unsure of what just happened. He must have felt the *innulum* as strongly as she did, stronger even, if he found her.

And he had been ordered to kill her.

Yet, he hadn't even tried. There had to be hope for that. Or maybe he left to report back to Darroc. Or worse, to get the Flame before coming back to do the job.

She screamed her frustration into the night, so devastated that she couldn't think of what to say to keep him there. How would she know, though? She was a parent for an hour and at the first moment, she lost him. She didn't deserve the honor of being his mother.

She tried to think logically. He looked well and he seemed well. If someone her age came up to her and told her she was her mother she wouldn't believe it, either. It was too fantastical, too outlandish. Perhaps he thought she was crazy.

And yet, the truth was there. He looked almost exactly like Hunter, right down to his green eyes, except a few elven features. He had sharper cheekbones, more rounded ears than Hunter did in his Val form. Maybe tracking was one of his gifts. If he found her a few miles away from the Gate, then he undoubtedly knew all the shifters were gathered there. Was he there for intel but then sensed her? Did he perhaps not want to hurt them at all?

Too many questions, too many answers she couldn't provide. Her own son—the entire reason for everything that had happened—thought her a liar. Willingly ran away from her.

"Are you okay?"

"For the Fates' sake," Faria hissed as she whipped around. The influx of emotion as she recognized who the voice belonged to was more than she could take. It was too much to see the son she had with Hunter and then be filled with infuriating excitement at seeing another man.

The Fates constantly fucked with her every chance they got. She was going to kill them when they next met, she decided. She'd had enough of it.

"How long were you standing there?" she asked, getting up off the ground. Queen or no, she would never be on her knees before a man.

"I just heard you scream and ran over. What happened?"

"He was here. The…person I've been trying to save from Darroc. The whole reason for all of this," she said. "He was here, and I told him who I was, and he ran."

Jamison furrowed his eyebrows. "Well, that's a really big deal. Where did he go?" His eyes shifted to the Gate and then the surrounding area. "Are we in danger?"

"Through the Gate. Another realm, no doubt, and I can't risk going after him. There is no telling where I would end up or how much time would pass. It's too dangerous and the Fates really enjoy giving me nothing but absolute shit to work with." She felt ashamed of letting her emotions get the best of her, but she found she liked using human cuss words. They felt freeing. "He isn't here with me, by his choice. That's all I know."

Jamison approached her and tentatively put his hand on her shoulder, the heat of him slowly seeping into her. It wasn't the first time they had touched. They had trained together almost every day for weeks, but this touch was different. She bit her lip, contemplating if she should remove his hand or not, but decided against it. He took it as a sign and wrapped her in his arms.

Wanting something to be comfortable was not the same as it actually being comfortable. The relentless buzzing of the Gate already had her on edge and now having him so close, smelling his wood and snow scent, feeling his breath on her neck, was overwhelming. She shimmied out of his embrace.

"I have to go prepare. I'm leaving in the morning for Blue Plains."

"Me, too," he said.

"You too, what?" she asked as they headed back toward the campground. He was silent, and as they continued, the buzzing of the Gate lessened. She felt her body ease back into a relaxed state, rather than flight. It was so easy to walk beside him and allow the cadence of his voice to soothe her.

He bumped his shoulder into hers. "I'm coming with you tomorrow."

"Wh-why?" she stuttered. "You're a clan leader, you should be here with your people."

"Just as you are queen but you are not with your people?" he countered, raising a brow.

Her frustration rose. "That's not even close to the same situation!"

"I am coming with you," he said, moving a branch aside for her, "because there is no one else from my clan that I would trust to be with you. Luck is my second, he will lead the clan just fine in my absence."

"Why can't he come then if he's good enough for your clan?"

"Because he's not good enough for you."

Jamison stopped moving and she took a moment to collect herself before facing him. She didn't know what she was doing with him. He was nothing but a balm to her ache, wasn't he? Still, it didn't stop her from boldly asking, "And you are?"

They looked at each other, the only light coming from sporadic shafts of light from the moon. Their breath mingled, heightening the tension between them. She could smell mint and the spice of nature coming off his skin, and she noticed fine laughter lines around his eyes. Faria could feel his every movement, knew when he shifted closer, could feel his touch before his hand cupped her face.

"You expect something from me that I cannot give," she whispered, looking at the delicate curve of his lips.

He smirked at her. "I expect nothing that you don't *want* to give. I know you will leave us soon. I only want to be there for you while I can."

"This attraction is animalistic. It isn't real. I belong to someone else."

"I don't want to own you." He shifted closer and put his lips against her neck. "I just want time with you and the honor of protecting you."

He released her, the chill of the night quickly enveloping her. He walked ahead, giving her a minute to catch herself.

Great, she thought. *But who will protect me from you?*

TWENTY

HUNTER

Hunter paced across his cabin as fury and jealousy rose within him. He had awoken from a restless sleep, and in the time it took for him to become fully aware of his surroundings, he had suddenly seen through the eyes of someone else.

He was in an unextraordinary forest, surrounded by pines that were common to the human realm. His heart quickened, hoping he finally had a true connection with Faria. He knew they should have one, but he suspected it never fully formed because she believed he was gone from this life. A few times he felt her grief pass through his body as if it were his own, the feeling so overwhelming he could hardly breathe. He had prayed to the goddesses to allow her some a reprieve from her ache or for the bond to fully form.

Hunter watched as Faria shot arrow after arrow into the surrounding tree trunks, then whipped daggers—his daggers—right after them. He felt the depth of her grief and, he was surprised to realize, her confusion. He wondered what she was feeling conflicted about.

He directed his thoughts toward her, wanting to comfort her. He didn't know if it would work, but he could try. "Looking good, Princess." He felt her heart beat double time. "I'm still here."

His own eyes opened and he was back in his cabin, sweat pouring down his back. *She's alive. She's safe. She's still training. That means she hasn't given up, and Darroc doesn't have her yet.*

He yanked off his covers and started toward his bathing room when a sharp pain flittered through his head. He clutched it, feeling as though it would split open at any moment. Tears prickled his eyes and his jaw clenched as he yelled against the pain. Hundreds of tiny pinpricks stabbed his brain from above his eye straight back toward his neck. Just as he thought the torture would never end, it was gone.

He slammed to the ground on all fours, breathing heavily as he tried to regain his bearings. Fighting through a wave of nausea, he wrestled to keep the bile down, and was thankful when he finally had a reprieve.

He pressed his forehead onto the cold wood floor, waiting for his heartbeat to return to normal. Just as he regained enough of his senses to stand back up, he was in that same unremarkable forest, this time standing in front of a male he had never seen before.

He was in Faria's mind again. Instead of the grief that consumed her moments before, she was filled with regret, hope, and…lust?

His nails scratched against the hard wood and corded muscle and veins pressed against his skin. She could not possibly lust after another. It didn't matter that she believed he was dead. Or that it was only a few months since it happened. How long was it for her in the human realm? Days? Years?

No, he couldn't think like that. He was a territorial bastard—he knew that, given how he was so quick to prevent her from sleeping with anyone besides him at *Inhibitions*—but to know that she was still alive and well, to know that she so thoroughly believed him gone was unacceptable…but what could he do?

How long had he begged the Fates, the Elders, anyone who would listen to allow him access to Faria? And now, just when he believed it would never happen, he finally was able to see through her eyes. What was that human phrase? Be careful what you wish for?

Rage consumed him, his control slipping further from him. A stinging, pulsating ache thrummed along his arms as his skin changed from a glimmering golden color to a pale white and then back. He stopped, mesmerized as silvery runes shifted under his skin.

Could the Elders have heard his prayers? Were they returning him to his Val body?

He marveled as the runes changed to black, as if pools of ink danced in his blood. He closed his eyes and concentrated on Faria again, and once again he was in her mind. He watched as the other male approached her. Watched as she said she belongs to another. As the male dared to touch her and said he had no desire to own her, but to be with her however he was able while he could.

Spikes of white-hot pain tore through his mouth as his canines lengthened into deadly, killing weapons. He was going to murder that human. He was going to flay the skin off his bones.

No. I am not this person. I do not harm innocents.

He needed the bond to snap in for Faria. He needed to let her know he was still alive and doing what he could to get to her.

He stumbled to the bathing room and looked into the full-length mirror hanging on the wall. The halo around his irises glowed, though the green was still muted. His canines receded back into his gum line, and his thirst for blood slackened. It had been a long time since he felt such bloodlust. Centuries, perhaps, or even longer. The Val were a perfect mixture of the gentle, loving elves and the cruel, animalistic Fae. Add in the blessing of the goddesses and they were truly formidable creatures.

I am a ship on the sea. The crashing waves move for me.

He repeated the mantra he used whenever he felt his control slipping. He'd often said it over and over again in the language of the Val whenever he was around Faria, when he felt he would shatter if he didn't succumb to her advances. After a few moments, he returned to his normal, muted, human self.

The bathing pool bubbled gently behind him, luring him in to wash away the confusion of the past hour. He waded in, sinking to his shoulders, and relaxed his back against the wall. There was no way he'd be able to sleep again tonight. His breathing wavered as he thought of how he'd nearly lost control, and he thanked the three goddesses no one was around to feel his wrath.

As the water lapped around his skin, Hunter formulated a plan. He needed to be more proactive. It wasn't enough that he passed time in

Anestra training whoever made the journey to *Mentage*. It wasn't enough that they built more weapons, concocted more potions, or did scouting non-stop looking for signs of Darroc. They needed concrete answers. They needed to know exactly when he would be back, what manner of beasts he would bring, who he allied with. They had no intel at all from Faria and Nellie, and they were sitting on their asses while they waited.

It was unacceptable.

While the thought of torturing Crispin for information still filled him with a delicious sort of anticipation, he tamped down on that feeling and thought of what else he could do for intel. They had questioned everyone in Athinia already, to no avail, though perhaps they could go back and visit Taps—the tavern warlocks often frequented. Maybe someone new had come in. They were waiting to hear an update from Enis about Mercy Bay's fortification efforts, as well as from Crescent Point to see if there had been any movement across the Barren Plain.

Really what they needed was a quicker way to travel throughout the country. Hunter envied the human realm and their technology. Driving or flying would have surely sped up the process and they would have spent less time waiting around before news came in for them to adjust their plans.

He would take Endo into Athinia with him after the morning work was completed. He knew of one place where he might get a few answers, though they had tried a few weeks ago. It didn't matter. He would try again. And if Endo would be willing to help, maybe they could start to be in a better place as well. He really needed an ally, rather than just an outlet for the darkness inside.

Or maybe both. Definitely both.

THE CHILL OF THE WINTERY air meant layers of clothes, layers that would only get in the way if something were to happen sooner than they expected. They had only three weeks until the new year. That meant three weeks until Darroc would return to Anestra with his army, according to Endo's intel. Three weeks to finalize their plan, to find allies among the dwarves and warlocks from Wendorre, perhaps even the Fae. Three weeks to train those still coming in from the far reaches of the country.

Three weeks until he hoped to see Faria again, with their son in hand.

He had to keep believing that it would work out. That if all else failed, at least he would see them together again. If he didn't keep the faith then three weeks from now would look very grim indeed.

He hadn't heard from the Elders, nor did he expect to, but he knew they were watching and listening to his every move. They needed to make sure he didn't go back through the Gate for any reason, that he would be there for Anestra. As if they had given him any other choice. He knew they bound him to this land. Their watchful eye was pointless. He needed to get out of their grasp. He didn't know how their powers held onto his so tightly, but there had to be a way to break free of them.

Hunter sat in the barracks, cleaning their weapons for the millionth time. It was cathartic, the routine. It stabilized his wayward thoughts and gave him something to focus on other than the lack of control he had over what was to come. Not for the first time, he wished they had access to *Drogosterra* blood, and wondered if Nellie would be able to provide once she returned home.

"Is there something I can help with?" Endo's voice interrupted his thoughts. Faline trailed behind, recovering well from the battle weeks ago. She had fallen into a coma two days after the attack, and after much convincing, Hunter allowed Endo to try to heal her again. Thanks to both his efforts and their serums, she seemed stronger than ever before. Hunter had to admit, he couldn't begrudge him as much anymore.

"Do you still have your healing ability?" Hunter asked.

"I haven't tried, but I believe so. I still have all my others."

"Do you think this means he's getting stronger? That your people, your land, are getting back their power the way he said you would?"

"I don't know, but probably not. It felt like something that was always inside me suddenly burst open. If we were getting our power back wouldn't everyone feel the surge? We'd be able to move quicker, create more powerful potions, clear this land of the foulness that runs through it. We haven't been able to do any of that."

Hunter nodded. Small things to be grateful for, at least. That was one way to know that they haven't lost this war, yet.

"Do you have news?" Endo asked. "Of Nellie? Of our queen?" Thunder rumbled in the morning sky, the threat of a winter snowstorm on their doorstep.

"Is she your queen?" Hunter asked, wondering if Endo truly felt any loyalty toward the Agostonnas.

"Yes," Endo said, more confidently than Hunter expected. "Faria was always my sovereign. Her marrying Darroc changes nothing. She is now Queen of the Warlocks as well, so she is my queen doubly so. That will not change."

Hunter paused midway while reaching for an arrow. He hadn't thought of that, of Faria being queen to the warlocks, too. "Faline? Is he correct? Is she queen to the warlocks as well?"

"Oh, I suspect so." Faline seemed lost in thought. "He never taught her anything…what to expect, what to watch out for. I suspect that she had some sort of surge of power, but she most likely hid it. After what happened, Faria became…different. Closed off. Unbearably sad. You remember how she hid herself away for half her pregnancy, then maniacally volunteered nonstop in Athinia until she was too swollen with child to do so. He only visited her often enough to know the baby was growing well. To ensure his child was healthy."

A firm crack sounded as Hunter broke the arrow clean in half in one hand. *His child.* His fury at the Elders and the hopeless regret he felt at not being there for her filled him with the same rage as the previous night.

He remembered how he had to watch her dance with Darroc at their bonding ceremony, watch as his hands slid possessively over her body. Faria sensed Hunter had watched, and she stared at where he remained hidden. He revealed himself to her, only to her, as a way to let her know he was still there and would protect her when he could. But then she silently begged with everything she had for him to save her. To come back to her. To make her his instead. And he'd turned away.

He'd felt the severed connection between them deep in his core, felt the pain so fiercely it nearly made him vomit. The intensity of it pushed their power out and played among the guests before Faria passed out from the strength of it.

Were they perhaps bonded before he left her? Before he seemingly rejected her? Had she been unwilling to accept him for longer than he thought, because of the perceived rejection he had given her?

"Have you had luck contacting the Keepers?" he asked Faline, needing his line of thought to be somewhere else.

"Not really," she said, picking up a sword to sharpen. "I was able to reach one, but the old methods of contacting them aren't working. It hasn't felt safe to send messages these days. We don't know who is a spy or not. He could have a shifter here impersonating anyone."

"Can't you smell them? Shifters smell different, don't they?" Endo asked.

Hunter tried to remember what Nellie smelled like to him and Faline scrunched up her face as if she were doing the same. "When Nellie was in her human form she smelled as a human does."

"Not entirely," Endo said, more to himself than anything. "She smelled mortal, of the earth, the way humans do. But there was always a lingering… perfume. A flower, or something pleasant just underneath."

Faline and Hunter looked at each other. They didn't smell anything different with Nellie, and he didn't think Queen Amira had either. Although, their former queen held on to Nellie's secret far longer than they had realized. Perhaps that was how she knew what she really was.

Faline's face had a rippling dawn of realization and looked curiously at Endo, a smile playing on her lips. She kept whatever she realized to herself and instead asked him, "So are there shifters, then? Here?"

"I don't think so," he said. "I do know that the evolved shifters, the true shapeshifters, not the weres, are all still on Earth. Those are the ones he's hoping to add to his army here. So where do we go from here?" Endo looked to both Hunter and Faline for answers. Snowflakes fell gently from the sky, covering the earth in a soft blanket of white. It was early, still only a few hours after dawn. The scent of breakfast cooking in the kitchen reminded Hunter of his hunger. "We can't just wait and hope for Nellie and Lady Faria to show up."

Hunter considered his question. He was glad Endo was willing to take charge, especially since he had every intention to bring him into town with him that afternoon. "With her being Queen of the Warlocks… is there any chance we can get any left in Wendorre to come here to fight for us?"

"Not likely," Endo said. "They're sick there, unhealthy. They stayed because they're loyal. Not to mention it would take a few weeks for them to travel here."

"I wonder if it would be worth it…" Hunter trailed off, lost in thought. Endo had mentioned the caves where this book was hidden, on the outskirts of Wendorre.

"Worth it to what?" Faline looked sharply at him, already disliking the plan he had. But it was better than no plan at all.

"What if I went to the caves to retrieve this Book of the Dead. I could bring some warlocks with me, those that are familiar with the land and who can convince their brethren of the truth… perhaps I can come back with the answer to two of our problems. How to unmake the weres, and warlocks to help enhance our army."

"We need you here," Faline said slowly. "You are our best fighter, not to mention you have connections that we desperately need."

Hunter nodded, relenting, but still the wheels were turning. There had to be a way to get to Wendorre quicker. Something had to be done.

"Endo, meet me at the front gate in a half hour," Hunter said, placing the weapons he cleaned back on the rack. "We're heading out."

Hunter made his way to the Council Chamber. With any luck, he would catch King Dennison just as he finished his meeting with Thuuk, leader of the dwarves of Caranek Peaks, and hopefully he would be in an agreeable mood.

He paused outside the doors to the Council Chamber, and his heart sank as Johanna and Enis stood at attention. "I take it his meeting isn't over?"

"Not yet," Johanna said, her face tight with worry. "Can't tell if that's a good thing or not."

"Probably not," Enis hissed, glancing back at the door as if scared she would be overheard. "Do you want us to announce you?"

"No, I'd rather not interr—"

The door was thrown open and Dennison stood in the threshold, his face severe. "Hunter. Perfect. Come right in."

Hunter had no choice but to enter the Chamber. He was immediately hit with the warmth of the fire, the logs giving off a cinnamon scent. The maps that once lined the walls had all been removed and were piled neatly onto the table. Thuuk stood in front of the fireplace, his stance casual, though Hunter could read the tension between his broad shoulders. Hunter bowed to him, and Thuuk nodded back before an easy smile donned his face. Hunter had trained Thuuk himself years ago. He had always known that Hunter was different, and he loved to play a game where he tried to guess Hunter's heritage. Every time he got it wrong, Hunter would stop holding back from hurting him in their training sessions. That dwarf really loved to get pommeled, but it helped him become a stronger warrior.

"Nice to see you, old friend," Thuuk said in his gravelly voice. He was about a head shorter than Hunter, but thick with muscle, and his long blond hair was braided back from his head. He wore casual clothing, a loose tunic and pants, and there wasn't a weapon in sight, though Hunter was sure he had something hidden somewhere. No dwarf would be caught without a weapon. "Not a day older than I last saw you…how many years ago now was it?"

Hunter glanced at the king before giving Thuuk an easy smile in return. "About fifteen years or so I think."

"Hm," Thuuk grunted. "Fae?"

"Nope," Hunter laughed. "But I'll do you a favor and not make you look bad in front of my king."

Thuuk let out a boom of laughter as King Dennison cleared his throat. "Thuuk was just refusing my request for aid," he said.

"I'm sorry, Dennison," Thuuk said as he sobered up. "I cannot risk my people on a war with almost no positive outcome. We live in the mountains for a reason. It's the only place we're safe. The Caranek Peaks are its own territory that happens to rest on your land. Unless we are directly involved, we stay out of all arguments. I don't think we've helped to fight in—"

"One thousand years," Hunter cut in, leveling his old friend a look. "Your people haven't fought since the Great War."

"Right," Thuuk grunted. "And we can't do it now. I'm sorry." Thuuk made to leave the room but Hunter blocked his path.

"What if I told you there would be someone there who could help tip the scales? Someone you could only dream of fighting with. You'd be a legend."

"I'm already a legend, boy," Thuuk said. "But go on then. Who is this mystery person?"

Hunter glanced at the king. It would be the first time he voiced it out loud to anyone other than Faria, and he risked the wrath of the Elders if he admitted his longest held secret.

"A Val. What if a Val were to fight beside you to protect Anestra?"

Thuuk ran his fingers along his beard. "Well," he said, holding Hunter's gaze, "That would be interesting, wouldn't it?"

"It would," Hunter nodded in agreement.

"Would there be more than one Val?" Thuuk asked. Hunter scoffed his frustration. Of course, fighting with one Val wouldn't be enough for the dwarf.

"Not likely," he said. Though they might be able to convince Ander to their side, he didn't know enough about his loyalties, nor did he have the proper training. It would be just brute force and raw magical abilities, and that wouldn't serve well in the long run.

Hunter waited for the king to say something, but his face was carefully blank as he sized Hunter up.

"I will still have to say no," Thuuk said slowly. He did have the decency to look regretful. "If what Dennison said is true about the brutality of these monsters and the unpredictability of what is to come, I don't think having one Val would change the tides."

"Not even if he were a Val Prince?" Hunter tried to keep the desperation out of his voice. They needed the numbers. They needed anything. "A commander?"

"Would this Val Prince have access to all his powers?" Thuuk looked at him as if he knew the answer to that. As if he could possibly know the Elders were keeping him locked down.

"Look, I'll discuss it with my own council members when I return to the mountains. Maybe I can give you an answer in a week's time."

King Dennison opened the door as Thuuk and bowed his head. "Please consider that your mountain rests on this land which Darroc wants to rule. He will not rule kindly, and he will not leave you alone. He will blast that mountain apart if it means he can control you."

Thuuk's face darkened. "I will keep it all under consideration. It was good to see you, old friend," he said as he clapped Hunter on the arm.

Dennison shut the door on his retreating back and turned to face Hunter again. "So. A Val."

Hunter nodded. "I thought you might have figured it out by now."

"My queen took her secrets to her untimely grave." The king barely masked his anger. Hunter didn't blame him. He was trying to rule a country where it seemed he was the last to know every piece of important information. "What did you come here for? I assume you wanted to ask something?"

"If all had gone well with Thuuk, I wanted to ask his assistance to find a way through the Peaks."

"I see. For the Crystal?"

"Yes. We're running out of options and I think we need it more than ever."

"You're not wrong," the king sighed. "If it even exists, which we don't know for sure that it does, then trying to obtain it would make sense, if we had the time. Which we do not."

"I'm running out of ideas here," Hunter said. "We train our people night and day. The warlocks are making new potions. The injured are healed and ready to fight the next round. No one will go back to Athinia because of the threat of danger at *Mentage* and we still have no way of knowing if Endo's intel was correct. We're planning for a battle that might not come for months still, or might be here tomorrow. I don't know what else to do." He ran his fingers through his hair, letting his frustration show. "I need to find Crispin. He has to know something more."

King Dennison sighed heavily. "You can take the afternoon off to question the warlock establishments in Athinia again, but I don't think you'll find him. I meant it when I said we would discuss it again if the Fates deign to place him in our path, but you can't waste more time than that to search for him."

Hunter nodded. "Thank you."

"And Hunter," the king said as he turned away. "Don't think to keep more secrets from me. If you want to fight to defend this country, in my army, under my leadership, you will tell me everything I need to know about you that will tip the scales in our favor. You don't command an army anymore. Not yet, anyway. Everything goes through me. Understood?"

Hunter nodded. It was a reasonable request, and one the king shouldn't have had to make to begin with.

At least he got what he went there for—permission to search for

Crispin.

Once he found him, he could finally release some of the darkness taking over his thoughts and attempt to control his actions. He could enjoy the sweet release Crispin's torture would provide for him.

He could finally take back some semblance of control, or else may the Fates save whoever got in his way once the darkness bled into every part of him.

TWENTY ONE

NELLIE

Dawn came sooner than she wanted it. Birds chirped though the sun was not yet up, the scent of damp, burning wood ever present in the air. Nellie yawned, stretching the kinks out of her shoulders and neck. If there was one thing she would not miss when she returned to Anestra, it would be sleeping on a cot in a tent. She glanced over at Faria, already dressed in human clothes, hiding daggers where she could.

"It's probably best if you don't bring weapons with you," Nellie said, shivering as she took the covers off.

"Not a chance," Faria replied, tucking weapons into her boots.

"It's kind of frowned upon in America."

"I cannot have blades longer than my palm. None of what I am bringing fits that description. It'll be fine."

Nellie decided not to say anything, and instead prayed to the Fates to keep them away from the police or anyone else that would cause trouble.

"Did you say your goodbyes?" Faria asked.

"To whom? Anyone I actually like is coming with us."

"To Thomas."

Nellie huffed, shoving her legs into her jeans. "I don't need to tell him we're leaving. We'll be back soon anyway."

"But he is in charge. Don't you think…?" Faria's voice trailed off. It was unlike her lately to press for information and Nellie welcomed the familiarity so she decided there was no harm in answering.

"After he pulled me aside the other day…I don't know. We're on good terms. I don't feel any particular way toward him anymore, except maybe a bittersweet sadness. But a small amount. Like, miniscule. It's too bad his new mate is such a wench, though."

Faria snorted. "That's the truth."

"So to answer your question, no. I don't care to say goodbye to him. I'm just eager to get this all over with. And to be honest, I want to get back home. I need to know if Endo is okay."

Faria looked at her with what Nellie could only describe as empathy. As if she knew exactly what Nellie felt, wondering if the people she cared about were safe.

"Hey, have you… are you okay?" Nellie asked. "I mean, we haven't really talked about you. How you're doing."

A wealth of emotions crossed Faria's face. Confusion, sadness, anger.

"Let's go."

Nellie cursed herself but she wasn't really surprised. Faria was queen and she made it clear many times over the years that she wouldn't always share her feelings or her burdens. Either that, or she still didn't trust her.

The rest of their group made their way over, looking infinitely more awake than she felt. An excitement buzzed around Marisa, as if she were actually looking forward to the hours-long trip they were about to take.

Nellie eyed Jamison then looked behind him, confused. "Where's Luck?" She loved having Luck around. His good mood was so infectious, and she had a feeling it would be needed to cut the tension between her and Faria.

Jamison threw her an easy smile. "He opted to remain here with the clans."

"Really? He seemed like he was looking forward to it."

"And now I get the pleasure of looking forward to it," he said as he opened the car door for the girls. Faria followed Marisa into the backseat. Nellie shut the door after her and leaned over the hood of the car, lowering her voice to a rough whisper.

"What do you think you're doing?" she asked Jamison. "She is still grieving."

"No one is getting in the way of what she needs. I am simply here for her in whatever way she wants, however she wants it."

"Really," Nellie said, knowing exactly what he meant, "*however* she wants it. How interesting. Just so you know, I will not let you take advantage of her."

"Excuse me—"

"Actually," Faria said, opening the car door. "Perhaps you both have forgotten I have far superior hearing than either of you, not that I needed it with how loud you were." Jamison had the decency to look embarrassed. "The thing is that I will never allow anyone to take advantage of me again. So," she looked pointedly at Nellie, "if I decide that I will allow him to be there for me, it *will* be in whatever way I deem and *however* way I want it. And the only thing I want or need right now is to sit in the front seat. I find I get sick sitting in the back."

Nellie stepped aside and allowed Faria the front seat, replacing her in the back. Marisa shook her head at her with a smile.

"What?" Nellie mouthed.

Marisa glanced at the two in the front. "I'll tell you later," she mouthed back.

Nellie felt, not for the first time, that she was missing something. "Let's go over the plan since we all need to be on the same page."

Jamison raised his brows at her in the rearview mirror and winked.

"We're heading to the train station. We should be able to beat the morning traffic, but then it'll be another few hours until we get to Blue Plains."

"What are the likely dangers we will encounter?" Faria asked, running a hand over one of her daggers. "Besides the chance of catching the virus."

"Blue Plains is a city, so it'll be nothing like the town you went to yesterday. Your senses will likely feel overwhelmed by all the stimulation. Plus any type of random crime. Mugging or something. We'll just do our best to stick to the plan and stay discreet."

They parked in a garage at the train station, unsure of how long they would be away from the clans. Nellie paid for both her and Faria's one-way tickets to Blue Plains, due to leave in ten minutes. They walked out to the platform and Nellie was grateful to see that the morning rush wasn't quite there yet. It was strange to not smile at the strangers around her even though she tried. The crinkle in their eyes let her know if they smiled in response. The masks they wore were going to take a while to get used to.

Faria stared down the tracks in the direction the train would be coming from. She was covered up more than the rest in an attempt to hide all her features. She wore jeans that molded to her curves and a loose black hooded sweatshirt. She carried a small backpack that held snacks and water for the two of them. A faraway look rested on her face, as if she weren't really waiting for the train at all but seeing beyond it. Nellie sidled next to her. "What are you thinking about?"

Faria gave her the side eye then said, "Sometimes I think I can feel him."

"Ander you mean? The *innulum*? Right now?" Nellie looked around as if she would see the very person they needed to, but she knew the Fates wouldn't make it that easy.

"Hunter. He has been invading my dreams lately, and I swear a breeze shifts and I can smell him, or feel his fingers run down my back." She peered over Nellie's shoulder at Jamison, laughing with Marisa about something. Faria lowered her voice even more. "Do you think I'm feeling guilt? For entertaining thoughts of comfort from another male? Am I hallucinating him?"

Nellie bit her cheek. She wanted to tell Faria that it was perfectly normal. She understood missing someone who was no longer there, the grief supplying memories in every place, every object, making the feeling palpable.

"It's more than that," Faria went on. "I know I have this healer's mark but there is another, hidden below it. I saw in a mirror the other night when Marisa put makeup on me. It looks like a mating mark but…how? It's so faded but it didn't show until I came here…do you think it was never really Hunter that I was meant to mate with but maybe someone else?"

This time they both looked over at Jamison who was in conversation with Marisa. His stance was relaxed, but Nellie could tell he was listening by the way he cocked his ear toward them.

"That…I don't know the answer to that," Nellie said. She had nothing against him, but she was definitely a Faria and Hunter stan, even if he was dead. "I think the Fates really like to mess with us. Do you feel Hunter when you're thinking of him?"

"No. It's when I stop. When I finally have a reprieve from the relentless ache inside me. When I am consumed by new feelings I never had before."

"So, do you think it's the guilt?"

"I don't know, maybe more than that," she said. "Last night when I was training, I felt his touch on my face, heard him tell me he was still here. It's almost like he knows I have the potential to move on, even though I'm not ready yet. It's only been three weeks that we've been here and I feel like I need a lifetime more, but there have been more moments lately where I almost wish it would happen sooner. The healing. The distraction is tempting."

The train's horn blasted as it made its way down the track. It pulled into the station, briefly letting some people off while others got on. Nellie led them onto the train, and when they found an empty car, she proceeded to pull out an antibacterial wipe and cleaned of the bars and seats. Faria raised her brows at her.

"Listen, the world is in a frightful state. I don't know if anyone was sick and I'd rather not risk being a guinea pig for my species, and you shouldn't either. We have no idea how this affects elves, or Val." It was the first time she voiced the idea of Faria being a Val since their argument a week ago, and she could have been more tactful, sure, but it wasn't really her style.

"That would be a cruel twist, wouldn't it, for the Fates to allow me to die by slowly wasting away and never fulfill my prophecy."

"Yeah, well not on my watch," Nellie said as she whipped out some Purell. She gave some to Faria as they sat down, Marisa sitting behind them and Jamison in front. Faria didn't deny being a Val this time. That was a good sign. Maybe. Maybe she didn't hear. Should she bring it up again? But how would she say it? And now way too much time had passed for her to bring it up again. Honestly, she needed to stop overthinking things.

No one else joined them in their car which was just as well, since Nellie would rather they keep their distance from strangers. This whole plan felt risky, and the closer they got to their destination, the more her nerves grew.

Nellie dozed off until she heard a low rumbling voice. She slanted open her eyes and saw that Faria had moved to sit next to Jamison. She pretended to be sleeping as she eavesdropped on their conversation. Just because she was older and wiser didn't mean that she needed to change *completely.* And, if they didn't want to be overheard, they shouldn't sit so closely to her. Faria knew better, at least.

"Would you like to tell me about him?" Jamison asked her. "Your son?" Nellie wondered when he figured it out, but she supposed it wasn't hard to put together.

"Ander? I know nothing about him, really. For me, I gave birth to him three weeks ago. He turned out to be the spitting image of his father, who only had the chance to briefly hold him once before he was murdered. Three weeks ago for me, but what looks to be much longer for him. He is a stranger to me."

"That must be hard." Jamison tilted his body so he faced Faria more. He looked around then lowered his voice. "Do you really think he'll do what Darroc wants? Try to kill you?"

Nellie was more than a little irritated that Faria had confided in him rather than only her.

"No, I don't think so. He had the opportunity last night and didn't, and I have a feeling he has been spying on me for quite a while. I think he'll hold off as long as he can. It isn't easy for elves to kill each other. It really goes against our nature to kill our families. But he also isn't full elf, and he seems to have the warrior spirit of his father, so I don't know. Maybe."

"You know it's dangerous, what you want to do. For us and especially for you. Risking your life with the hope that Ander will have good morals. Maybe you should think about a way of disabling him rather than trying to appease to whatever good nature he might have."

"I don't recall asking your opinion," Faria said coolly. "But since you are so willing to give it, can I ask you something?"

Nellie shifted a bit to hear better.

"Say you had a friend, who was more like a sister or a brother. Someone who you would die for without hesitation. Something happens to you and instead of them trying to listen or understand, they abandon you. For a long time. Then on top of that you find out that she lied to you for years about what—who she was. How do you forgive her?"

Jamison pursed his lips, considering his answer. "She is so loyal to you, Faria. More so than any in my clan would be to me. It really is enviable."

"Her being loyal to her queen is without question. It is expected of her, and I have no doubt in her ability to do so. But the lying…the abandonment."

"On whose orders was she lying about who she was? In a place where we now know all our kind were persecuted. And especially someone of her power, being what she is…I'm certain there are more than a few of our own clan members that do not trust her and wouldn't mind putting her down."

Nellie inwardly scoffed in offense as Faria said, "If any of you harm her, you forfeit your lives. No tribunal, no permission. And I would not be swift about it."

"No one will. Goodness knows she would gut us before we had a chance to do it," Jamison said with a laugh. "What I'm saying is, can you blame her for keeping her secret? And to remain held onto that secret after what I'm assuming was on your mother's orders, the queen? Which you just said was an irrefutable fact that all must be loyal to their queen without question?"

Faria didn't want to admit that he had a point. She knew he was right, and had argued with herself over the same thing. It was just so hard to let go of the hurt.

"She is a natural leader, she is incredibly useful, and the amount she cares for you is envious. I would give anything to have anyone be that loyal to me."

"What about Luck?" Faria asked, changing the subject.

Jamison let out a bark of laughter. "He's probably as close to my own version of Nellie that I'm gonna get, but at the base of it all, we are all made from humans and the human instinct is to look out for themselves. To find shelter for themselves. To eat for their own survival. To kill if it serves their interests. Our core is human and having an animal live inside us makes our survival even more predatory. We are not like you are."

"Nellie is like you, is she not? Human at her core."

"Don't worry," Jamison said as the train stopped and Nellie finally had a reason to stir from her pretend sleeping position. "Nellie is not like us. It's why her leader was so threatened by her. I don't know what her core is, but she can be everything and nothing. She is completely at the will of her choices, and she already chose you. If I were you, I would think about that and not anything else."

Marisa yawned loudly, dramatically stretching the kinks out. She winked at Nellie, letting her know she heard the conversation, too.

Nellie couldn't help but feel a burst of thankfulness to Jamison, no matter how irritating she found his charm. What he said was true and he was able to give voice to everything she felt to the person she felt it for.

For the first time in a long time, Nellie felt that perhaps not all shifters were so bad.

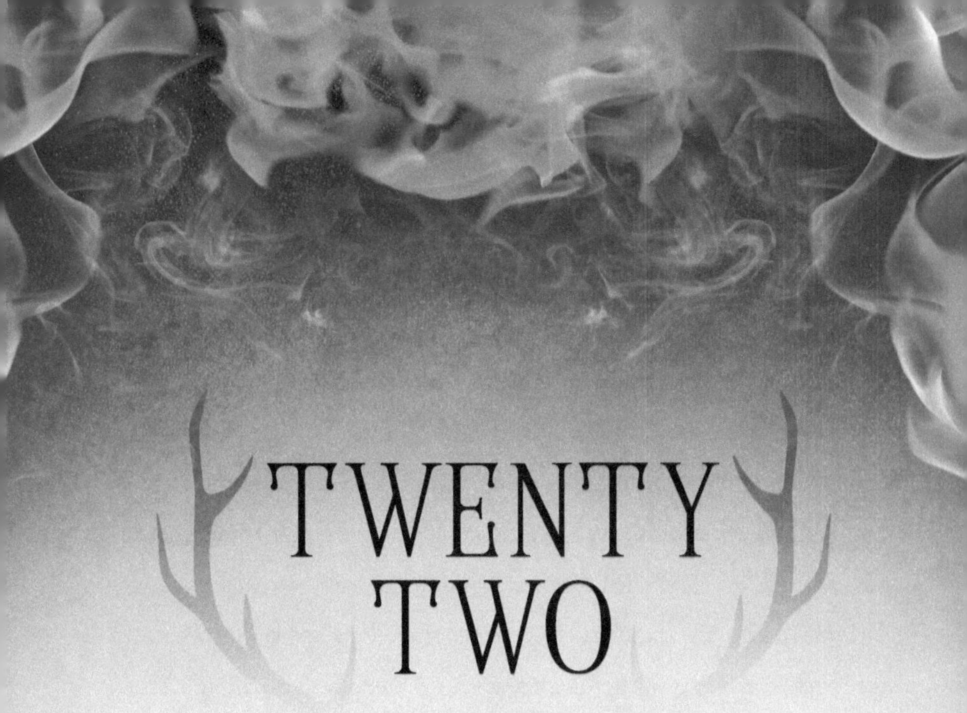

TWENTY TWO

FARIA

The heat radiating from the train hit her as she descended onto the platform, immediately squashed between her three companions as they guarded her from the onslaught of humans trying to board the train. She had never seen so many humans at one time, not even in the town they visited the other day. They came in all sorts of shapes, sizes, and colors, and though they were covered in masks and winter wear to protect against the brisk morning, Faria could tell they were all beautiful. Their differences were all so unique.

She was particularly interested in someone with purple hair and ink stretched all over her arms. She was filled with a longing to have something similar. There were a few tattoo artists in Athinia, but she had never visited their shops. She made a note to herself to go if they survived this war.

Pinpricks slid down Faria's arms and up through her hair, as though tiny ants marched across her skin. She looked at the edge of her ponytail wrapped around her shoulder and saw her hair change from black to the color of mulled wine, deeply red and exotic looking. She looked around her, making sure no one noticed the color change. The last time she purposely changed her appearance was in Anestra, one of the first times she snuck out. She had barely turned seventeen and her powers were just presenting. This particular one hadn't surfaced since then. Perhaps it was because she approached the end of the Change with her twentieth birthday just a few short weeks away.

"Now's not really the time to play chameleon," Nellie said to her from behind. Faria looked over her shoulder at her friend. Her sister. Jamison was right; she should find it in her heart to forgive Nellie. She had been following the queen's orders, which anyone was expected to do. Goddess knows all the things Faria had to do under the queen's orders. They still had to air out some grievances, but she could see a mending start.

"Although, I thought the only power that worked on Earth was your healing ability. It's been a while since you could do that, hasn't it?"

Faria shrugged nonchalantly at Nellie, though she felt anything but casual about the thought of her abilities returning. Excitement thrummed through her.

She followed Jamison down something called an escalator and through a huge lobby filled with what looked to be marble. The riches that humans had were incredible! She wondered why so many were disheveled and seemingly penniless. If they had money for huge marble and gilded lobbies, certainly their government had money to help their citizens.

They stepped outside into the bright sun, just barely starting to warm up the brisk late fall day. Huge buildings crowded them, taller than even some of the trees in the enchanted forest lining her home. Metal and glass surrounded them on all sides, from the buildings to the vehicles on the road. It was pretty, in an iron jungle sort of way, though it made her feel horribly uncomfortable to be enclosed by such cold structures. She missed the fresh air the woods afforded her.

Nellie led them over to a side alley next to a restaurant, the smell of fried oil in the air. "I'm thinking maybe we should go over our game plan a little bit. We really shouldn't get too close to anything."

"Too close to anything? Everything is crowding in on us already," Faria said. She was starting to feel claustrophobic. She almost voiced her concern but was distracted by a person walking by with spiky black hair, wearing chains from his hips to his ankles. "I can't believe how different and creative everyone is here! So many personalities that are shining through and all the different colors! It's just marvelous."

Marisa hid her laugh behind a cough as Jamison shooed them back out of the alley. "Let's just find that shop Stacey owns. That's priority number one."

Tall buildings lined the busy street in neat rows, though Faria could barely appreciate their beauty. The screeching of car horns ratcheted up her heartbeat, causing her head to pound behind her eyes. She attempted to block out the noise, but something caught her attention. Faria cocked her head to the side. She could hear shouting and jeering coming from her right. She veered in that direction, leaving her group behind in her haste to see what was causing such a commotion.

"Where are you going?" Nellie asked, not bothering to hide her annoyance at running to keep up with her.

"I can hear voices chanting in this direction."

"Yeah, we really don't want to be running into an angry mob," Marisa said. "I'm all for getting the next thrill but I have a feeling I know where we're heading and we can be positive there is a crowd, which means we're more likely to catch something we don't want to catch. I'm not really in a hurry to be near them."

"We don't have to get too close. I just want to look," Faria insisted. She had to go in this direction, she knew it. It wasn't a pull necessarily, not the way there was when she sensed Ander. It was more like a feeling of déjà vu, like she knew she was in the right place at the right time, doing what was expected of her. She'd had many moments like that in the past and accredited them to the Fates guiding her. As much as she wanted to end their existence, she still followed when they nudged her. The need to head in that direction possessed her.

She rounded the corner and was bombarded by the sound of horns and alarms, a sea of color, lights flashing, and fireworks exploding. Waves of emotion suffocated her and made it hard to breathe. Chaotic streams of people wove around her.

"What is this about?" Faria asked, confused at the field of mixed emotions she saw. "Why is everything so…much?"

"Looks like a game just let out," Jamison said as he elbowed people out of the way. "Everyone's leaving the stadium."

"But why are they shouting at each other? Why are they blaring those horns? Is this normal human behavior?" The horns reminded her of large gatherings often held at *Mentage*. Its discordant sounds were often associated with celebratory parties for new babies, weddings, and birthdays. They were always used with excitement and good feelings, but what she heard now felt antagonistic and wrong.

Faria hadn't dealt with much aggressive behavior in Anestra, but it seemed to be coming in spades in the human realm. It was one thing to be surrounded by shifters, whose animal sides warred with their human halves, but it was another to see humans filled with such animosity for no apparent reason.

"That's just how they deal with the win or loss of their teams." Nellie grabbed her arm, meaning to push her back in the other direction. "It's meant to be fun, but some people are more aggressive than others and I'm sure some are wasted. Let's go back this way."

A chant rang out as a group of men shouted at the top of their lings. They held tin cannisters and with the press of a button, fire erupted. Streams of people shrieked and fled in fear as those who controlled the fire continued laughing.

"What the..." The crowd increased as more people left the stadium and Faria got swept away from her friends.

"Faria!" Nellie called, elbowing people out of the way. "Push back this way!"

"I'll get her," she heard Jamison say. "Go wait at the coffeeshop!"

Faria was jostled from people as she worked her way down the crowded road. She felt as though she were a fish moving in the opposite direction of a current. The group of men shot off their cans of fire again, laughing as more people screamed and scrambled to get away from them.

These humans had no idea the precious power behind the element they played so casually with. As if it wasn't damaging the earth upon which it burned. It reminded her of another time, another fire that scorched the earth. She swallowed down bile, disgusted at the way these humans were so carelessly indifferent.

In Anestra, flame was a revered gift reserved for chosen people with magic. Its power sustained life, it provided warmth, it guided the way. It was precious, and to handle it was a privilege. In the human realm, it appeared to be about nothing but destruction and instilling fear in others.

"Hey!" Faria yelled at them over the noise. "What are you doing?"

"Oh look at that, boys, she's wearing black!" A boy in a bright orange shirt said. "You feeling sad princess? Want me to make you feel better?"

The guys around her laughed as an oily feeling slid over her. She'd dealt with people like this in Anestra. Crispin Jakfour was king of the creeps and she'd had to put him in his place more than once.

"You don't respect the element you're playing with. Why are you trying to scare innocents?"

"Element?" One of the guys snickered. "Innocents? Who are you?"

They crowded around her, effectively sealing her in. A few picked up their chant again as they set off more fire. Faria could hear shouting, people yelling that they're the police. That they need to back up. She tried to push her way through the group of men but they wouldn't let her go. One held her back while another tried to remove her sweater.

A blur of color whirled in front of her, followed by a string of curses as the men who held onto Faria toppled over and landed bleeding on the ground. She felt a pair of strong hands grip her arms, effectively shoving her back through the crowd and down an alleyway. The world righted itself as Faria turned in circles. Her adrenaline rushed and she knew if she had her full abilities, she was likely to spurt fire at whoever dared to touch her.

"Are you out of your mind?" an angry voice said. Ander towered over her by at least a head, his dark hair and glittering green eyes pale compared to the glow of his golden skin. She was reminded once again of the first time she saw Hunter in his Val glory, all of the avenging angel they were fabled to be in plain sight. Faria stared up at him, surprised to see who her knight in shining armor was, and found herself unable to speak once again. She inspected him for injuries, for something she could fix. His clothes were so very human—jeans and a long-sleeved shirt that Nellie had once called a Henley. He wore sneakers this time, giving off the appearance of casual, though he was anything but. His muscles were outlined through his shirt, and she noticed his knuckles were scarred as though very recently bloody.

"How can you be so irresponsible to antagonize those assholes?" he asked her. "Don't you know what kind of trouble you could have gotten into?"

"They were abusing their use of fire. They needed to be dealt with."

"Well they almost dealt with you," he said. "And it could have been worse. Again, what were you thinking?"

"I was thinking to protect, which is the natural instinct of a queen. And a mother," she added quietly. "Are you hurt?" she asked, indicating his knuckles.

"No."

His shortness stung her, but she ignored it. She didn't want to argue with her son, not now that he was right in front of her again. "Well, thank you, at any rate, though I had it perfectly under control."

He made a face at her. "I'm sure you did."

"How did you find me then?"

"I followed you."

She snorted. As if what he said was the most obvious answer in the world. "How?"

"GPS."

"I don't know what that is."

"You are like a beacon to me, I don't know. I just always know where you are."

"Like a tracking spell?" Her heart stuttered. Had Darroc put one on her? Had Ander? Or perhaps it was something far less sinister. "Or do you maybe have the *innulum* as well? I'm not sure how it works with Val children. I can feel you, but I can't tell where you are. I just know that you're alive."

He was quiet for a moment. "Is that why you didn't come for me?"

"What?" she gasped. "I came for you immediately. I told you that already. You have been my sole purpose. My reason for living."

"It's been years." His voice shook and Faria's heart shattered. "I have felt you for years."

"It has only been three weeks for me. My love, I gave birth to you weeks ago. I went through the Gate hours after he stole you from me and ended up on Earth. There was no way for me to know it was longer for you. Where have you been?" She implored him to believe her, to know and understand that she was doing everything she could to get him back.

"Everywhere."

She felt almost a sense of jealousy at that, at how much he learned and experienced through Darroc when her own mother had barely let her leave Athinia, let alone Anestra. But she now understood the reason why.

Any absurd amount of jealousy she felt was immediately eclipsed by overwhelming sadness. "Has he harmed you?"

"Depends on your definition of harm."

She was going to tear Darroc's flesh from his bones and then set him on fire. She couldn't begin to fathom the type of abuse Ander might have suffered at his hands. There was so much that Faria wanted to say but she didn't know how to form the words. Her sadness, her anger, her anguish all threatened to undo her.

"I wish you could have known your father. You are so like him. Your looks, the infuriating way you give such short non-answers."

His jaw clenched. "I do know my father."

"Darroc is *not* and he never will be your father," she hissed. That he would even say such a thing was offensive.

"I know."

"What do you mean, you know? You know who your father was?" Faria was startled by his answer. He knew Hunter?

"I've seen him training with a warlock friend in your land."

"In *our* land," she corrected. "When was this? In the past?"

"I came here as a warning," Ander said, changing the subject. "He intends to attack in two days."

"Anestra?" Faria breathed, alarmed at how little time they had to figure out the wasting disease or find more information on the Flame. How would she get Ander on her side in time?

"No, he will attack the clans."

"Did you get the Flame, then?" Faria asked, her heart bottoming out. If Darroc had the Eternal Flame, nothing mattered anymore. There was no hope for them.

"He sent me to create chaos, to distract the humans while he did what he needed to do. He will send me to the fire realm soon."

She had so many questions. "How can he intentionally send you there? The Gate does not let you choose." She paused, not wanting to give voice to her fear but she knew she had to. "Did you start this wasting disease?"

Ander hesitated as he stared in her eyes, his mouth a grim line. "Wasn't your hair black?"

"Yes, I can change it," she answered distractedly.

He nodded as if that answer was enough. But she couldn't get enough. She wanted to touch him, to hold him, to apologize. She still couldn't reconcile the fact that her baby, the one that left her three weeks ago, was now the man standing before her.

"You will have to make a choice," he said suddenly. "Between staying and fighting for the clans or stopping me from getting the Flame. I might not have killed you yet but…I am loyal to him. The one that raised me. And I have a duty to follow through on this task for him."

"You don't have to do this," she begged. "I am your mother. Your father is—was—a good person. A protector. A brave male who fought until his last breath."

Ander scrunched his eyebrows at her then cocked his ear to the side. Faria heard it, too. Footsteps running toward them. He moved as if to block her, to protect her from whatever was coming but then he quickly shifted away.

"I have to go," he said. "I need to know something first." He paused, contemplating his words. "Why do you waste your time with him?"

"With whom?" Faria asked, though she had a feeling she knew who once she caught the approaching scent of woods and snow.

"The shifter. I would think your mate would be upset."

"Mate?" Faria asked, alarmed. "What do you mean?"

"I know what the mate mark is. I've seen it on him, too."

"On who?" she asked. Ander backed into the shadows of the alley and walked away from her. "Who did you see?" She called at his retreating back.

The shock of seeing her son once again, this time so much more willing to speak to her, was eclipsed by his implication. Hunter was dead. She looked into his lifeless eyes. Saw his neck broken in an impossible way, the bones ripping through his burnt skin. There was no way he was still alive.

And yet, Ander was so sure. Unless…*Darroc*. She knew he had done something evil to her, aside from his attempt at impregnating her against her will. The potion he had given her after teaching her to read his magic must have nurtured a seed of darkness within her. Could that have formed some type of bond? No. She refused to believe it. It couldn't possibly…but she didn't know what Darroc or the Fates were capable of.

"There you are!" Jamison said, shaking her from her thoughts. "Are you okay? You look like you've seen a ghost."

"I have, in a way," Faria mumbled. She looked at Jamison, at his eyes that crinkled when he smiled, at the dimple in his lightly bearded cheek. She felt such attraction to him, to his ruggedness and the way he seemed to adore and respect who she was, though she was not his queen. It confused her on a normal day, and now even more so.

"What do you mean?" he asked, removing a stray hair from her forehead.

It was such a casual and intimate gesture, but she couldn't bask in the feeling of it just then. She stepped away, needing space from him and what he represented. Was Ander to be believed? She couldn't deny what haunted her memories, just as she couldn't deny the electricity that flowed between her and Jamison. He made her feel like she could finally breathe.

"Nothing," she said. "Where are the others?"

"Waiting outside a coffee shop a few blocks up. Nellie was up in arms when I said I would find you, but I am clearly the far superior tracker."

"I doubt that," Faria laughed, making her way back out into the sunlit street with him.

"Well, when she's in her human form at least," he mumbled.

They walked side by side, their arms casually brushing against each other. Strolling along in companionable silence as though they had all the time in the world felt so normal, so easy. Faria was loathe to disrupt it, but urgency called to her.

"We have to go back," she said, fiddling with a loose string on her shirt. "Back to the clans."

"You mean abandon the plan to find Stacey?" he asked.

"Yes. No. We came all this way, and it's still important to see if I can heal this disease before the shapeshifters are extinct, but we must hurry. Darroc will attack the clans in two days."

Jamison abruptly stopped walking and two passersby knocked into him, grumbling under their breath. "How do you know?"

"Ander just told me."

He cocked his head to the side, considering her. "And you trust him?"

"He just saved me." Raucous laughter poured out from a nearby bar and Faria wished they had time to join in and forget the world for just a moment. "He is my son."

"Raised by the enemy, who was ordered to kill you."

"And I've already told you he won't. He may not know it, but the *innulum* prevents such violence. If I am to die then it will be at Darroc's hands, not his. And he wouldn't have warned me if he wasn't looking out for me."

"Of course not, unless he wanted to get you in the prime position for Darroc to do so."

Faria shook her head. She knew that wasn't the case but didn't bother explaining it to him. "When does the next train leave?"

"Not for two hours," he said. "We're going later to avoid the rush from the game."

"Then we need to hurry and find Stacey's shop."

Jamison grunted and led her in the opposite direction, rippling through the bustling pedestrians.

Faria stepped off the sidewalk, intending to cross the road but a loud horn slammed down, freezing her in place. Jamison snatched her around the waist and held her against him, exhaling harshly. "You almost got yourself run over," he said. She looked into his hazel eyes, realizing they were only inches apart, and though the mask he wore covered his face, she could envision perfectly where his lips would be. If they weren't covered, she might have had half a mind to go for it.

Get your hormones under control, Faria. It's just the adrenaline speaking.

She was lying to herself, she knew. It wasn't just hormones that had her picturing a different type of future for a moment. One with someone who accepted her despite her title, despite the mistakes she had made, despite the tangle of self-loathing feelings she continually expressed.

And, she reasoned with herself, Hunter had left her over ten months ago. They had only mere moments together before he was killed. She had worked herself into moving on from the second he rejected her at her bonding ceremony, and now it seemed even easier to do so knowing he would never come back. It helped that she had an admirable distraction in front of her.

Despicable, she thought. *You are absolutely despicable.*

"Um," Jamison laughed, removing his hands from her waist and setting her firmly back on her feet. She instantly felt the cold air rush between them and missed his warmth more than she should have. "Gotta watch where you're going, Your Majesty," he said.

Faria breathed out a chuckle of her own and mumbled a soft thank you. He grabbed her hand, running his thumb across her knuckles before helping her cross the street.

"I'm not an invalid," she said with the feigned air of annoyance. "I can cross the street on my own, you know."

"Obviously," he said, bumping into her shoulder.

Nellie paced in front of a coffee shop a few feet away, her eyes zeroing in on their hand contact. She gave Faria a look, and Faria stuck her tongue out at her, though Nellie wouldn't see it with the mask on. Faria decided she rather liked the masks and the secrecy they afforded.

"Well, here you are," Nellie said, ceremoniously whipping out hand sanitizer and squirting it on both of their hands. "Clean off all those germs," she said, giving Jamison a pointed look as she rubbed Faria's hands vigorously for her.

Marisa laughed into her coffee, its steam reminding Faria how cold she actually was. She shivered to emphasize the point. The café they sat outside of had a few iron tables and chairs, but Faria opted not to sit on them, worried they would cause even more of a chill.

"I bought you a peppermint hot chocolate," Nellie said. "Another favorite of mine that I've missed."

"You missed melted chocolate? We have the same thing back home." Faria pulled down her mask and blew into the open lid, relishing the minty steam spreading over her face. She took a hesitant sip then made a face at the artificial taste of the peppermint and sugar.

"Nells," Faria said. "We have much better chocolate in Anestra. And real peppermint, not whatever this is."

"Yeah," Nellie agreed, sighing after taking a sip of her own. "But nostalgia had me missing this one."

"Where to now?" Marisa asked, chucking her cup into a nearby garbage can. She put her gloves back on and jumped in place to keep warm. "Stacey's store?"

"Yeah, and we gotta hurry," Jamison said. "According to the Maps app, it should be one block down from here."

They hastened their way down the block, their sense of urgency spurring them on. Faria winced as sirens raced down the road, their piercing shriek making her teeth clack together. An uneasy feeling nestled into her. She sped up, quickly outpacing her friends. Something wasn't right. She knew it.

She smelled the smoke before she saw the flames consuming a brick building with the name "Blood Moon Emporium" written in blackened block letters on the front. Faria broke out in a sprint but strong hands wrapped around her waist, holding her back.

"Not on your life would I let you run into that fire," Jamison said through clenched teeth. "Don't even think about endangering yourself now."

"Get off me," she snarled at him. "I can help. I have water…"

"Water magic? The thing that doesn't work in this realm?" His anger was palpable, but her fear for what might have happened to Stacey, for the loss of answers, spurred her own fury.

"Release me. Now." He removed his hands from her body but he still didn't give her space. She scoffed at his audacity. "We need answers. It's too much of a coincidence that this happened."

"But Faria, look," Nellie pointed at the firemen rushing to put the fire out. "Even if you could help, there would be no way to mask your powers in front of all these humans. This fire is large enough to burn any hope away. We have to go."

"This can't have been for nothing," she hissed. "We have to look.

Maybe there's a clue?"

"We knew it would be a long shot anyway," Marisa piped in. "Mo said he hadn't heard from her in a few weeks, and she was sick. It was always a slim chance that we'd find her alive."

"Now we have almost no opportunity to see if I can heal this disease. No chance to save more shifters." Frustration laced her words. "Let's get back to the clans. They need to be warned." She quickly explained what she learned from her son, surprised that neither of them questioned his intel. She had turned around to head back toward the train station when a blur caught her eye.

Down a side alley and leaning against a brick wall was Ander, his face covered in sweat and ash coating his clothes. He shook his head at her, either to tell her to keep quiet or to confirm Stacey was dead. She didn't know which. Had he started the fire? How could he have known where they wanted to go? She took a step in his direction, but when she blinked, he was gone.

They had about an hour left until their train was set to depart, and the events of the day were taking their toll. She looked forward to the quiet train ride to process all that she learned. The human realm was too overwhelming for her. She needed to come up with a way to get Ander on her side, prevent Darroc from getting the Eternal Flame, and still go home to fight again.

She felt someone sidle up next to her and smiled. She appreciated that Nellie was less hesitant to approach her. She knew Nellie had heard her conversation with Jamison on the train ride down. Call her a coward, but she wasn't sure how to voice how she felt to Nellie's face. Having her listen to her feelings was easier.

"So, you saw him again?" Nellie asked quietly, timidly, as if she were scared to not receive an answer.

"Yes."

"And you trust him?" she asked.

"Unequivocally." She paused for a moment. "I trust that his information about Darroc is correct. I trust that he will not murder me simply because I know he cannot."

Nellie searched her face, as if she were plucking hidden pieces of information directly from Faria's brain. "Did he say anything else?"

Faria thought about telling her more. About Ander's claim that he knew who her mate was, or about how she'd seen Ander outside of Stacey's store.

She decided against it. "I have a choice to make. Either I stay and fight with the clans or I stop Ander. I have to choose between protecting the shifters or stopping him from getting the Flame."

Nellie laughed. "More of the same impossible choices. Those freaking Fates." Nellie's laughter died down, her face turning serious. Faria wished she could laugh as well. She felt so many emotions that none of them would come out.

"Yes, basically." She looked around them, at the iron jungle surrounding her, at the humans bustling from one place to another, their heads down in their cellular devices, hardly paying attention to where they were going, let alone to each other. There was a deep sadness among them, such dissatisfaction with their lives. She understood and related to them more than anything. To constantly be a slave to forces beyond their control just as she was. The need to make money and work jobs they didn't enjoy had seeped the life from them, all to make sure they had health care or food for their family. Doing their duty and what was expected of them to survive.

It was miserable. Every decision being made not by them, but those who controlled them. Every one of those decisions affecting the outcome of their lives.

So, what would she do? Abandon the clans the way she did her people? Go after Ander, and fail again? Did she stay and fight, to help secure their loyalty to bring back to Anestra? How would she even ensure they got to Anestra?

"What do you think I should do, Nellie?" she asked. "This is your former family. Are we to abandon them?"

"You go after Ander, don't you? It's the reason for everything. We won't survive if he gives Darroc that Flame." She was quiet as she thought out her next words. "But if we protect the shifters then maybe they will fight for us. I can't imagine Darroc intended only the shifters to fight for him. What was he doing in other realms? We have to assume he's amassing a bigger army than what we think." Nellie shook her head. "He can't get that Flame."

"And ignore the risks? You heard Moira describe it to us. A fire realm? Where one is supposedly killed the moment they make contact?" Faria wasn't afraid of the danger necessarily, but she would like to find a solution where everyone except Darroc survived. "I don't know that realm, I don't know how much time would pass. I don't even know that I would survive, if it's specifically Ander being a chosen one."

"But maybe Ander isn't the only Val who would survive there. It's time to recognize that part of you. I don't know much, but the way you used blood magic, the way you healed Moira, the way you are still constantly finding new powers. It goes beyond being a chosen of an old elven prophecy. I think you were somehow made to be Val. And if that's the case, only you can survive the fire realm and stop Ander."

If she was right, then Faria would need Nellie to lead the clans in her place if she decided to go to stop Ander. Nellie noticed her hesitation and continued. "Say you choose to stay and fight with the clans. To what end? Watch their numbers dwindle and then somehow convince them to do it all over again in a realm unknown to them in a land they could not care less about?"

Faria snorted. "That about sums it up."

They were quiet for a while as they entered the station. Nellie purchased their return tickets from the machine and hastened to the platform, Jamison and Marisa trailing behind. The stench of pollution coming from the exhaust of the trains suffocated Faria, as much as the city did. She couldn't wait to be back in the open air. Her head was killing her. She felt as if it would split open and all her treacherous thoughts would spill along the ground. She closed her eyes and rubbed her temples and dreamed of the clean air and freedom she'd soon have.

Warm hands pressed against her shoulders, massaging the tension in her upper back. Jamison was taking his liberties with touching her, but she couldn't say she minded. She felt the tension in her muscles melt away. The hum of humans speaking around her dimmed, and she enjoyed a welcome reprieve from all the stimulation. A sigh of relief escaped her.

You're going to be okay, Princess. I'm waiting for you.

Faria's eyes shot open as a cool breeze shot past her, bringing with it the scent of spice. She whipped around, expecting Jamison behind her but he sat on a bench in between Nellie and Marisa, laughing at something Nellie said. She turned in a circle, desperate to find the source of that voice, to see who had touched her. She knew it had to be a hallucination but still, the touch felt so real. She needed it to be real. Her eyes searched the crowd around her as she looked for a hint of russet hair or golden skin. Anything. She would take anything.

"Lose something?" Marisa asked.

She huffed a breath. "I lost everything."

Marisa gave Nellie and Jamison a pointed look. "Oookay," she said as their train approached.

She followed Marisa onto the train and waited as Nellie wiped the seats clean. She sat and looked out the window, searching again for someone who wasn't there. But wait…bright green eyes with a golden halo stared at her from the platform. She wiped a streak of condensation from the window, pressing her face closer to the glass to see. She stared straight into the eyes of Ander. She turned fully toward him, pressing her hand against the window. He nodded at her before drifting back into the crowd.

Did he just ensure that she would return because it was part of a trap, or for her safety?

"Here, you need some more of this," Nellie said, extending her sanitizer to Faria.

"What for?" Faria asked.

"You just touched that gross window. Who knows how many germs are on that thing?" After a moment, Nellie spoke again, her voice quiet. "I think you should do what your mother would do."

Faria paused her ministrations, staring hard at her hands rather than at Nellie's face.

"I mean," she quickly continued, "she would do what was best for her people. I think ultimately you should make the tough choice, the way she would have."

"And you think I would not make the choice that is best for my people?" Faria asked.

"No, that's not what I mean."

"Both choices are best for my people," Faria said, trying to avoid an argument. "Either I risk my life for this alleged Flame, unknowing if I can behold it or even survive in that realm, or I stay and protect the lives of people that are not mine in the hopes they will come fight again for us. Both are incredibly difficult decisions and incredibly crucial to the survival of my people."

Nellie nodded then went to sit with Marisa, understanding that she struck a nerve. Faria readjusted herself and closed her eyes, ignoring the sting of rejection as she was left alone with her wretched thoughts again.

THE SYMPHONY OF ANIMALS FIGHTING and weapons clashing met their ears long before the campground came into view. Faria was surprised the clans were still training. She had expected them to be sitting around their campfires eating dinner and having fun with each other. She smiled, marveling at how much more in sync with each other they were from when they started.

Activity bustled around them as Marisa, Nellie, and Jamison headed toward their own clans to give their reports. Faria leaned against a tree off to the side, watching the younger children help prepare dinner, the scent of roasting meat filling the air. The older children helped organize their weapons as the elder clan members gave them more tasks to do. These shifters and the humans of the realm were in grave danger from Darroc. He wanted to whisk them away to fight in Anestra just as much as she did.

Was she any better than him, really? She was willing to risk their lives for the sake of her country, exactly the same as what Darroc wanted to do. What made her different? The love of her people drove her the same as his love for his own people. She did believe that Darroc wanted Wendorre's power to be restored and ensure the warlocks' survival. He was doing whatever it took to make it happen. Wasn't she doing the same?

Her eyes roamed the camp until they landed on Moira, the mysterious teenaged girl she had healed. The one who was strange, who knew things no one else knew, who had a power unlike any she had ever seen.

The answer shot through her as her vision cleared.

She knew what she had to do.

IT WAS ANOTHER MISERABLE NIGHT. Another night dreaming of him, wishing he were there, wishing the Fates hadn't decided to take him away from her.

This dream was more vivid than the others. They had stood in the Forest of the Dawn, facing each other. Hunter looked so much older than she remembered. His russet hair was longer and he had scruff on his face as if he couldn't be bothered to shave it off. His arms were crossed and the runes that normally hid themselves in his human form writhed a luminescent onyx beneath his skin. Faria would have been surprised if she wasn't distracted by the thin white markings that stood out in stark contrast along his golden forehead.

Tears sprang to her eyes. The mate mark.

Would her grief know no bounds? Was this a trial the Fates thought was necessary she go through? To have to see someone she had hoped for so long would be hers as nothing more than a figment of her imagination?

She couldn't breathe. She didn't want to. She longed to perish and let herself drift into the Beyond to join who was meant to be her other half.

But she couldn't. Ander was her first priority and always would be. To be distracted by the conjuring of a ghost wasn't an option.

"Why do you keep haunting me?" she asked, barely able to keep the waver from her voice. "Why can't I get a moment of peace?"

"I'm still alive, Princess." His voice rolled through her, melting into all the spaces he once occupied. The ache in her stomach built. "You know why you keep seeing me."

For the love of the Fates, please wake up, wake up, wake up.

"Because of grief. Because you're dead and you won't let me forget you." She didn't know why she answered him, why she chose to pay this game of the Fates any attention at all. "Because of guilt."

His jaw clenched and his runes thrashed chaotically as though he wore licks of shadow as a second skin. His nostrils flared and for a moment Faria felt a sense of danger coming off him. She breathed it in, allowing a bit of her own darkness to bask in the power he released.

"*Do you feel guilt, Princess?*" he asked, finally taking a step closer to her. She couldn't take being inches apart, but she refused to touch him, to give sense to her insanity. "Do you feel guilty when you think about him?" He circled behind her, closing the space between them. "I can feel your lust for him." He scraped his teeth along her neck, his canines causing just enough pain to make her shiver, to make her believe he was real. "I know what you want to do with him."

"I'm not going to reason with a figment of my imagination," she huffed, trying to keep some semblance of control. "I need you to leave me alone. I can't do this with you."

"You have the same mark as me, love," he said, his voice softening. His words soothed her and acted as a balm on her shredded heart. "You know what that means. Why you can see me. Why you can scent me. Why you can feel when I touch you." His hand trailed along the side of her hip, but she stepped away, not allowing herself that pleasure. He scoffed. "You need to accept the bond."

"No. What I need to do is to get Ander to trust me, to convince him to leave Darroc, and to save my people."

"Your people are okay for now, Faria. If you accept the bond, we will at least have a way to communicate. I can't hold this connection for long."

His image shimmered like a mirage, putting truth to his words, but Faria wouldn't accept it. She couldn't accept it.

For the Fates' sake, wake up.

"I can't do this, Hunter. I can't focus on our son when you haunt me. Please, just stop."

"I'll prove it to you, Princess." His voice faded just as his image did. "Soon."

She tossed the blankets off her, the cool air kissing her sweat-slicked skin as she rolled off her cot. Nellie's gentle snores helped ground her back into reality.

Faria slipped on her boots and grabbed a sweater before leaving the tent, desperate to clear her mind.

The canopy of trees provided protection against the light misting of rain that threatened to break through the remainder of autumn's leaves. There was too much cloud coverage to see the moon, but with the occasional chirp of a bird, Faria could tell dawn wasn't far off.

She wandered along one of the paths that led away from the camp, trying to shake the remnants of her dream. She cursed whatever forced her to repeatedly endure it.

You must endure. You must survive.

Her mother's words echoed in her head. She had known that Faria would spiral into the suffocating darkness that took root in her, would seek comfort in what would numb her enough to move forward.

Footsteps against fallen leaves crunched their way into her thoughts. She scented the air, wondering who else would be awake so early in the morning. The scent of snow and wind nestled against her skin. She sighed inwardly. Of course he would find her.

"What are you doing here?" she asked, not bothering to turn around to face him. "Shouldn't you be sleeping?"

"I could say the same to you," Jamison answered. He stopped close enough for her to feel his heat press into her back.

Faria squeezed her eyes shut, fighting to keep her warring emotions under control. How lovely it would be to lose herself in the cold swirl of darkness she felt in her core, to allow it to soothe the fire building under her skin.

She faced him and felt his alpha power ripple against her. She had started to recognize the different levels of authority among the shifters, and Jamison was one of the most alpha among them. She breathed him in, enjoying the hint of influence that lapped at her. She tried to stifle the shiver that threatened to tear through her.

"I don't want to talk about it."

Jamison shifted a stray hair off her forehead, his fingers lingering along her cheek. "What can I do to make it better?"

She didn't know why he asked. They'd already had this conversation. He knew exactly what he was offering, just as she knew exactly what she would be taking. "I would just be using you."

"I want whatever you want to give me. Whatever will give you a reprieve from what you feel. Whatever will make you feel alive rather than stuck in the purgatory you've been putting yourself through."

He closed the distance between them, but waited for her acceptance before he did anything more. She tried to resist the temptation but the guilt and her dream was still so fresh, she couldn't deny it. If it chased away her demons then maybe, just once, she could get a break. She could sleep through the night. She could refocus her attention on their mission, instead of haunting the ghosts of her past.

"Just once," she whispered.

Jamison grabbed her waist and pressed her against him. His mouth possessed hers but it was her tongue that sought entrance, needing to claim him before he could claim her. She would never give anyone that privilege again.

He moaned when she pushed him against a tree, fumbling as she hurried to unzip his pants.

She felt a breath whisper against the back of her neck, felt hands slide across the front of her stomach and caress her skin as they slipped under the loose pants she wore. She stiffened, though Jamison didn't notice. He unzipped her sweater and worked on the clasp of her bra.

A soft growl in her ear raised the hair on the back of her neck. Faria bit her lip as she sank further into the apparition behind her. Jamison was supposed to get rid of him, not bring him to life. She needed to escape the agony.

What Jamison was doing sent shivers down her spine, but what her hallucination of Hunter was doing was even better. She didn't want to stop. She would never stop this madness if it meant she could be with him one more time.

Sharp teeth nibbled along her neck, the sting of the pain heightening the pleasure she felt as his fingers drifted lazily down. "Do you think he can give you what you need, Princess?"

Her eyes flew open but Jamison continued, unaware of another's presence. Hunter's fingers reached her slit and circled around her most sensitive area. "You're so ready, Princess. Is this for him?" He bit her neck harder. "Or for me?" His tongue soothed the aching bite.

Faria shook her head, trying not to think about the depths of her depravity that encouraged her willingness to have relations with a ghost.

"I'm still here, Princess."

She rocked her hips against his hand as he bit her shoulder and pushed his finger inside. A burst of pleasure shot through her and she pressed back against him, silently begging for more. His finger slid into her again as he forcibly added another, heightening the sensation. A moan escaped her.

She reached back for the buckle on his pants, desperate for more, but before she could touch him, he disappeared.

The sudden emptiness swelled inside her as guilt and rage warred against each other.

"Stop," she said, fighting back tears. "Jamison, we have to stop."

Immediately he stood back, concern filling his eyes. "Did I do something wrong?" He brushed the hair back from her face and forced her to make eye contact.

"No, it isn't you. It's me. It's…I just…I thought this would help but I can't anymore. This can't happen."

Tears poured down her face as Jamison pulled her sweater back on and held her to him. He ran soothing circles along Faria's back and she sobbed against him.

"It's okay, Faria. It's okay."

But it wasn't okay. It would never be okay. Until she Faded into the Beyond, she would never be able to rid herself of the agony of missing him.

TWENTY THREE

HUNTER

The low lighting in Taps would only work to his benefit. Soft murmuring of the few patrons along with the clanging of cooking materials from the kitchen were all the noise they heard inside. The snowstorm Hunter and Endo just trudged through muted the world around them.

Hunter normally loved snowstorms. They made for terrible hunting conditions, but it was so easy for him to find peace in the serenity of gently falling flakes.

Now it was easy for him to find that quiet darkness swirling inside him, yearning to come out and play.

He tossed his head, indicating for Endo to wait at the bar. "Go see if Jones is available."

Endo eyed him, but Hunter ignored the look. He was focused on the far corner of the tavern, the one where shadows fought the flickering firelight. A figure slumped on the table, hood pulled tightly, covering their facial features. The skin of the person's hand was badly scarred. *There.* That was who he would start with.

He casually strolled over to the corner with his hands in his pockets, the picture of perfect ease. He cocked a half smile as he slid into the chair opposite the man.

"Hello, Anwyn." The human shrank back from Hunter, removing his hood slowly. The entire right side of his face was covered with scars, their deep grooves made even more harsh in the dancing light. His hands circled his tankard of ale as he surveyed Hunter, careful not to make eye contact for too long. Humans weren't normally afraid of him but this one had a special reason to.

Anwyn had participated in several riots that resulted in fires and loss of properties when the warlocks first started their so-called rebellion. He was, in fact, the culprit of a barn fire just outside of Athinia that had resulted in the loss of three mares, and its entire structure was unsalvageable. Hunter had questioned him nearly a year ago, forcing him to confess. He said he had been bamboozled, in his exact words, by some influential warlocks. The queen and king forgave him, given that he suffered greatly from his last arson job, but he had to do five months of community service. Hunter hadn't thought that was good enough. Most of Anestra ran on the barter system, anyway. Everyone's lifestyle was a form of community service.

"What brings you out in the storm?" Anwyn asked with a slight shake to his voice. Hunter chuckled bitterly. The darkness in him stirred at the scent of Anwyn's fear, though he kept it on a tight leash. Anwyn wasn't who he would lash out at.

"Felt like a walk," Hunter shrugged. "You?"

Anwyn lifted his tankard and took a long gulp for good measure. "What can I do for you?" he asked after a moment.

"See anything unusual lately?"

Anwyn shook his head.

Hunter raised a brow. "No? Hmm." He let the silence fill the space between them and received another tick of satisfaction when Anwyn shifted under his stare. "Heard anything unusual lately?"

"What do you expect me to be hearing?" Anwyn asked. "I live alone. People are scared and hiding or visiting their relatives in the countryside, thinking it's safer. No one wants to be around here. There's nothing to hear."

Hunter could sense the truth in his words. While some flocked to *Mentage* to train and fight in the next battle, other families chose to leave to try to protect themselves. He didn't blame them. No one was forced to fight for their country, though most chose to. They normally had more than enough to protect and defend Anestra, but with Darroc's beasts and his unpredictability, they needed more.

Hunter nonchalantly ran his finger through a ring of water left on the table. He had to play this carefully. Anwyn was like a scared doe. One wrong move and he would bolt. "So you haven't had contact with anyone?"

"Who am I supposed to be having contact with?"

Hunter stared at him. He could see his reflection in the dark pools of Anwyn's eyes, could see the gold shine around his pupil glow. Anwyn swallowed hard. "Who is it that you're more afraid of?" Hunter asked softly.

Anwyn let out a curse on a harsh breath. "I don't know for sure, but I think Crispin has been around."

Hunter's heart beat quicker, but he made sure to keep his features neutral, almost uncaring. "Why do you think that?"

"I don't know. I've felt like someone has been watching me. I get an oily feeling running down the back of my neck."

"A feeling," Hunter said. "You are human…what is this *feeling.*"

"Fucking intuition!" Anwyn growled. "I just know it."

"I see." It was all the confirmation Hunter needed. He knew Crispin would be lurking around. He was too much of a narcissist to not wait and see the results of his scheming.

"Everything okay here?" Endo said, edging up to the table. Hunter shot him an annoyed look, but the concern on Endo's face cooled him down. Hunter knew he was in that dark space in his mind. The sound of Crispin's name sent him diving headfirst into the chaotic storm inside him. It wouldn't be right to take it out on Anwyn.

He flipped a coin onto Anwyn's table as he got up. "Next round is on me."

The tavern was still empty and as the storm outside rattled the windows, Hunter was satisfied—it was unlikely any other patrons would come, at least until the snow let up.

The bar top was little more than a slab of wood, with caskets of wine and ale lined up behind it. Jones, the warlock barkeeper, busied himself rubbing a liquid salve along the wooden top.

"Hunter," the barkeep said. "What brings you all the way out here in a storm like this?"

He chose not to say anything, staring the man down instead. He found he was more likely to get the answers he needed when he said nothing at all.

Jones looked at Endo then back to Hunter again, shifting on his feet. "Would you like a drink?"

Hunter made sure to keep his expression unreadable, waiting for the moment he would crack. Jones was a likeable enough person, but when it came down to it, Hunter knew he would defend his own if he had to. He was what Hunter referred to as a 'neutral,' someone who could tip the scales in favor of either order or chaos. He knew this because he was a neutral as well.

"You want some food or something?"

He had to hand it to Jones; maintaining eye contact with him when his eyes glowed an eerie color took a lot of guts. But he knew if he just waited another moment…ahhh…*there*.

Jones wiped a thin sheen of sweat from his forehead with a tremoring hand. "I don't know where he is," he blurted out.

Gotcha. "Where who is?" Hunter asked, feigning innocence.

"He isn't here right now, I swear it."

"Hmm." Hunter removed a blade from one of his many hidden pockets and admired it in the firelight. "That is unfortunate."

"Hunter," Endo said, his voice low, "what are you doing?"

"You see," Hunter said, ignoring Endo, "if you did know anything…about anything, you would be very useful to me." He pricked his finger along his blade and let the blood run down his palm, displaying how sharp his dagger was and how quick he could make Jones bleed. "But seeing as how you don't…well, then that means I wasted my time and I do hate wasting my time."

"Now, now," Jones said, backing up a step. Idiot. Didn't he know not to retreat when he had a predator glaring him down? "There's no need for threats."

"Threat?" Hunter asked. "Did I threaten you?" The darkness was trying to escape. It fed on chaos. On blood. It was a gift from the gods, the Elders had told him. A gift to lose a sense of morality.

He had kept it locked up tight for decades, but with the events of the past few months, well, he found little reason to keep it caged.

Being good didn't win wars. Being powerful did.

Even still, if he harmed every person he wanted to, he would be no better than Darroc L'Azare or any of his ancestors before him. He had absolute control. Goddess help the day when that control disintegrated.

"I don't know what you want from me," Jones said, his voice shaking. "Please. I'm just trying to stay alive."

"What are you doing?" Endo murmured. "I feel nothing but hatred pouring from you."

Hate? Is that what he felt? He supposed it was. Hatred for his situation, for Anestra falling apart, for the queen's death, for the loss of his mate and his son. He hated a great many things, but did he hate

Jones? Well, that would depend on Jones.

"One more time," Hunter said, his voice soft. "Where is he?"

"I—" Jones looked to Endo, pleading. Endo, bless him, crossed his arms and stood united with Hunter, even if he didn't agree with his approach. "I don't know, I swear."

"Pity."

Hunter flung his dagger at Jones, pinning his sleeve against the wall. Before Jones had time to react, two more blades fixed him to the wall.

"Wait," Jones cried out. "Hunter, please. Wait. There might be something."

Tears leaked out of Jones's eyes, but it didn't faze Hunter. He knew the old warlock had information. It was his own fault he tried to keep it to himself.

"He came in about a month ago," Jones said through his tears. "Crispin. He put a tracking spell on Endo. Said he didn't trust him. That he knew Endo was sympathetic to the wrong side. He put the tracking spell before the attack on *Mentage*. He's been trying to get Endo alone since."

Hunter crossed his arms. It was better than he hoped for. He was not only reassured in his assumption that Crispin hung around, but now he also had bait to lure him in. He casually walked behind the bar and clutched Jones's neck. Jones scrambled against the wall, trying desperately to get away from his grasp.

"Is that all?" Hunter asked, as calm as if he were asking about the weather.

"Ye-yes," Jones gasped out.

"Gods!" Endo said. "Hunter, what the hell are you doing?"

He felt Endo next to him, but he didn't release his hold on Jones. "Don't think of lying to me again," he said, leaning in close to the barkeep. "I do hate being lied to."

Jones nodded frantically. Hunter waited another moment until he was sure Jones got the message then released his hold. He ripped his daggers from the wall and walked back around the bar as if he had all the time in the world. He removed another coin from his pocket, placing it on the counter. He smiled at Jones. "For your shirt," he said as he winked and headed for the door.

Endo muttered apologies before he followed Hunter outside. The winter air and the scent of freshly baked goods from the shops surrounding him couldn't calm him. The snow gusting into his body did nothing to wash himself from what he'd just done. He didn't regret any of it.

That was the problem.

Endo growled behind him, "What the hell was that about?"

Hunter shrugged. "We were there to get information. We got the information."

"Like that? Like…like," Endo stuttered. "Like we've lost all sense of morality?"

"Interesting choice of word," Hunter chuckled. At the moment, he cared little for morals. "Was it moral of either of the two to lie to me? To think they could hide an enemy to the Agostonna family? Which makes them an enemy to our people? Our land? Our peace? They were lucky I didn't harm them. They deserved much more than what they got." His darkness flowed into his veins a little more freely, its power sending tremors of ecstasy down his spine. "I would do anything to keep this land safe for Faria's return. And I would tear down the barriers between the realms to bring her back to me."

Endo huffed next to him as he struggled to keep up through the drifts of snow. "Be careful, Hunter. You're starting to sound like the same villain we're trying to destroy. This isn't who we are," he tried to reason. "This isn't you."

Wasn't it?

"You don't know me at all," Hunter said. No one did. He didn't even know himself.

But he was starting to remember. And he liked it.

A HOLLOW KNOCK ON THE door echoed within the cabin, taking up the silence with its gonging sound. Hunter sat in the tub, letting the hot water soothe his aching muscles and relax him enough to think. There were two days left until Darroc was due back with an army, barring any unforeseen circumstances, and they were barely in better shape than after the first battle with his monsters.

And try as he might, he wasn't able to connect to Faria again. He felt her confusion in passing, he felt the stress pouring from her, but he had no context. He tried to reach out to her, tried to comfort her as much as he could, but he didn't know if she felt it.

The knock sounded again, this time more urgent. He heaved himself out of the tub with a sigh, grabbing a bathrobe to stave off the sudden chill. Even with fires lit, it was still freezing in the barracks.

"Coming," he said, trying not to wince as he made his way to the door. He and Endo had sparred that evening after their training duties, and he wasn't as quick as he normally was, distracted by thoughts of how to trap Crispin.

He swung open the door and looked into the steely blue eyes of King Dennison. Their ire reflected as the flames from the hearth hit their icy depths. "My king," Hunter said with a slight bow. He moved aside so the king could enter.

He seemed both out of place and at home in the barracks. King Dennison was the commander of their army and used to spend most of his time running missions or training in the field. Lately, however, he had taken over the role of ruler as well, and the title seemed at odds from the rest of him. He wore a simple tunic shirt and pants, his hair pulled messily out of his face. Though the king himself was an excellent commander and could rough it with the rest of them, the air of confidence and power he gave off was at odds with such casual clothing.

"Hunter," the king said. "We must talk."

It was nearly midnight and Hunter had been looking forward to sleeping, but he indicated toward the bare table and chairs situated in front of the fire and waited for the king to sit.

"My wife knew what you are," he said without preamble. "Faline knows, though given her connection to the Secret Keepers, I'm not surprised she didn't say anything. But I have to assume Nellie knows as well, given how many missions you were on together."

Hunter still said nothing. There was no need to. He let the king run through his stream of consciousness, waiting for the moment where he would have to respond.

"Faria, I presume, knew what you are?"

Hunter nodded.

The king hesitated. "I will not demand you, as your king—if you do view me as your king—to give me all your secrets. I ask you as a friend, a companion for the past five years that I have known you. You came upon us right when we needed a weapons master, filled with knowledge of the other worlds. You do not age. You carry with you the burden of a thousand men. You leave, usually with extremely short notice, and return sometimes months later if it suits you. I think we have been more than amenable with you."

"You are right," he said. "You heard what I told Thuuk. You deserve an explanation." He took a deep breath. "I am the last Val Prince from the Great War, and am now protector to the Elven Royal Bloodline. After my family and brethren sacrificed their magic and were slaughtered, a group of beings known as the Elders took me in. They told me that I was chosen by their gods to survive, and that the three goddesses ask that I protect the Agostonna family in whatever way I can. I've done that discreetly for a thousand years. Faria was the first Agostonna I had close contact with in centuries."

The king drummed his fingers on the table, letting that information sink in. At last, when the silence grew nearly intolerable, he said, "Can you prove it?"

Hunter blinked. "Prove that I'm Val?"

"Yes."

Hunter shifted uncomfortably in his seat. "Not at the moment. The Elders wanted to unmake me as punishment for the part I played in changing Faria's fate…one of them came to my defense and as a result I am here, but without the full strength of my powers. With the exception of a few elven-type gifts, I am barely more than human, stuck in this state until they see fit."

"Hm." King Dennison kept his face blank.

"You will see when Faria returns with our son."

"And you are certain it is yours?"

"He is the spitting image of me in my Val form," Hunter said with an offended edge to his voice.

The king's glacial eyes took on a darker shade, piercing through his soul. "Have you sired others?"

He wanted to laugh. It was nearly impossible that after centuries of life, he never procreated. He had always thought that perhaps when the Val sacrificed their magic, something happened to make him infertile.

Until Ander. "No, I believed I was unable to."

"You have never bedded any others?" The king's voice was dubious, though Hunter had a feeling he was trying to make him squirm with this questioning. It almost worked.

"Of course I have," he said. "None that resulted in a child."

"I see. Can the Elders help us?"

Hunter let out a dark chuckle. "They could, maybe. But they are extremely angry with me. My orders are to stay here. I have no way to contact them, I wait for them to summon me."

"So what you're telling me is that though you are the last Val, and a prince, you have no way to give us the protection we need."

The truth was a bitter taste in his mouth. "Just my natural gifts, yes." Hunter shifted in his seat, preparing to reveal another truth about himself. "This brings me to one of the things I wanted to discuss with you. The Book of the Dead will have an unmaking spell, as Endo told us. I am eager to get my hands on it now that Darroc undoubtedly knows I am still alive. I can only die by the spell of unmaking. He will want to use it against me."

The king sat back in his chair and rubbed a hand through his beard. "I see."

"If I were to get it, we could also use it against his monsters."

"This is the book in the caves lining Wendorre," the king said. "That's at least a week's ride out if you don't stop."

"Yes."

"Is it within your abilities to travel quicker than the average elf?"

Hunter desperately wished he could say yes. He had a nagging feeling that he was forgetting something, but after nearly a millennium of life, his memories were dark spots in his mind.

"No," he said.

"So you are suggesting…what? That you wish to leave us days before the next battle is supposed to start?"

It sounded ridiculous, but Hunter didn't know of any other way they could survive this.

"If we unmake the monsters then we'd be left with just Darroc to contend with, unless the spell worked on him, too."

"We will put our trust in Faria," the king said. "And pray to the goddesses, the Fates, whoever else will listen that we get the help we need."

The king rose from his chair and showed himself to the door. "I will see you at six o'clock tomorrow on the practice field." The finality of the door slamming felt as though his Fate were sealed.

They would not survive the coming war.

HE WANDERED IN THE DARK for miles consumed by the nothingness around him. It was more than just darkness but the absence of light, of sound. He wasn't even sure if he was walking so much as floating.

It felt familiar, this space, and he thought after a while he must be dreaming. Or perhaps, he thought, he was unmade and this was all that was left; consciousness bumbling around, lost forever in a void.

He wasn't sure how much time had passed, if time existed where he was, but after a while he began to feel as though he were being watched.

There was nothing else to do except continue on, until he became aware of a pinprick of light in the distance, hovering in the middle of nothing. When it grew near, he stopped in front of it.

A tiny bell whispered through the vast empty space, so quiet he wasn't quite sure that he heard it at all. As it rang its final note, the light grew large enough that it swallowed him whole.

Sound rushed over him and with it came the scent of the ocean, burnt wood and trees swaying in a harsh breeze. He opened his eyes, the sun burning brighter than he remembered it, and before him stood Jacobi, the Elder who had convinced the others to give him one last chance.

"My son," Jacobi said, removing his cowl and embracing Hunter. "I hope you will excuse the theatrics. You would not believe the hoops I've had to jump through to get to you without the Fates or the others being alerted."

"Where was I just now?" Hunter appeared in a relaxed stance, but he felt as though he were balanced on a razor's edge. He didn't like how the place he just left settled under his skin, nor did he spare any warm feelings toward any of the Elders, whether they chose to spare his life or not. He felt murderous toward all of them.

"In the dreamscape. It took you quite a while to fall asleep and then it was so fitful, I wasn't sure I would be able to reach you. We must hurry before they catch on to us."

"Return me to my true form," he demanded.

"Ah, I wish that I could! They would surely know my involvement then, if they haven't figured it out already. If the Fates deem it, my son, they will return to you. Do not fret."

"The Fates haven't exactly been on my side lately," Hunter said, furious that he still had no control over his situation. "So, why the dramatics? Do you have news for me? Is it Faria?"

The Elder waved his hands away, as if the thought of giving news on Faria was nothing compared to what he had to say. "I know you are trying to find your way into his lair, but I must warn you that he has more dark magic surrounding that place than you would believe. You would need his blood, need to know the proper enchantments. I'm afraid it is all but unreachable."

The frayed string of hope Hunter held onto disintegrated. He wasn't surprised. What villain would leave their front door unlocked? Still, it was a blow to their meager offensive plans. "That is unfortunate."

"Yes, but there is some good news, and I implore you to think of it as such when I tell you. Centuries ago, when you landed quite literally in front of us out of thin air and we discovered what you were, what happened to your species, and what the gods intended for you, we made the decision to lock your mind from both the horrors and the secrets of the Val."

He fucking knew it. The feeling he'd had the past few months of things he couldn't quite remember had to be a result of what the Elders did. Rage made his body tremble. "You did what?"

"Please understand, we believed you were still being hunted, and you knew too much about the secrets of both the Fae and the elves, and they couldn't fall into enemy hands. We had to do what was best to protect both you and those you swore to serve."

He had been violated so much more than he thought possible. "Why are you telling me this now?" Hunter had a hard time controlling his fury. For centuries he lived by the Elders' rules, doing what he was told, coping with the loss of his entire species. He felt alone, desperate for real companionship, and unable to find it because he didn't age and everyone else did. But to find out the people who helped "save" him also put him in a tighter cage than he imagined…it was deplorable.

"There is a Val ability locked away in your memories. It will allow you to pass through space and time. It was how the protectors of old were able to get to their charges whenever and wherever they were in trouble, without the use of a Gate. I want to undo part of what we did to you so you can reclaim that ability."

"You want to loosen the leash?" Hunter scoffed. "You think it wise to give back powers you deemed too dangerous for me to keep? For what purpose?"

"My child," he answered, surprised at the question. "I want nothing more than to see you succeed."

Hunter stared into Jacobi's black eyes, noting his graying hair and skin just starting to sag after more than a thousand years of knowing him. This didn't feel right, all this secrecy. Why risk the other Elders' wrath? Was it because they knew he would fail? "Give me all of it back then. All the Val secrets. *My* secrets. There is no one to hunt me anymore." He didn't mention that he thought some of his powers were returning anyway. He had suspected it was the Elders but given all the secrecy, he knew whatever forces at work were much more powerful than them.

"Darroc is hunting you and I will not see you harmed because you couldn't handle the onslaught of pain releasing all the locks would cause. No, just this bit will do for now."

Before he could protest, Jacobi placed both his hands on either side of Hunter's head, sealing him in. Searing pain, sharp and hot smashed through his brain and a moment later information slammed through him, incapacitating his movements. Hunter's jaw clenched with the impact and after a few seconds he couldn't take it anymore. This was worse than any torture he had undergone, worse than being unmade. He'd beg for it to stop if he could only use his voice.

But then it all did stop and as sweat beaded down his forehead, he realized that he was laying horizontal in his bed, the fire only just turned to embers. Clutching his sheets, he willed his heart to calm and for his surroundings to make sense once again.

It was dawn. Hunter's eyes burned from exhaustion and he stared longingly at the bathing chamber, hoping he had time for a hot bath to soothe his aching body.

A slight popping noise sounded in his ears and he felt as though he were being squeezed through a tube. The pressure released and he found himself off kelter, standing precariously close to the edge of the sunken tub. Surprise tipped him into the steaming water.

Coughing, sputtering, he stood up and wiped his face. Was this the ability Jacobi unlocked? He'd expressed his wish to be in the bathing chamber, and so he was.

He let out a breath of laughter. He still had no memories of ever having this power. It was how the Fae moved about—there one minute and gone the next. And as a Val, he was a mixture of Fae and elf with the power of the goddesses, so it made sense to have some shared abilities.

He washed quickly and dressed himself in his usual attire of plain tunic and pants and put on thick winter boots. He found breakfast on the table, undoubtedly delivered while he was in the bath. Shoving a biscuit and some fruit in his mouth, he pocketed the nuts and made his way to the practice area, not fifty feet from his door.

The king was already there, warming up with some slow stretching exercises used for centering himself.

"I have some news," Hunter said. The king listened as Hunter told him what Jacobi had said about Darroc's enchanted lair, and how the king was right—there would be almost no time to figure out how to enter even if they did make it there quickly. He left out the part of having one of his powers unlocked. He wanted to understand how to use it, first.

The king nodded. "I have some news as well. Endo was just here to warn me. He could feel something happening among the warlocks. A warning, like a call to arms. It's Darroc's way of telling them to prepare for him. He described it as immensely painful when he tried to refuse."

"I see. Do all the warlocks feel it, or just those that went to his side?"

"Just the ones who left."

Hunter thought for a moment. They expected Faria and Nellie in the next day or so, or at least they trusted the Fates to bring them together before the battle. Darroc wasn't supposed to come until the following day. He hoped it didn't mean the worst for his mate. "How much time do we have?"

"Hours, perhaps."

He nodded. "Let's do a final count, then."

The king didn't move. "This will be the last time they will sleep in for an unknown number of days. We are as prepared as we can be. We can at least wait until the sun rises."

Hunter bowed his head in supplication then grabbed two swords off the rack. "If that's the case, then let's get one last practice session in."

He tossed a sword to the king who gave him a grim smile and got into position.

"Your highness!" a voice cut through the early dawn. "King Dennison!" Wil and Reed ran onto the practice pitch. "You must come quickly!"

"What is it?" the king asked. Hunter steeled himself for bad news. It would make sense if the Fates were continuing to throw them off. It seemed like it would amuse them.

"It's Crispin," Reed said, his breath coming in short bursts. A trickle of blood dripped down from his temple. "We found him lurking along one of the secret passages onto the grounds."

Hunter's heart stilled as the darkness in him practically purred at the news. He fucking *loved* the Fates.

The king's brows drew down. "Where is he?"

"Enis has him detained where we found him, sir. She didn't think it would look well to have him walking through *Mentage*."

"Have Johanna clear the Council Chamber at once and bring him there. We will be there shortly."

Wil and Reed nodded then started jogging back up to the house, dodging the early risers who thought to get started on their morning practices. Hunter's skin thrummed and it was all he could do to hold back his power that longed to come out.

"I see that look in your eye," the king said. "You will not harm him. That's not who we are."

So many thoughts rushed through Hunter's head. He remembered having to do horrible things to protect the Agostonna line. He murdered, tortured, spied, seduced, all over Anestra and beyond, all to get information, to stop a threat before it started.

"We must become who we have to in order to make it to tomorrow."

The Council Chamber was cleared of everything by the time they arrived. A threadbare rug covered the old dirt floor, and a fire roared in the hearth. Crispin kneeled in the center of the rug, looking worse for wear. His normally coiffed hair fell in greasy strands around his face, his clothes were ripped and soiled, and his nose had a steady trickle of blood running down it.

Johanna stood behind him with a sword pointed at his kidney, while Enis stood close with a dagger at his throat.

"Thank you, Johanna. Enis. You may leave." The king's voice held no room for argument. The two hesitated slightly before bowing to him and leaving the room. A blade was drawn from the shadowed corner of the room. Endo held his sword at Crispin, his face a mixture of disgust and hate.

"Just in case," Endo shrugged, never taking his eye off Crispin.

Their prisoner, whose arms were bound behind his back, spat on the floor in front of them. Even in such a sorry state, Endo had the audacity to sneer at them as if they were nothing but children who hadn't yet realized they'd lost the game.

"Endo," the king said. "Would you be so kind as to drag Crispin off my rug for a moment, please?"

Endo grabbed the rope binding Crispin and jerked him off to the side, making sure he wasn't too gentle about it. Hunter smirked. For all Endo was worried about the way Hunter had acted in Athinia, he seemed to have no problem getting in touch with his rougher side.

The king dragged the rug back a few inches, revealing a small wooden door in the floor. A rush of memories flooded Hunter's mind.

A trap door with ancient runes surrounding it, and a crude stone stairwell leading into darkness. A room, much like the one he stood in, but with chains lining the wall. A single stone slab in an upright position. Blood of his latest victim drenched the floor. The smell of iron and rust assaulted him.

He glanced over at the king who seemed to be waiting for Hunter to react in some way. "Do you know of this?" he asked.

Hunter nodded, unnerved. "Bits and pieces. Are you aware of what's down there?"

The king's jaw clenched. "My wife told me much about *Mentage* when I first arrived here."

Hunter waited for the king to lift the hatch, wondering how accurate his broken memories would be. A cold wind burst into the room from below, along with the musty scent of earth, decay, and a hint of rust.

"I'm not going down there," Crispin said, the first hint of fear shadowing his face. He licked his lips. "You can kill me just fine up here."

Hunter strolled over to Crispin as if he had all the time in the world, though he knew the clock was desperately winding down. "You will go wherever the king says."

Before Crispin uttered whatever scathing reply he was bound to make, Hunter punched him on his temple, effectively knocking him out. The king let out an exasperated sigh.

"What?" Hunter said innocently. "He'll be easier to carry this way."

King Dennison shook his head but waved his hand, allowing Endo and Hunter to lead them into the chamber below.

The darkness stirred within Hunter and he felt a sense of familiarity as they crept slowly down the stairs. "There are torches along the wall," he said. "They will light automatically in a few more steps."

Sure enough, a path was lit for them until deep shadows flickered along the walls, and eerie luminescent runes flared to life. The heavy pull of magic pressed against his skin.

Just as his broken memories told him, there was a large stone slab with cuffs standing in the center of the circular room. Next to it was a table with sinister looking instruments, ranging from knives and smaller scalpels to hooks and liquids within bottles of various sizes.

Endo grunted from Crispin's weight as they cuffed him to the slab. "What the hell is this place?" Endo whispered.

Hunter chose not to answer. He slapped Crispin a few times, attempting to rouse him.

Crispin opened his eyes, looked around, and then chuckled darkly. His teeth were stained red from an earlier beating. The king stood behind Hunter and they waited calmly for Crispin's laughter to die down.

"You fools," Crispin's voice croaked out. "You cannot win this." He rolled his eyes over to the king. "He controlled Callum. Did you know? He made that pathetic waste of a human walk right up to her and slash her throat. She didn't even fight it. She knew it was her end. That was your queen. Not even willing to defend her life. How pathetic."

King Dennison shook, his fists curled in rage. Hunter kept his face blank, waiting.

Crispin swung his head back over to Hunter. "You know he defiled your princess. He told us all about it in delicious detail. About how after that blast killed you, she was knocked out from the power of it. And while the babe screamed, he tore her pants down, and relished the feel of her—"

"Enough." The king's voice cut through Crispin's. He looked at Hunter, his wrath palpable. Every line of his face was etched with grief and vengeance. "Get the information you need." The king began to walk away, Endo following close behind him. "Through any means necessary."

Once he was alone with Crispin, Hunter moaned as he allowed the darkness to lick his skin, as intimate as a lover, until he was just on the cusp of losing control.

He smirked at his victim and picked up a tiny instrument from the table that resembled a toothpick. It was the perfect place to start.

"Let's begin."

TWENTY FOUR

NELLIE

The quiet among the clans cast a tension-filled afternoon as the shifters spent much of their time sharpening weapons, going over battle plans, putting in last minute practice with different maneuvers in their animal forms. The sun hid behind the clouds, making a chilling day even more so, and though plenty of fires were lit among the encampment, the heat hardly staved off the shivering of those filled with fear or anticipation.

Spending the afternoon passing out bowls of oatmeal was the only way she knew how to stay busy. The plans were drawn. Nellie had her orders from her queen to stay the line, no matter what, and that was what she intended to do. Most of the shifters refused the food, or else took it with a small smile but didn't eat it. She couldn't blame them for not wanting to eat when nerves were at an all-time high, but she reminded each person that keeping up their energy could be the difference between life and death when fighting.

Moira came to her after a time, insisting she help as well. Nellie didn't like the thought of her remaining here and told her as much, suggesting she leave with those who were too old, injured, or young to fight, but she adamantly refused.

"I am meant to be here," Moira said, a small smile playing on her lips. She acted whimsical, as if she were detached from what was about to happen. "I cannot go."

"But why?" Nellie asked. "I know you're different. You can show us your memories, you lived in Anestra for a time, but what exactly are you? Why do you think you need to be here?"

"Hmm, what I am is hard to describe." The young teen chuckled. "I was part warlock, part something else. I was made to be this way long ago, and then when I gave up the last of the power I could, I became a little less warlock and a little more something else. I have a role to play just as much as you do, and as Faria does."

"But you could die," Nellie implored. She was frustrated at these riddles. "You're so young."

Moira placed her hand on Nellie's arm as if to comfort her. "If I die, as I imagine I will, it will not be forever because it never is. Do not worry, Nellie. I will do what I can to help you and our queen."

She drifted off to deliver more food to the clan members, gliding away serenely. It upset Nellie to see a child knowingly go into a battle to the death. It wasn't right. None of it was.

"Hey, Nells." Callie walked over to her with a backpack and a set of keys in her hand. "I've just come to say good-bye."

Nellie was relieved Callie wasn't staying to fight. She wasn't trained, and this wasn't her battle. Still, she was sad to see her friend leave. "Where will you go?"

"The Angels of Fate are guiding me out west. I've only seen flashes, but I might have a way to slow the spread of the wasting disease. I have to see what I can do before the humans go to war."

The thought chilled Nellie. She hoped it wouldn't come to that. "Will I see you again?"

Callie enveloped Nellie in a warm embrace, her strawberry scent filling her with bittersweet nostalgia. "Yes, I imagine you will." Callie pulled away then gasped, her fingers grasping onto Nellie's shoulders. "Oh, wow. Nellie. He's cuuuute!"

"Who is?" Nellie breathed. "Endo?"

Callie winked at her. "I'll see you soon."

Tears filled Nellie's eyes. Endo was alive, and if Callie was swooning over him, that must mean he went back to the right side. Relief was a short-lived beast as the pressure built in her chest. They needed to survive and return to Anestra. She didn't know how it would happen, but she vowed to do whatever it took.

The sun set quickly and the wind picked up, making conditions for fighting unfavorable. Nellie walked back to the tent she shared with Faria to prepare herself for battle, anticipating the heaviness of the elven armor after weeks of wearing jeans and sweaters. Folding back the flap, she entered a suddenly quiet tent, realizing she had interrupted a conversation.

Jamison sat on the bed next to Faria with Moira kneeling before her. His easy smile ticked her off. How dare he sit next to Faria, on a bed *with* her, no less. She had to remind herself that Jamison was not a citizen of Anestra and though he knew Faria was a queen, he was not under any obligation to treat her as *his* queen. It still felt presumptuous and rude.

"Should I leave?" Nellie asked more forcefully than she intended.

Faria shook her head. "Moira was just telling me a bit of what she knows about jumping between realms and the unpredictability of the Gates. Did you know that the Gates stopped working properly once the Val disappeared?"

Nellie shook her head, surprised that Moira would know a thing like that. "That's an interesting theory."

"Yes, apparently their magic helped stabilize time. It's why the Gate doesn't work properly. Apparently, it used to bring you to wherever you wanted to go. She said it was a power unique to the Val, gifted by the Fae and blessed by the goddesses. Time also used to pass in a predictable manner between realms. Now, as you know, it's all a mess. She was saying that perhaps a resurgence of Val would set it right again."

"Hmm," Nellie said, stripping off her clothes. She didn't care that Jamison was there. Maybe he would be uncomfortable enough to leave. She peeked behind her shoulder and saw him wink at her behind Faria's back. She should have known he wouldn't have minded. She sighed inwardly.

"Well, I would hardly call one Val a resurgence, unless you're ready to admit that you could be what I think you are," Nellie said. "And it would take a while for Ander to procreate, unless he's been up to more activity than causing chaos and doing Darroc's bidding."

"Ew, Nellie. Don't talk about my kid that way."

"He will be here soon, my queen," said Moira. "It is an honor serving you and I hope you will allow me to do so again in my next life."

"Please don't speak like that, Moira," Faria said. "You will be fine; I'll make sure of it."

The young girl winked at Nellie and headed out into the night. Nellie stared pointedly at Jamison, now relaxing back on his elbows, a little too at ease on Faria's bed.

"Well, I guess I should go as well," he said. "My clan will want some words of inspiration from me."

"Yes," Faria said. "Remember what I said about your position," she called to his retreating back.

"I'll stick close by, Your Majesty," he said with a bow before he left the tent.

Nellie and Faria got ready in silence, Faria strapping on all her weapons, now donning the same elven tunic and pants she'd had on when they first arrived. Nellie buckled her armor in place and stretched, making sure she had all movement available to her.

"Do you have feelings for him?" Nellie asked.

Faria snorted. "I hardly think we have time to talk about feelings, do we?"

"No, we really don't, but I do need to know where your mind is. Do you like him?"

Faria cocked her head. "My heart is shattered in a million pieces, my queendom is under attack by my psychotic *husband*, my son is now practically my age and the spitting image of my dead lover, and my *best friend* can turn into a dragon. Jamison and I have a connection and he's been able to provide me with a necessary distraction. He knows my feelings cannot move forward."

Nellie nodded, unsure of what else to say. She didn't have time to figure it out, though, as a horn rang out through the camp. The shrillness of it died down, followed by shouts and the echoing beat of war drums.

Faria and Nellie looked at each other for a moment longer before Faria moved to her side, embracing her in a deep hug. "Remember what I said, Nellie. We must win. Stay the line."

She released her quickly and ran out of the tent, her bow in one hand and her quiver of arrows slung across her back. Nellie was so shocked by the sudden affection and at the way her command felt like a goodbye, that it wasn't until another shrill of the horn sounded that she exited the tent as well.

Activity erupted around her, this time far more organized than the last attack. Clan members lit pyres around the perimeter, effectively creating a ring of fire around them—their first line of defense. It would do little more than give the monsters pause, but those might be the few seconds they needed.

The clans fell into line behind, Tommy, Jamison, and Marisa all at the front lines. Faria was at the back, guarding the archers, along with Moira, Samantha, and Luck. Nellie nodded at each as she made her way to the front to stand as close to the fire as she could get without burning herself.

In the distance, she heard trees collapsing, much larger than the first time they fought the monsters, and the snarls and growls sounded fiercer, more guttural, almost entirely inhuman. A shudder ran through her, but she squelched it. This wasn't a time for fear, but to protect. Fear meant she would make mistakes and she couldn't—wouldn't—risk it.

She cracked her knuckles and moved her neck in slow circles, willing her breathing to stabilize. She turned around and looked at Tommy, Jamison, and Marisa once more, and then at the hundred or so shifters lined behind them, each getting ready to change into their animal form or fight as humans. She wanted to say something, but words failed her. This was likely a suicide mission; most of them would die. So no, there were no uplifting words she could say.

But as the growls grew and the screeches reached an all-time high, a breeze picked up carrying with it the acrid scent of carrion, she smirked and said, "Try not to get in my way," and shifted into a *Drogosterra*.

TWENTY FIVE

FARIA

The fire blazed in a circle around them, the roaring flames doing nothing to mute the sounds of the monsters on the other side. They had only moments, if not seconds, until the beasts jumped over the flames and the slaughter began.

Faria made the signal for her archers to nock the arrows they'd dipped in *Drogosterra* blood the previous day. Arranging them to stand north, south, east, and west, she yelled for them to release once, then twice.

A loud snarl snapped from behind her, letting her know the monsters had started to breach the area. At her command, the archers changed direction, each one alternating their position so half would shoot from the front and the other from the back. The first of the monsters on her side broke through.

And then she was cast into darkness.

The world was silent and completely void of anything. There was no sound, no scent, no light. She had been here before, she realized, and was filled with a certain kind of dread. *Gods*, she didn't have time for this, not now.

Voices hissed around her as the Fates made their appearance. She didn't want to hear anything they had to say.

"It is time," They said. "You must face your trials if you are to become queen of Anestra."

"You cannot be serious!" she yelled at them. "Do you understand what you just took me away from?"

"This is not up for negotiation," They said. "If you think to rule the land your ancestors have passed on to you, this mussssst happen."

There was no point in arguing. She had no way to return.

"The first trial already came to passsssss."

"How could that be?"

"It was the losssss of your son." The words echoed around the void she stood in. "You endured. You did not stop fighting. You followed the path you were meant to. You could have given up and did not. The losssss of a child is one of the greatest hardships a parent can face. It shows your strength and ressssssilience. This is important in a queen."

"Are you telling me," she said, seething, "that you purposely had my son taken away from me, had him live his entire life without me, just to see how I would react?"

"The second trial," They continued, ignoring her, "is not something you have control over."

"Oh, did I have control over any of this?"

She knew it was the wrong thing to say. Their voices lashed out and she felt a burning on her skin, as though she'd been whipped. "Do not disrespect ussss. We can remove you entirely from existence if we choose."

She knew she should keep her mouth shut. She really wanted to. She told herself she wasn't going to respond. "Really? Then do it."

The silence that rang out was so profound, Faria wasn't sure for a moment if they did. If this was what it was like to be dead, to move into the Beyond.

"If you wishhhhh," the voices whispered, the words like snakes slithering down her spine. "Or we can wait and see what is in store for you in the battle to come."

"No, I spoke too quickly," she said. She hated the idea of apologizing. "I want to know what the other trials are."

"The second trial is one that you must endure, no matter the outcome, for his Fate lies with yours. You must watch your son choose his own path. And you must learn to deal with the consequences of either."

"What is that supposed to mean?" Trepidation filled her. Consequence sounds like a bad thing, and the only bad thing he could choose was to kill her or side with Darroc, right?

"The last trial will be most interesting," They said. She could almost hear the mirth in Their voices. Did they think this was funny? Was this all just a game to them, a way for them to pass the time? She held her breath.

A bright light flared, and a scene appeared before her, as if on one of those human's screens. Images flashed so rapidly. She recognized *Mentage* covered in snow. She saw her father fighting against monsters. More pictures flickered as if she were flipping through a book. Ships on the sea. A dark cave. A dungeon. Fire. The images blurred the faster they went, dizzying her until they settled onto one.

Crispin. She recognized him even through all the blood dripping down his face. His body was broken, skin torn from his muscles, breaths no longer escaping him.

"Do you know thissss person?" the Fates hissed.

"Yes," Faria breathed, horrified at the image. "Did Darroc do this?"

The Fates twittered and she got the impression that they really were laughing at her. "No, he cannot take the claim for this."

"Who, then? How?"

"Four months have passed in Anestra to your three weeks. They have been waiting for you, for Darroc L'Azare. It is the eve of battle for them. What happens here will greatly affect what happens there."

"Who did that to him?" she asked again. Why wouldn't they answer her?

"There is another evil that comes. One larger than the warlock king. One that is pulling the strings hard enough to bring down the wrath of the gods."

"Is that who did this?"

"In a way, but not."

They were so infuriating. She didn't have time for this.

"If you are so powerful, why not change the fate of whatever evil you're talking about so they don't come to power?"

More laughter flittered through her, its discordant sound scraping her insides, changing her bowels to water. "It is not our job to prevent such a thing," They said. "It will be your tasssssk to see that Anestra does not fall. Your tasssssk to prove that you are a worthy queen. Thissss will be your final trial."

"You didn't show me my future until I fade," she said, desperate for more answers. "Isn't that what you are supposed to do? Isn't that what you did for my mother?"

"Too much dependssssss on others. We shall sssseee."

She lurched back into her physical body, suddenly surrounded by utter chaos. Arrows flew from all directions toward the pus-filled faces of the monsters that had broken through the ring of fire. The scent of the carrion on the breath of the beasts was suffocating and all consuming.

They stood at least six feet tall when on all four legs, more than twice that if they stood on the back two. Their grotesque bodies looked like an experiment gone wrong. They could have been beautiful once, if they weren't patched together in such unnatural ways.

Screams tore out in the night, but Faria shut out as much as possible, trying to empty her mind of all she had learned. She ran and tumbled in between dead and dying bodies of both shifters and beasts alike, snatching as many fallen arrows as she could. She needed to conserve her energy for Darroc.

An unnatural silence fell upon the forest. The frenzy of the monsters dulled, the fire seemed to cease its roaring, and the wind, which had been thrashing violently, calmed itself.

Darroc L'Azare strolled onto their battlefield, as if he had little care in the world, Ander standing at his side. His red eyes blazed and unholy canines peeked through cracked lips. His skin was sallow and his entire frame looked more like a wraith than warlock. They were similarly dressed in fitted black combat clothes. One clawed hand held onto Ander's shoulder, as if proving that he possessed the very thing she wanted. Faria wanted to vomit from the sight—but she had to trust that Ander was on her side and that the *innulum* would work, that Ander wouldn't murder his own mother.

Faria was struck by a sudden memory of when Darroc told her the legend of the warlocks' demise. How the son murdered his father for power after his mother flew away in a phoenix's body, taking away their source of magic.

The juxtaposition of past Darroc and current Ander struck a chord deep within her. Fire licked her veins, begging to be released, to strike in vengeance for the murder of Hunter and the contamination of her son.

Still, her power could not be released on Earth. It was as if she needed to scream but had no vocal cords. Instead, she concentrated on her elven accuracy, the Fae-blessed gift that fortunately did work on this world, and whipped a dagger straight for his eye.

To her disbelief and dismay, Ander threw one of his own and knocked hers out of the air. His aim was just as good as hers. She tried again, and again he knocked hers out of the air. She refused to feel indignant, refused to feel anger toward her son for defending Darroc's life.

Darroc turned his deep red eyes on her, a smile playing across his face, sharp teeth pointing through. His smug demeanor at Ander's behavior ignited her fury. Fates be damned if she would allow her son to protect his captor. She let her emotions best her as she let out a frustrated scream and ran toward him.

Faria was vaguely aware that no one was fighting now, but rather watching her race toward the very person who had caused such anguish in all of their lives. She nocked an arrow and aimed for him, and this time Ander didn't strike it away. He didn't need to. Darroc burnt it to a crisp on its way to him. Though she kept trying, none of her weapons struck him. Frustration grew, both from not being used to missing her target and from the reminder of how much stronger than her he was, especially in this realm.

Nellie, back in her human form, ran up behind her, but Faria barked a quick, "Not your orders," as she sped up, less than twenty feet away from Darroc. She sensed the hesitation, but Nellie fell back, leaving Faria alone once again.

A sudden yank behind her neck drew her up short of Darroc, a raised dagger frozen in her hand. She rose slowly in the air, her entire body out of her control, as Darroc lifted a single clawed finger. She struggled to move, to talk, to do anything, but instead she remained immobilized, suspended in the air before him.

"You, my fiery wife, have been a naughty girl killing my friends."

She glared at him, the most she could do with no control. She cursed the Fates for allowing this moment to happen. She cursed whatever gods thought it funny to render her powerless but allow Darroc the full use of his magic.

"It has been, what, nearly eighteen years for me since I last saw you?" His voice grated against her spine. "Of course, it has only been a few weeks since you last saw me. Did you miss me, or did we need to separate longer?"

She visualized a vulgar gesture and flung the image at him, trying to convey it in her eyes.

Darroc threw back his head and laughed, its chilling sound echoing above the moaning of the injured and dying.

"I have such a tale to tell you, my pet, though I suppose you don't particularly want to hear it given your undoubtedly painful position. Suffice to say, I have raised my son quite well, if I do say so myself. He has made a most excellent student. So much more…*willing* to do things I couldn't even dream of when I was his age."

Faria tried to shift her gaze over to Ander but was unable to do even that. He stood just outside her vision line, unwilling to move closer so she could lay eyes upon him.

"Well, anyway," Darroc continued, "I wanted him to kill you because how beautifully poetic would that have been? Alas, I already have you in my grasp and a simple snap of my fingers would have you in a million pieces. I don't think I want it to be quite so quick, though. My son," Darroc reached behind him and gripped a claw-like hand on Ander's shoulder, leading him to face Faria head on. "Perhaps we should show her what you've been learning the past few years, since she missed out on so much."

Hatred burned from Ander's eyes and Faria wished desperately it was directed at Darroc rather than at her. He stepped a little closer, removing a long, thin blade from a side pocket of his leather armor. He was only a few inches away from her when he paused for a moment and breathed, "Be brave."

Ander slid the blade under her fingernail and sliced it off, removing it entirely from the bed. Blood flowed freely as she fought to scream, tears springing to her eyes at the sudden pain.

"Good," Darroc said. "Again."

Once more, Ander flicked the blade and another nail popped off. Tears flowed freely down her face now and she was almost grateful she couldn't move; she would have to hurt Ander to defend herself.

A strangled cry behind Faria turned her blood to ice as she heard Nellie shout, "Leave my queen alone!"

Darroc smiled at someone behind Faria's shoulder and breathed in. "Well, well. What have we here?" He took another deep breath and held it, as though savoring the taste he scented. "You smell deliciously familiar."

"You are such a coward," Nellie spat. "Torturing her while she can't move a muscle to defend herself. You must be so proud of yourself."

"You would be most interesting to cut open and experiment on. In fact, I daresay I did cut open one of your kind before. A woman who tried so hard to hide from me, but I caught her scent in the end. It would be fun to add you to my collection, but unfortunately I now have to use you as an example."

He raised his fingers and snapped. A silent scream tore through Faria as bile threatened to climb her throat. She prayed to the goddesses and Fates to spare Nellie. She looked deep into Ander's eyes, searching for an answer, begging for him to tell her that Nellie was still alive but he only stared back at her, stricken.

A small hand reached out to grasp Faria's and though she couldn't see who it belonged to, she knew it was Moira. She felt, rather than saw, a fire grow next to her though no heat licked through her clothing. She searched for a reflection in Ander's eyes but it was indistinguishable. A bird? Faria shifted her eyes back to Darroc whose blood had drained from his already pale face. The monsters that were lined up behind him whimpered and backed slowly away from the fight altogether.

Her limbs tingled as if tiny bolts of electricity shot through her before Faria realized she had control over her body again. She collapsed in a heap on the ground, both Nellie and Jamison reaching to lift her. She hissed against the shock of pain that burned through her fingers as her bleeding nail beds scraped along the rocks and dirt beneath her. She turned her stiff neck to look at Moira and froze, paralyzed by what she saw.

The young girl, normally petite, scraggly, and red-haired, was now as tall as a human woman and surrounded by fire. No, Faria amended, she was *on* fire, as brilliant green, purple, silver, and blue flames consumed her body. She smiled a cruel slash of a smile at Darroc, then bowed her head to Faria as if in reverence.

The queen didn't know what to do, for she couldn't possibly believe she was bearing witness to a real phoenix. If Darroc's legend were to be believed, she was now gazing into the eyes of his centuries missing mother. The true Warlock Queen.

Faria scrambled to her knees and placed her forehead on the ground as Nellie did the same on her other side. Moira bent down and placed a fiery hand under Faria's chin, raising her up out of the gore that lined the forest floor.

"You shall never bow to me," the phoenix said. "You are a queen, in more ways than one." Then Moira bent to whisper in her ear. "You must kill my son," she said. "He is far more twisted and evil than the balance will allow. I fear if you do not, all realms will be tipped over to the end of days."

"Will you help me?" Faria asked. "I have no power here."

"You have power everywhere," Moira said, kissing Faria's brow. She felt a blaze of heat scorch inside of her from where Moira's lips touched. Her pool of magic stretched as if awakening from a long nap as it flared to life. The bracelet she wore, the one with the last kernel of warlock power, glowed brightly as it molded itself to her flesh. "Hurry now," Moira said. "He makes his escape to Anestra."

Faria looked in alarm at Darroc, who indeed appeared to be retreating slowly away, his face still pale in the flickering light.

A tsunami of fire burned in her blood as she called upon an orb of flame—one so similar to what he'd used to kill Hunter weeks ago. She flung it at him, putting the weight of her fears and frustration behind it.

It soared through the air, just missing him and setting the tree behind him aflame. She called another, this time putting the power of ice into it. It flared a brilliant blue and white as it struck him hard in the chest. He froze, stunned by the impact, then curled his mouth. "Did you think your tricks would defeat me?" His voice thundered throughout the clearing. "I am the most powerful warlock that has ever lived. You cannot—"

Moira flared her wings and enveloped him in a fiery embrace. His shouts smothered against the loud crackling of flame until he was no longer there, seemingly incinerated.

Faria almost forgot they were in the middle of a battle when sound rushed back at her. The cacophony of the dying and the braying of beasts surrounded them. Darroc's monsters seemed confused whether or not they should continue without their leader there to direct them. She saw several clan members take it upon themselves to attack the monsters again and admired their ferocity and endurance.

"He is not gone," Moira's voice echoed in her mind. "But I give you this time to prepare for the next."

"Where are you going?" Desperation soaked Faria's voice as she responded in kind. "Will I see you again?"

"If you have need of me," the phoenix said as she continued her transformation into a brilliant bird, "sing the song and I will come."

"What song?" Faria shouted, but the phoenix took flight and disappeared again.

Ander reached for her hand and a healing warmth washed over her. "I'm sorry," he said. "I had to do it."

"I thought you might kill me," she said. He tried to pull away but she grasped his fingers, not wanting to sever their connection. Despite his ministrations on her, she was filled with an overwhelming gratitude that he was alive, that he wanted to heal her, that he cared about her at all.

"He changed his mind about me retrieving the Flame first," he said. "I don't know why. Said there was something he wanted you to see. He probably wanted to show you how he controlled me."

She felt a hint of trepidation at that but then again, she now had a phoenix on her side. She didn't know where Darroc went, but the new ally they gained could tip the scales in their favor.

Luck, Nellie, and Thomas ran up to her and Ander, forming a protective circle around them. The rush of beasts slowed to a trickle, the battle nearly coming to an end. Bodies littered the forest floor.

"What are the losses so far?" Jamison asked.

"Too many," Luck reported. "But enough will survive through their injuries."

Nellie stood wide-eyed, a bleak look on her face. They still needed to convince the shifters to fight in Anestra, and now seemed like the only time they could. Faria began to ask the dreaded question but movement in the trees caught her eye as another round of monsters came, this time smaller, quicker. Ander let out a pained groan and fell to the ground, clutching his stomach.

"Ander!" Faria yelled, reaching for him.

"It's the blood command," he grunted, face scrunched in pain. "I must finish his orders. It's part of the magic he placed on me."

"The what?" Faria gasped, furious.

"I have to get the Flame," he said. "I have no choice."

Faria clasped her son's arm before he could disappear on her, so like when Hunter did a year ago. She felt his muscles bulge as another wave of pain washed over him. She would not let him go. She refused.

Faria looked at Nellie and yelled, "Lead them!"

Faria felt her body start to flicker, felt the shift as though her body were being squeezed through a tube. She gazed between Nellie then to Jamison. A horrified look crossed his face before his hand grasped onto hers and the three of them popped out of existence.

TWENTY SIX

NELLIE

The space her queen once occupied was now empty and Nellie felt disoriented, scared, and immensely unprepared. Moira was a phoenix? Where did she go? Where did Darroc go?

Most importantly, she felt utterly empty without Faria. It was her one task to stick with her, to help her survive, to find her son. She only completed half of her mission and as the queen's protector, she failed by letting her get away.

They thought the battle was over, but another wave of monsters appeared. These were smaller, quicker, although considerably dumber than the larger beasts, as if they had no idea what their purpose was. They were chaotic and unorganized, which made them even more dangerous than the others.

She went after them along with the remaining shifters. The gravely injured were still lying on the forest floor and now the monsters made their way toward the fallen. Their numbers appeared to be half of what they once were.

Nellie changed herself into a fox, needing to end this quickly. She bit and swiped with all that she could, attacking creature after creature. There were so many of them and the shifters seemed to be tiring after already expending so much energy on the larger beasts.

Nellie's endurance was waning, too. The beasts trickled through, one after the other and her thoughts wouldn't cease. Was Darroc dead? Where would the phoenix take him? How much time had passed? Could he be in Anestra now, attacking her home?

Would they all survive this?

Most importantly, she needed to convince the others to follow her to Anestra, but how could she when there were so few left?

An opportunity presented itself as she changed back into her human form.

She removed a sword from across her back, clashing with a monster who spit foam as he snarled and snapped at her. She drove her sword into his neck, then moved on to another, then another. She saved Marisa from being attacked from behind, then turned and recognized Samantha in her wolf form who was clamped down by the jaws of a monster. She flung a dagger straight for its neck. It collapsed on Samantha's body. Nellie ran over and pushed it aside, looking into Samantha's pained eyes.

"Are you okay?" she asked the wolf. Blood flowed, but it looked as though Nellie had gotten to her in time. The wolf nodded, then ran off to fight another beast.

A scream rent the air.

Nellie whipped around in time to see Luck, who had been protecting the gravely injured off to the side, clutch his stomach as he slammed to his knees. Blood splashed on the fallen leaves. His insides splattered along the ground.

"NO!" Nellie cried, running toward him.

The light left Luck's eyes. Jamison had left with Faria, and now his second, so full of laughter and jokes, lay dead at her feet. She couldn't wrap her head around the fact that a once fierce, playful, caring soul was gone, and the Air Clan had no one to lead them.

A renewed sense of vengeance and anger washed over her as was overcome with a second wind. She didn't know how long they'd been fighting—an hour? More?—but now she had no choice but to stay and protect those who couldn't protect themselves.

She'd expended too much energy by now to shift, so she continued fighting in her human form, flinging dagger after dagger at the feral beasts as they approached, brandishing her sword at those who got too close.

She lost sense of time as she fought through angry tears, the heavy loss to the clans pouring through her. She seethed at the Fates, at the death of Queen Amira, at Faria's disappearance. She yelled and screamed as she brandished her sword again and again, attacking anything that got too close. She had to protect the others. The injustice of it all consumed her. She had to make it right.

Nellie heaved in a deep breath, trying to control the heavy sob fighting its way out of her chest. She would have time to break down later. Her work wasn't done. She had to do more.

She had to *be* more.

Tommy approached her, his wide eyes and cautious stance letting her know she must have looked just as crazed as she felt. Sticky grime coated her face, threatening to run into her eyes and mouth.

"Nellie," he said gently. "It is done."

She looked around, wild and fierce, as if she didn't believe him. There had to be more. There had to be more for her to let her anguish and confusion and fear out on. More to hurt so she could take away the pain, but he appeared to be correct.

Animals shifted back into their human form as more of the clan members walked toward her, shock on their faces. She looked into the eyes of so many she didn't recognize, so many she never cared to know, and felt the gratitude toward them, for them choosing to fight against Nellie and Faria's demons.

"Thank you." Her voice was raw, broken. "Thank you for fighting for us."

"You're thanking us?" Tommy said in disbelief, shaking his head. "It is us who need to thank you, for protecting our injured and fallen. For respecting our dead, our land, and our ways."

Nellie was confused. She may not be a part of the clans anymore, but she was still a shifter. She was raised on these ways, and him thinking that she wouldn't respect where she came from almost offended her. She would have said as much, if he hadn't gotten down on his knees—in the thick of blood and gore soaking into the ground—and bowed to her.

Others followed suit, until every remaining shifter was kneeling before her. These people who had once wished her dead, who voted her off the island, who threatened to kill her when she returned, were now bowing to her out of reverence and gratitude. Another sob welled up inside her. She stood tall, or as tall as she could on shaky legs, and bowed her head to them in return.

They slowly got up and stood at attention, waiting for her to say something.

"Thank you," her wrecked voice croaked out. "I don't deserve this honor. I was unable to save so many." Her voice cracked at that, but she swallowed a sob and continued. "Thank you for putting your trust in me and my queen. I don't know how we can repay you."

"On the contrary," Marisa said, tear tracks running through the blood spatters on her face. "It is you who saved us. We would have been decimated if it weren't for you."

"We will honor our dead. Now, before the dawn light awakens the forest," Tommy said. "And then we will go."

"Go?" Nellie asked confused. "Go where?"

"With you. To Anestra."

"With me?" she asked, still dumbfounded.

"You saved our land," Marisa said. "It is time for us to save yours."

Nellie did break into tears then, and she sobbed into Marisa's arms as the clan mates gathered the dead and started to build their pyres. She cried as the bodies burned. She mourned their loss, the way she was unable to protect them. She cried for her past, for what they all went through to get to this point. She cried for the uncertainty of their future.

When the fires burned down and the ashes of the bodies were carried into the Beyond on the breeze, when the tears finally dried, she addressed the group who gathered around her, weapons in hand.

"I don't know what we will be returning home to," Nellie said. "I'm not even sure how we will return. The Gate has a mind of its own. But know this—no matter what happens, I am with you. I will honor and protect your lives to the best of my ability and fill each moment with gratitude that the Fates have reunited us."

Shifters pounded their fists to their chests as one, both an acceptance of what she said and a call to arms to prepare themselves for whatever came next.

"And now," she said, her eyes misting. "To Anestra."

TWENTY SEVEN

HUNTER

Hunter removed first his gloves, then his shirt, and dropped them on the cavern's floor. The sound of his clothing plopped as they hit the pools of blood leaking from Crispin's dead body.

He was drenched in sweat and exhausted. He knew the darkness inside was satiated, but that did nothing for the weight against his conscience. He learned almost nothing from Crispin as he spewed his lies. He knew Darroc hadn't touched Faria in that way, but the image wasn't any less horrifying. The only thing of value that he did learn was that Darroc had found a way to obtain the Flame. They had to assume when he arrived back in Anestra that he would carry the Flame with him.

Time was running out. They had hours, maybe, before they needed to be ready. There was no way they could get the Crystal of Light. No way that they could get the Book of the Dead for the unmaking spell. There was almost no chance at all that the Fates would change their design.

The wait for news, for anything, was nearly unbearable. The stillness in the air was palpable. It almost felt like the night that he and Faria had changed the direction of the Fates. They were all on some sort of precipice and he didn't know which way they would fall.

Hunter walked through the halls of *Mentage*, unconcerned if anyone should see him blood splattered and without clothes on. They would all soon be in some state of bloodied undress. He made it to his cabin uninterrupted and quickly washed his hands and changed into fresh clothes. He didn't bother looking at himself in the mirror. He knew he'd be sickened by the sight.

His vision swam and once again he found himself in the human realm standing behind Faria and…that shifter. Her body was pressed against his, her tongue down his throat as he dared to run his hands over her breasts. Jealousy consumed him as his possessive nature fought to take over. If Hunter hadn't just fed his darkness, he was certain the force of what he felt would crush the barrier between realms. He'd want to kill the male for daring to touch what didn't belong to him.

He closed the gap between him and Faria and ran his hands over her hips, pressing her back against him instead. He felt her stiffen and he knew that this time she couldn't ignore his pleas to accept the bond. To accept that he was alive and real. He knew she felt the pressure of every touch he gave her.

He nipped her neck and dipped his hand inside her pants. He couldn't tell if her slickness was for him or not and it only spurred his anger further. "Is this for him? Or me?"

Hunter gasped as he reappeared in his cabin before he heard her answer. Fury like he had never known filled him. It went beyond rage, beyond all rational thought.

I am a ship on the sea.

He repeated the mantra over, but it didn't work this time. Pressure as the air distorted and stretched around him made him feel as though the veil between realms was thinning. As though he really could shatter them if he wanted to. The runes on his body writhed and his canines slashed through his gums so hard they bit through his lip.

The sting of the sudden pain sharpened his vision. He couldn't lose control. He needed to remain focused, patient. The time for murder would be there soon.

Taking one last inhale, Hunter left his cabin and went out to meet what little of the king's army was waiting to fight.

It seemed as though every citizen of Anestra stood in the field in *Mentage*. The same field that was burned black by Darroc's evil fire. The same field that grew bloody under the beasts' dying bodies.

It was also the same field that yielded plentiful food year after year. Where gatherings were had for the people. Where parties were held, weddings were celebrated, memories were created.

Hunter vowed to never let Darroc taint it and what it represented again.

The king placed his hand on Hunter's shoulder. "Did you complete your task?"

Hunter nodded.

"No word from your Elders?"

Hunter didn't bother to hide the grief he knew was etched on his face.

The king swallowed. "Let us honor what has come before, and pray for what comes after."

Hunter walked up to Faline, who insisted on being on the front lines with everyone else, and held her eye. She nodded at him then faced forward. They stood shoulder to shoulder along with the citizens of Anestra. Emotions ran over each of their faces, but fear was not one of them. It made Hunter proud. He knew he trained them the best he was able. They would deal with what came next, together.

A sudden shout from down the line came from Enis. "Movement! Movement from the forest line!"

"Ready your weapons!" the king shouted. As one, the people grasped their weapons or readied their magic, the sudden surge crackling in the air as they waited for the call. "Steady!"

Another moment passed before Wil shouted, "WAIT!"

Hunter scanned the trees, willing himself to see straight through them. His hearing, though exceptional, provided no answers. He could hear movement but it was barely there, just a whisper of steps, not like the monsters' clomping disrespect of the land.

A figure emerged, followed by another and another.

"It's Nellie," Faline breathed on the other side of Hunter. Tears poured from her eyes as she took off at a run.

"Hold steady!" the king yelled to the others as he followed Faline, along with Hunter, Enis, Wil, and Endo.

Nellie sprinted toward them with a huge smile on her face. Fresh tears streaked down her face, and though she was spectacularly covered in grime and blood, none of it seemed to belong to her.

She collapsed straight into Faline's arms and wept freely. "Thank the gods!" Nellie yelled out. "Thank all the freaking gods!"

The king grasped her shoulder looking her over. "How much time passed for you?"

"Three weeks," she said, breathless. "I brought backup. It isn't much—we barely survived. They will follow your direction."

They turned and watched as shifters poured from the forest, cautiously walking toward them. Hunter counted several dozen. Like Nellie said, it wasn't much, but it was infinitely better than what they had. He looked among them but didn't spot the one face he wanted to see.

"I thought we would be too late," Nellie said. "How much time passed here?"

"Four months," Endo said. Nellie whipped her face to him and smiled a brilliant smile at him. She shrieked as she jumped into his arms.

"I knew you would come back!" she exclaimed as she wrapped her legs around his waist. He tightened his arms around her.

"Nellie," Hunter said, not caring that he was interrupting their reunion. "Where is Faria?"

Her smile fell. "You mean she isn't here?"

"What do you mean?" the king asked. "You were to stay with her. Where did she go?"

"I-I don't know." She looked at Hunter. "Ander. He's under some sort of blood command of Darroc's. He was tasked to get the Flame. He disappeared and Faria and Jamison disappeared along with him."

He couldn't entertain the thought of that shifter with his mate because a true fear poured over him. She couldn't mean the Eternal Flame—but she had to. Crispin had said as much.

He cursed to himself. The Flame was ancient lore. Something to do with the ultimate creator hiding away that which gave birth to all living things, all planets in all the universes. The power had been too great, so the creator split it into millions of tiny pieces, the only surviving of which was said to be a single flame, whose power would give the wielder everlasting life and success in all their endeavors.

Hunter had mentioned the Flame weeks ago. Endo had even said something about it. It would be absolutely devastating in Darroc's hand. He hadn't wanted to believe Crispin, but there was no denying it now.

"I must go to her," Hunter said.

"No!" the king replied. "We need you here. And you don't know if you will survive there." The king looked pale as if he, too, knew the implications.

He met Faline's eyes, her face stricken. She nodded at him, a sign of approval.

He risked everything—the wrath of the Elders, of the king. The possibility of ultimate death. But he could not wait around to see if Faria would be successful. He wouldn't lose her, not if he had the chance to be with her. To help her.

"Is he dangerous?" he asked Nellie.

"Ander saved her life twice and tried to give her information, but he is sworn to do what Darroc wishes. He healed her, though. He has that ability. And he looked abhorred at having to torture her."

"At what?" Hunter shouted. "My son did what?" Perhaps the darkness ran through his bloodline.

"He didn't want to!" Nellie said quickly. "He tried to stop it. He shook so hard with the effort. Like I said, he healed her afterwards."

Hunter's resolve crumbled. His son would always be dangerous to her, to all of them, for as long as he was under Darroc's control. He needed to leave.

He looked at the group, at the shifters approaching them, at the people of Anestra holding the line.

"Are we correct to think Darroc is on his way?" he asked her.

"A phoenix appeared," Nellie said. "It's a long story but he's gone for now. We assumed he would come here but since he hasn't, I would say that he's probably nursing some pretty grueling injuries."

He nodded, taking it for the answer he needed. He looked at the king. "Forgive me," he said.

Hunter gathered his strength and envisioned Faria's location.

I wish to be at her side.

He didn't know if it would work, if he could jump between realms. Sudden darkness engulfed him before agonizing heat blazed his body.

He stood on a hardened piece of rock, a river of lava flowing before him. The heat seared his lungs and it took a moment for him to adapt, for the haze of ash to clear. He looked across a desolate landscape, barren of any life. The sky was tinged in gray. The wind scorched his face as he lifted an arm to shield himself from the violent onslaught.

"It exists," he breathed as it cleared away.

The realm of fire.

TWENTY EIGHT

FARIA

It was a new sensation to her, to disappear as she had with Ander. The squeezing and flattening sensation of her body was overwhelming and she thought she might perish in that way. When she landed, she no longer felt herself holding on to her son. She coughed, breathing in rancid, sulfuric air.

She squinted her eyes against the rush of heat blasting at her from all sides, as though she were in the middle of the largest pyre, slowly being roasted from the inside out.

Jamison helped her up, still gripping her now sweaty hand. His face dripped with perspiration and he had a pained expression.

"Why did you come?" she barely breathed out. "We don't know that you'll survive."

His breathing was staggered, as if he were being choked. "To protect you. Until the end."

She shook her head. "That's a mistake," she said. "I cannot give what you need."

"Suck it up, buttercup," he rasped, giving her his best attempt at a smile in the scorching heat. "Where's Ander?"

Faria looked around at the barren landscape. Lava flowed around them, bits of hardened rock here and there scattered along a river of fire. There was no sign of life, which came as no surprise. She tentatively stepped forward. It was hard to see through the fog and steam.

A blast of searing wind came at her from behind, clearing a path before her. She saw a body, tall, broad shouldered with brown hair.

"Ander?" she called to him. She walked forward a few paces when he turned. Her steps faltered.

He stared down at her, searching her body, devouring every piece of her he could before his eyes landed on her hand holding another's. The intimacy she once felt with Jamison was replaced with despair, disbelief, hope. Perhaps this was the Fate's way of being cruel with her again, giving life to her hallucinations. Perhaps she'd moved on into the Beyond, only her version of Beyond was a land of hell where she had to stare at his face forever.

Fire reflected in his shining emerald eyes.

She couldn't believe she was about to ask this question, couldn't believe he was standing before her, whether it was a mirage or not. Couldn't believe the Fates would be so cruel. But still, she gathered her strength, feeling her heart shatter over again, as her lips cracked in the blazing heat, and she finally acknowledged the one truth she refused to believe since his death.

"Hunter?"

EPILOGUE

S ilence.

It had been silent for years. Centuries.

Millennia? Forever.

Always.

There was no way to keep track. No way to know.

Fits of slumber and quiet were her only companions for longer than she could remember.

Darkness was her lover, caressing her, intimately lulling her into her suspended state of…

Sleep.

She had been sleeping so long. Why? Why was she not living? That was surely what she wanted to do?

But she was so tired. So lost. So confused.

Who had she been, in the Before? Why was she here, now?

"Farrahhhhhh…."

That voice. She knew it, once.

It settled within her, calling her name. Was that her name?

It willed her to remember…what?

"Farrahhhhh…"

A deafening roar shook the darkness, vibrating through her essence.

It was familiar, that feeling. She felt it before. Before her sisters left her.

Before *he* left her.

The power that used to reside within her was gone now, wasn't it?

What happened to it?

"Farrahhhhh…arise, sweet love."

Sweet love. There it was again. The feeling.

The darkness changed its pitch and she could see a light shining through.

How could she see? She gave it all up didn't she?

Her life.

Her body.

Her soul.

Where did she put it?

"Farrah, sweet love. It is time."

The voice was closer, clearer.

She remembered it. Remembered him.

They created something together once, didn't they?

"Arise, now, before it is too late."

Yes, that's right. They agreed to this. To rest, to let their creation play out as it would.

Then why was she being disturbed? She didn't care any longer. She wanted to sleep, to stay suspended within this darkness. That was where it was safe. Where there was no pain. No memories. No hurt.

Just bliss.

"Farrah, my precious. We must save them."

He was incessantly stubborn, this voice of the being she once loved.

"They come, my love. I need you. Arise!"

The darkness shifted but something was different, off. It no longer roiled through her but around her. It helped her take shape and she felt heavier, denser.

She didn't want it. But how could she prevent such a thing from happening?

She did not want to rise.

It hasn't been long enough to erase the pain. The memories were still there, haunting her.

The command was sharper. Clearer. Intentional.

"NOW!"

She tumbled as the darkness pitched her toward a light as the air around her trembled, the force of the movement thrusting her further away from where she sought sanctuary for thousands of years.

A thunderous crack resounded and sunlight poured in, blinding her. She gasped, gulping a huge lungful of air. The temple around her crumbled as the dirt dragged her further into the life she desperately tried to escape.

Inhale. Exhale.

She had to remind herself to breathe, now. Remind herself what it was like to survive while confined in this body.

She opened her eyes.

Lady Farrah, Goddess of Light, has awoken.

ACKNOWLEDGEMENTS

To say this book was a journey would be a vast understatement. When I finished *Chosen to Fall*, all I knew was that I needed Faria in the human realm and Hunter alive. I had no other specifics, no road maps to guide me. I waited until I had a sign, until my characters demanded I tell their story, piece by piece, until I finally got it right. In November of 2020, I decided to participate in NaNoWriMo and wrote out the first draft of Fated within twenty-five days. It had its bones, but I left it alone for seven months before adding in the muscle and blood that made this book come alive. The heart came last, minutes before writing this in fact, which made this book thrive.

There are so many people that have contributed to the making and production of this book, it's impossible to decide on any order of importance. I have been so insanely lucky to have the most amazing support system throughout this book's journey.

Thank you to my editor, Quinn Nichols. You played the role of both developmental editor and line/copy editor and I cannot express the gratitude I feel towards the magic you put into my story. You saw it when it was just bones, took your time to give me an in-depth analysis, provided endless explanation for all the changes, and turned this very rough piece of rock into a beautiful gem. This story would be nothing but a rough imitation of the real thing without you.

To my Beta readers! I don't know what great karma I've had in a past life to grant me the luck of knowing you all, but I am so eternally grateful. I have such a special relationship with each of you that I am so appreciative of; Jesse Broman, for providing me endless hype girl support; Nirmaliz Colón, for listening to my crazy last minute angsty ideas; Victoria A Pietsch, for providing such thoughtful and layered feedback that has done nothing but elevate my work to the next level; Lilian Sue, for the constant encouragement and always being willing to bounce around marketing ideas; Anakha Ashok, for always checking in with my mental health, making sure I'm getting enough sleep, and taking time out to rest; Kiraka Davis, for promoting my work at every opportunity and always being willing to listen to my problems and ramblings; and Jessica Grewe Glover, for providing me music to escape into and an ear to vent to, allowing me to dispel my chaotic energy and come back a little more stable than before. I am so lucky to have every one of you!

I really cultivated a special Bookstagram writing community over the past year, especially in the summer between when *Chosen* was released and when I spent manic hours drafting and editing Fated. The background support has been the foundation of my sanity and I am so grateful to every person who has supported and guided my journey. Two people deserve super special recognition for the amount of sheer chaos I made them endure:

Evelyn Mahony for penguin pebbling me with all of the memes, animal videos, hot story inspiration, astrology talk, TikToks, and constant

ABOUT THE AUTHOR

 Emmie Hamilton is a writer, mother, and amateur candle maker. Her favorite pastime is creating worlds others wish they were born into. She received her MFA in Creative Writing from Southern New Hampshire University and has been previously published by Pure Slush Press and various non-fiction outlets. *Fated to Burn* is the sequel to her debut novel, *Chosen to Fall*.

You can connect with her on Instagram @authoremmiehamilton or visit her website www.emmiehamilton.com for the latest publication information.

stream of support in both my professional and personal life. You bring me endless comfort and joy and I appreciate the heck out of you! Ily bby.

And JPM for being my anchor, my inspiration, my reminder that when you find someone you have an affinity toward, life is just better. Thank you for all the music, the laughs, and one of the most honest friendships I've ever had the fortune of having.

A super special shoutout to my Whimsical Writing Group. This summer was hard, but you ladies helped me endure. Thank you for the motivation, the support, and all of the laughs. You have truly helped get me through. So thankful for you all!

TO MY FAMILY—

To Michael, for once again allowing me the time to work late nights and every weekend so I can live out my passion, and for providing me the freedom to create whatever comes to mind.

To my mother for being my number one cheerleader. My father for purchasing twenty copies of my book though he is still awaiting the audio book. My sister and brother for always hyping me up. I am endlessly grateful for the love and your belief in me and my dreams.

Finally, as always, to Oliver. You are my reason, my being, my essential self. Everything I do is for you, my love, to show you strength, resilience, bravery, and love. You are mine, and I am yours, forever.